# Yesterday's Promise

## by

## Cassandra Bella

*The Grady Brothers Trilogy*

**Yesterday's Promise**

Cover Art by *Debbie Taylor*

The Wild Rose Press, Inc.
PO Box 708
Adams Basin, NY 14410-0708
Visit us at www.thewildrosepress.com

Publishing History
First Crimson Rose Edition, 2018
Print ISBN 978-1-5092-1935-3
Digital ISBN 978-1-5092-1936-0

*The Grady Brothers Trilogy*
Published in the United States of America

**"This is what we are.**
What is good between us." He buried long fingers in the soft fall of her hair, holding her captive, refusing to let go.

"You can try, but you will never be able to deny this. Deny us." Tightening his hold in her hair, he nipped at her bottom lip.

She moaned, low and desperate, swaying into him. Surrounded by the heat of him, she could only give in to what he offered. Taking it. Needing it. His scent—full of earth and sun—teased her. Drawing her to want more, knowing she would never fully be satisfied.

Cursing, he stepped away, leaving the chill of separation to jolt her back to awareness.

She looked at him, confusion running through her as she shook her head.

"I'm going to go." He brushed the pad of his thumb over her lips, swollen from his kiss. "Just as you asked."

He reached behind her, picking up her wine glass. "But, when you're ready to accept what's between us I'll be here." He gathered her shaking hand into his and pushed her Chardonnay into her hesitant grasp. "Ready for you. For everything that could be so good between us."

Not bothering to wait for an answer, he spun on the heels of his boots, never looking back as he headed for the door.

## Dedication

To Philip Westfall.
Nobody has ever been able to make me laugh,
protect me, and irritate me in the way you have.
I'm thankful every day that my life
and my memories are full of your friendship.
I love you, Sergeant Chuckles!

Prologue

Men were jerks.

No. Correct that...*boys* were jerks.

'Cause it didn't matter one bit that Keith Randall had just celebrated his twenty-first birthday. He was still an immature, crazy-hormonal, I must get laid or die, little boy.

Scowling at the long, dark road ahead, Gina Simms tucked a stray strand of long black hair behind her ear. She guessed she was a mile or so from the Double 'G' Ranch.

Lights had shimmered in the windows of the big house when they'd passed by earlier. Hopefully one of the heart-stopping Grady brothers was awake. Heck, at this point, she would settle for their old man, as long as someone let her in and gave her use of a phone since she'd dropped hers in the front seat of Keith's Camaro.

She'd refused to take a second more looking for it.

Hell no. She'd wanted out of that car, and nothing would have stopped her.

"Your own damn fault," she muttered, kicking at the pebbles scattering the dirt road. She'd been the one who'd said yes. Had crawled in eagerly beside him, feeling special that he'd chosen her for the prized first ride in his new ruby red convertible Camaro—a birthday gift from his parents.

Who could blame her?

Plain old Gina catching the attention of the hottest guy in Snow Ridge. Her friends had been green with envy. Keith Randall asking her out. She was nothing, nobody when it came to the same scale he operated on. Just a girl barely out of high school, wasting time until she figured out what to do next with her life.

And Keith—he came from one of the wealthiest families in town. A football star in his high school days. Sandy blond hair and brilliant blue eyes catching the attention of nearly every female he passed.

He could have had just about anyone sitting beside him for that first ride in his fancy new car. But he'd chosen her. And she'd been so starry-eyed and pitiful, she'd jumped at the chance. Giddy with the idea he wanted to spend even a second with her.

*Stupid. Stupid. Stupid.*

She kicked harder, creating a swirl of dust, as a double flash of light peeked over the crest ahead. A car. Hopefully not Keith's.

She wouldn't be getting into anything tight and confining with him again. The guy had hands that liked to roam in areas they didn't belong. And ears that refused to hear the word *no*.

Nope. She'd already made that mistake tonight. It was the reason she walked alone and chilled on the side of a deserted mountain road. Be damned if she'd repeat it. If it was Keith coming over that crest, he could just keep on driving.

But it wasn't Keith.

It wasn't even a car. It was a truck. One of those big brutes, riding high, sure to get through any terrain found here in the Rocky Mountains.

It moved slowly, inching forward as she hugged

the edge of the road tighter.

It slowed even more as it drew closer, headlights washing over her as it rolled to a stop.

The passenger door window slid down. "Bit late for a walk."

A sigh of relief escaped at the sound of the familiar voice. *Thank goodness*. Maybe now she'd get off this Godforsaken road.

"It wasn't a walk I was after." Wrapping her fingers around the mirror's thick frame, she stepped onto the running board. "Think you might be able to give me a ride home?"

"Sure." His smile flashed bright in the dark cab. The illuminated gauges in the dashboard danced shadows over his scrubby jaw. "Better than walking alone this time of night."

Yeah...well, some things couldn't be avoided. Stepping off the running board, she opened the heavy door and climbed into the big truck. "Thanks."

He waited till she had her seat belt in place before tugging on the gearshift. "No problem. Been a slow night. At least this gives me something to do to pass the time."

A slow night? For him? Gina eyed him curiously. She knew handsome when she saw it.

He was a bit too old for her taste but still, it was a Friday night in Snow Ridge. She figured there would be plenty of women willing to offer him up some entertainment.

Then again, she snuck another look over the curve of her shoulder, he *was* a man. Not a boy like Keith.

Not for her. She mentally shook her head. She was young and still craved young. Just a better sort than those driving fancy Camaros and unable to control the itch between their legs.

Through the window, she watched as the lights of Snow Ridge flickered up ahead. She'd be home soon. It had been one hell of a night. One she wanted to put behind her.

With the ease of one who knew his vehicle well, he guided his truck from dirt to pavement, speeding up for the final stretch between ranch land and town.

On the rise behind Main Street sat her neighborhood, her home, where her parents were probably already tucked away in bed for the night.

At the traffic light, she expected him to turn right. When he didn't, she realized she'd simply assumed he knew where she lived.

"You missed the turn." She gave a small smile. "I'm sorry. I should have given directions."

He didn't look at her. Didn't slow down. Just kept driving, his truck joining the handful of others working their way through town. "I don't need directions."

"Obviously, you do," she snapped, regretting it immediately. He'd been kind enough to give her a ride. It wasn't fair to get testy with him.

She looked at him again, forcing another smile. "Sorry. I tell you what, to make it easier, why don't you drop me off right up there at Grady's Pub. I can make it home from there."

He didn't answer. Didn't even acknowledge he'd heard a word she'd said. Instead, he kept on driving, staring straight ahead with a determined set to his jaw.

Well, now it made sense why he didn't have anything going tonight. His whole attitude probably went real far in chasing away any woman who might be interested.

She'd never thought of him as a jerk. But he was quickly proving her wrong. "Look. You can pull over anywhere and let me out. I appreciate the ride to get me this far. I'm good from here."

Still no answer.

*Jerk.* Scowling at him, she eyed the stop sign ahead. If he wasn't going to pull over, she'd get out herself. Wrapping her hand around the handle of the door, she waited for him to reach the intersection.

Intent on watching, waiting for him to stop, she didn't catch the black flutter of movement until he'd already reached over the span of the cab.

The prick in her neck was quick. "What the hell?" She reached up, flattening her hand in the curve below her ear. Pulling away, she found a small point of blood staining the fleshy part of her palm. "Did you just stick me with something?"

Again, no response.

Screw him. As fear began creeping slowly up her spine, she decided she wasn't waiting until the stop sign came around.

She tried pulling on the handle but couldn't get her fingers to answer the demand her brain sent. They slid helplessly off the metal, falling useless to the side.

What had he done to her? She turned, prepared to demand he tell her what was going on. She'd had more than enough of men for the night. Was done with them and their games.

Plus, she was scared. And the fear was increasing drastically with each passing second.

Opening her mouth to speak, her words escaped in a disjointed slur. Her jaw felt like it weighed a hundred pounds. And she swore her tongue must have grown three times its size.

Damn. This wasn't good.

Terror roared to life as a black shadow teased the edges of her vision. Behind the steering wheel, he continued to stare straight ahead, showing no signs of being aware of what was happening beside him.

What did he want with her? Why would he do this?

She needed to get away. Needed to end whatever sick plan he had in mind. But every struggle to move proved worthless. She was numb from head to toe. She couldn't speak. Couldn't move. She could only sit there and stare helplessly at the man she'd trusted, hadn't thought twice about asking for a ride home.

The black shadows swirled and danced. Her head pounded. Her body sagged under an unexplainable weight.

Trapped by her own useless limbs, she was unable to escape whatever horror awaited her.

And she knew, without a doubt, it was definitely a horror she faced.

She thought of home, of her bed, her parents, as the shadows took over, dragging her under and burying her beneath the dark truth that her life was about to take a tragic turn.

Chapter One

She'd sworn she would never come back.

Had vowed to stay far away from Snow Ridge, from the past and the memories she'd left behind a decade ago.

Yet here she was, surrounded by boxes of every size and empty shelves waiting to be filled, reminding her of how much she still had left to do.

With a sigh, Cara Bennett turned away from the large picture window gracing the front of the shop. Away from watching the slow crawl of Main Street. Plenty of work still needed to be done if she had any hope of Precious Gems opening on time.

Returning to the box she'd left open, half-unpacked, she committed again to sorting through the many handmade treasures she'd collected. From the Buffalo tapestry she'd discovered in Boulder to the stunning turquoise pendant she traveled all the way to Trinidad to claim.

She refused to feel regretful or remorseful for the turn her life had taken. She would still know the sweet taste of success. She'd just experience it here in Snow Ridge, rather than back in Denver inside the modern flat she adored. The one overlooking Denver and the exciting life of lower downtown she'd fallen in love with. Her home for so many years, now subleased to a newly married couple who, she knew, would enjoy it as much as she did.

"*Never expect life to journey without many turns.*"

Hattie told her that, her Irish brogue thick, when Cara was still a small child. She hadn't understood it then. She understood now.

The bell above the thick glass door broke the silence, pulling her from her thoughts.

"How can you work without coffee?"

As always, a burst of boundless energy followed her friend through the door, spreading like wildfire through the air.

*Jacqueline Eloise Schmidt.*

That's how she'd introduced herself all those many, many years ago. Back in First Grade. Ms. Robinson's class. Jackie's family had just moved to town, halfway through the school year. And there she was, a powerful slice of energy wrapped into this little ball of a freckled, red-headed girl. With big brown eyes and a smile stretching from ear to ear.

She'd been assigned the empty chair at the table next to Cara. Had stuck out her hand, introduced herself, and started the path leading to a friendship of over twenty years.

"Pure desperation." Straightening, Cara placed the intricate glass bowl she'd unwrapped on the shelf to her left before turning to claim one of the cardboard cups Jackie held out.

"And what about you?" She took a sip, savoring the shot of caffeine she'd been craving since long before Jackie left to fetch their morning drinks. "I know that's not real coffee you're drinking."

"Not for another month." She rested a hand on her swollen pregnant stomach. "But I find pretending it is

8

helps."

In her friend's sparkling brown eyes, Cara saw the love she carried for the little one growing inside. "You know, partner or not, you don't have to worry about this." She swept a hand out, circling the boxes closing in on every side. "Being pregnant gives you an excuse."

"Oh, don't tempt me. Peter will tell you, I've been using the pregnancy excuse every chance I get." With a devilish smile, so much a part of her, she sidestepped to the bowl Cara set down, running a gentle finger along its curved edge.

"This is what we're selling? What we're hoping all those rich snow bunnies will buy up and take home with them?"

"Yep." Cara nudged her aside, turning the glass bowl until it sat just right under the reflection of the light. "See that beauty? How the light bounces off the gold vein layered through the glass? That's one of a kind. It's unique. And it's everything we'll be selling. Original creations, made by and sold by those who call Colorado home."

"It's beautiful. I'm tempted to steal it myself. I have the perfect spot."

The sharp look in her eyes left little doubt she told the truth. "But I don't understand why you don't just open a studio dedicated to your paintings. You have to know you're good enough. You've got that fancy downtown gallery clamoring all over you."

"And it's a good ego boost, knowing that." Cara set her coffee on the counter and went back to the box she'd been working on. "But this place," she pulled a glass vase made by the same artist from the box, "needs to be more."

Setting it beside the bowl, she stepped back, admiring the beauty in both pieces. "For one, my work would lose something if I felt forced into completing it just to keep the shop stocked and running."

She returned to the box, grateful to find it empty. Kicking it out of the way with the toe of her shoe, she tugged another into the spot she'd cleared. "And I like the idea of helping out local artists by giving them a chance to showcase their work they might not get otherwise."

"Makes sense, I guess." Jackie collected the bubble wrap as Cara tugged it free from the box. "But, hell, if I had your talent, I'd be selfishly hiding all this other stuff away so my work had center stage."

Cara laughed, not believing a word she said. Selfish wasn't who Jackie was. Loud and pushy, yes. But not selfish.

Her arms overflowing with bubble wrap, Jackie disappeared through the back to the dumpsters waiting in the alley. Back in minutes, she stared down on Cara, a look in her eyes she knew all too well and usually ended up dreading in the end.

"So, with all this unpacking and creating this grand showcase for starving artists, you know you're going to need a break."

"Don't go there." Cara made an effort not to look up at her friend. "I told you I hadn't decided yet."

"Well, you might want to soon. The Spring Festival is tonight."

Cara sighed. Grabbing a set of hand-painted salt and pepper shakers, she pushed to her feet.

Part of her, a large part if she was truthful, longed to return to the festival. Moving away from Snow Ridge meant leaving behind many things from her childhood, including the yearly trips to the Spring Festival—an integral part of the town, its culture, and history.

Nestled in the heart of the Rocky Mountains, sandwiched by two popular ski resorts, Snow Ridge was a town with two tales. The snowy winters brought the tourists in a flurry of constant motion and excitement. They filled the hotels, the shops, the restaurants, and bars. Created the ambiance and flair the town was known for, made popular by those who thrived on their winter sports.

But, as warmer spring days caused the snowpack to melt and resorts to close for the season, the small mountain town returned to its residents. Life slowed. The excitement faded. And Snow Ridge returned to the small, ranching town it had been founded on.

And the Spring Festival was the residents' way to mark that transition. To celebrate a good winter season while being grateful for the break. For the slower pace of mountain life until snow began to fly again.

She wanted to go. She did. But—

"You can't hide forever." Though Jackie's voice was firm, her eyes held the softness of a friend who understood. "Especially not when you're about to open a store smack-dab in the heart of Snow Ridge. You should go, have fun, and forgive yourself for something you couldn't control."

She was right. Cara knew it and couldn't argue with her. But, even as an adult, the frightened, brokenhearted teenager who fled town all those years ago still existed deep inside. And it was that voice, that fear, causing the hesitation. Making her question what was right after all that happened a decade ago.

Knowing her friend's pain, Jackie reached for Cara, wrapping a comforting hand around her arm. "It's time to let go. Jacob would have never wanted his death to control you like this. He'd want you to be happy. You know that as well as I do."

The mention of his name rekindling old memories, Cara could hear Jacob's voice whispering in her ear. She could see his smile lighting the mischievous spark in his slate-gray eyes.

"And…" Jackie released her hold on Cara's arm and took the salt and pepper shakers from her hands. "He'd hate to be the one responsible for denying you a long overdue visit with Madame Luwiski."

Her smile was devious a second before she turned her back to arrange the shakers on a low-hung shelf.

"I can't believe she's still alive." Cara bent over the box, digging out a sapphire and iron picture frame.

The rumors and myths ran crazy when it came to Snow Ridge's personal psychic. Nobody could say for sure her exact age. Only that she'd been a part of many past decades in the town's history.

The accepted story of her past was one of a well-liked, respected Voodoo Queen from the Bayous of Louisiana who had fallen into bed with the wrong man…a married man. She'd been forced to flee her home and settle in a flimsy one-room cabin butted up against the mountain ridge to the west of Snow Ridge.

The very cabin where Madame Luwiski—the result of the torrid affair—continued to live, without the benefits of modern-day comforts.

From there, she'd supposedly learned at her mother's side from the time of her birth. Then, in turn, learned to take care of herself after her mother's death when she was still a child.

Nobody knew what was true or what was a myth. But they knew her and her claim to see into the future. Some believed it, daring the venture along the remote, beaten-up gravel road leading to her cabin for a private reading and a glance at what their lives might or might not become.

Others didn't believe at all, seeing her as nothing more than the crazy woman who lived outside of town. Pitied her for what they believed was a sad, mournful life.

And then there were those like Cara and Jackie. Who, through their childhood, made it a yearly tradition to visit Madame Luwiski's tent at the festival. Not because they believed or didn't believe. But because it started on a whim and never stopped, becoming as much a part of their friendship as the hours-long telephone conversations, ice cream to mend a broken heart, and swapping of clothes and shoes.

"I haven't been to her tent since you left." Jackie grabbed the hand not holding the frame. "I've missed it almost as much as I've missed you."

Though she ended with a wink, sadness teased her voice. And there, at that moment, Cara knew she'd be going.

Sidestepping her friend to set the frame on the counter, she brought the best smile she could to her lips. "I suppose, with you being pregnant and all, I'd be crazy not to go. After all, how many people get the chance to have free rein on Old Peterson's Crazy Cider because they already have a guaranteed designated driver?"

"Ah damn, didn't think about the Crazy Cider.

Luckily," she cupped her hands around her stomach and smiled softly, "this little one's worth it."

"So…it's a date." Jackie turned her big brown eyes on Cara. "Peter and I will pick you up at five. Then it's Crazy Cider for you, one of those huge turkey legs for me, and Madame for us both."

Yes. It was a date. A good one or not, Cara still wasn't sure. Wouldn't know until after the night was done.

\*\*\*\*

"I ain't going to no damn festival." Joe Bennett spun his wheelchair away from the worn, scarred table, waving Penny, his personal nurse, away as she stepped up to help.

With a frustrated sigh, Cara followed her dad out of the kitchen and into the front room where late afternoon shadows lingered. "You've always loved the Spring Festival. I can remember when you would look forward to it for months."

"Not a damn thing to look forward to anymore since I'm stuck in this thing." He slapped an angry hand against the arm of his wheelchair. "Should have just had the doctors put me down like an old, crippled horse."

Leaning over the side, he grabbed the remote, scowling at her and Penny before turning his attention to the television and the twenty-four-hour news channel he'd watched religiously over the past few months.

Cara pinched the bridge of her nose, fighting back a headache. This surly, cranky man was so far removed from the big, burly, loving father who could wrestle a bull to the ground one minute while softly smoothing Band-Aids over her scratched and bleeding knees the next.

The accident had changed him. Penny had warned her. And she'd seen it herself in her visits before making the move back to Snow Ridge.

"You should stop being an old grouch and go to the festival with your daughter," Penny scolded, stepping in front of him and his view of the television. "You might remember what it's like to be human again."

Shooting her an ugly look, he leaned to the right, looking past her to the petite brunette repeating the day's top news. "Can't be human when I can't even walk of my own doing. And I'll be damned if I'm going to show my face at that festival and let all of Snow Ridge cluck their tongues at me in pity."

Cara blinked back threatening tears. To see her dad like this, hear the pain and disgust in his voice, it was like a fist shoved harshly into her chest, yanking on her heart without mercy.

For almost three decades her father had been known and respected as the foreman for the Double 'G' Ranch. From the moment he'd moved his young bride away from New York, settling in the calmer, gentler ways of Snow Ridge, he'd earned his reputation as a vital part of the ranch's success.

His wife's tragic death, a year after Cara's birth, had left him with the full responsibility of a toddler as well as his duties to the Grady family. And yet, he never wavered. Never gave up. Refused to allow his daughter or the ranch to suffer.

Cara settled into the overstuffed chair next to her father. He didn't acknowledge her. Didn't so much as look her way. He just kept his eyes glued to the television.

It wasn't fair. Wasn't right. A man so vibrant and full of life didn't deserve facing a future where he may never have use of his legs again. A life void of everything he loved and thrived on. And now, she realized, she was starting to sound like him. Such negative thoughts wouldn't help. He'd given into them, but she refused to follow the same path.

"Why don't you go for just an hour?" She gave it one last try. "It might turn out it isn't as bad as you think. You have friends who want to see you and are worried about you."

He turned to her, finally, and for a moment, she saw past his surliness to the grief shimmering in his deep blue eyes. "I have no need to see anyone, friend or not. I'm fine right here." He turned back to the brunette and her news.

"Fine." Knowing it was worthless to continue trying, she pushed to her feet. Bending over, she brushed a light kiss across his sun-worn cheek. "I'll be back tomorrow to see how you're doing."

Still fighting the tears, she let herself out the front door. Stopping at the steps of the porch, she sucked in a breath of fresh mountain air, fighting against the darkness settling in her gut.

"Cara." The old hinges on the screen door squeaked in protest as Penny followed her out the door, joining her on the front porch.

"Don't give up on your father yet." She rested a gentle hand on Cara's arm. "He's an impossible old crank now, I know. Some days he tests my every limit with his stubbornness."

She shoved a hand through her short blonde curls, frustration shimmering in her green eyes. "But his doctors and his physical therapists are growing more optimistic by the day that he may walk again. That ugly stubbornness of his might be the perfect thing for his recovery."

"I hope so." Cara wrapped her arms around her middle, staring out over Penny's shoulder to the rise and fall of mountains butting up against Double 'G' Ranch.

"I had thought staying here, surrounded by the land he knows and loves, would be the best thing for him. Now, I'm not so sure."

A single tear escaped. She quickly brushed it away. "I'm afraid staying here, in this house and on the ranch, is a constant reminder of what he can no longer do. Of how much his life's changed, stuck in that wheelchair."

She'd debated moving him to Denver. Had rationalized the quality of care, resources, he'd have available as a reason to pack him up and move him in with her.

But she couldn't do it. Couldn't take him away from the mountains, the ranch, the town, he loved. He'd already lost the use of his legs, perhaps forever. She couldn't force him to lose his home and his very life, as well.

So he'd stayed, and she'd packed up the life she'd built in Denver to return to Snow Ridge. For him. For the father she loved and adored.

And missed terribly in the months since his accident.

Penny reached for her, wrapping her in a hug threatening to break down the last of her control. "Here is exactly where he needs to be. And I promise, someday he'll get past all that surliness inside and realize how much you've sacrificed."

"Nothing compared to what he's sacrificed for me." Cara sniffled like a little girl. Slowly pulling out of Penny's embrace, she swiped at the stray tears, forcing a smile to her lips.

"Thank you, Penny. Not just for this, but for everything you've done."

"It's my job. What you hired me for." She shrugged off the gratitude. "Plus, it helps that I knew and liked your father before his accident."

"And now?"

"Now, I see hints of him buried underneath his frustration and anger. Your father isn't gone, Cara. He's just hiding."

She could accept that. Needed to accept it.

"You go have fun." Penny flicked her hand in a dismissive wave. "You deserve a night with no worries weighing you down."

Cara could only nod, her throat too tight to push a word past. As Penny turned back to the house, she made her way down the steps, turning in the opposite direction of her car.

She needed to get home and get ready. But first, she had one more place to visit.

****

Other than a recent paint job, the breeding barn was just as she remembered. A crisp, clean white with emerald green trim to match the main house.

Sucking in a sharp breath, she stepped inside. Childhood memories flooded as the distinct scent of horse and hay mixed in a battle against the lighter smells of worn leather and aged wood.

Out of the sun's aim, shadows lingered, dancing

over the tops of the stalls lining both sides of the barn. The crunch of gravel under her shoes echoed as she slowly worked her way deeper inside.

It was quiet except for the occasional neigh of a horse or scrape of a hoof against the hard ground. But it wouldn't be for long. Not at this time of year. Not when the front stalls held the mares waiting to give birth while the back stalls held those who already had with colts on unsteady legs hovering close to their sides.

March through August always proved to be a constant rush inside the breeding barn. The ranch had a reputation for its award-winning Quarter Horses, created over a century ago. And here was where it began. From mating to births, these stalls held it all.

And her dad once handled it with grace, known for his way with horses and his ability to work with them on a level most would never accomplish in their lifetime.

She could still see him now, through the eyes of the child she'd been. So large. So strong. His worn and beaten hat pulled low over his eyes. His quick and easy smile creasing the deep lines cut into his face from the many years he'd spent in the sun.

If she closed her eyes, she could go back there. To the rides on his big, broad shoulders, looking down into the stalls at the new foals and fillies staring up at her with big, beautiful eyes. The quick winks sent her way as she sat on a wooden saddle hold, watching while her father worked with the horses. Always knowing what to say, how to soothe and comfort, easing them into doing what he wanted.

So many memories. So much happiness. And now—

Her steps slowing, her heart catching, she made her way deeper into the shadows of the barn to the stalls holding the stallions. To where everything changed.

Though she hadn't been here since her father's accident, she'd heard the story many times.

At the last stall on the right, she stopped. Curling shaky fingers over the edge, she looked inside at an empty space showing no signs of the horror that had occurred.

Nothing other than deep ruts cutting into the wooden planks where hooves had slammed, over and over again, when they weren't connecting with her father's head. His spine. His legs.

He'd known the stallion well. Had worked with him many times. But it didn't make a difference when the big horse was spooked. When the stall gate, left open whenever he tended to a horse, swung closed, trapping him inside the narrow space.

They said even as he was beaten by the weight of the frightened horse, flesh torn and ripped, bones broken and shattered, he tried to soothe and reassure him in his calm voice—known by many—that everything was okay.

Chilled by the thought, by the horror her father had faced, she wrapped her arms around her middle. Used the relief of her father's survival as the warmth she needed.

Having him and his anger was better than not having him at all.

"Cara."

Her name floated her way. The sound of the voice so familiar she closed her eyes against the swarm of memories it evoked.

Reluctant, she turned. Seeing him there, standing in the shadows with the bright sun streaming in behind him, he looked—

*Damn.* He looked like all she'd tried hard to forget. Like the dreams she couldn't chase away. The memories refusing to let go no matter how many miles she ran.

"Hello, Cade." Her voice held none of the emotions charging through her body. She refused to give a hint that seeing him again affected her in any way.

Step by slow step he moved closer. She resisted the urge to back away and head for the safety of the doors.

"Are you okay?" He stopped with only inches separating them. Close enough for her to see how the years had changed him. Gone was the young man she'd left behind. In his place was someone new. Someone she didn't know.

Except for his eyes, the rich gold-spotted hazel of all the Grady men inherited from their Irish ancestors. Weapons in their own right. Always burning hot. Never without emotion shimmering in their depths.

"I'm fine." She took a protective step back, uncomfortable from the heat of his body washing over her. "I just needed to see for myself."

He watched her carefully. His face was rougher now, lined from age and hardened by life. "We haven't used the stall since it happened." He wrapped long fingers around the top of the stall.

The sight of them sucked the breath from her lungs as she remembered when those hands had roamed passionately during a hot summer night that changed everything.

"You should." She chased the taunting images away, refusing to be affected by them or Cade. "It doesn't do any good to keep it empty. It won't change what happened."

He shoved a hand through the careless tumble of his whiskey-brown hair as he shot a glance inside the stall. "Doesn't feel right. Maybe someday it will."

Nothing felt right. Not like it once had. This had been home. The only one she'd known. The land had been hers to explore. From the mountains with their dark, mysterious caves and the cool waters of Blue River offering a wonderful escape during the hot summer months, to the groves of Pine and Aspen trees, perfect for climbing and swinging from their thick branches.

She knew it all. From one fence line to the next. The ranch had been her security, her comfort. Everything she needed. Until the night of her high school graduation. Until what she knew and counted on slipped away.

"I need to go." Feeling suffocated by Cade, by the memories she couldn't chase away, she inched around him and headed for the sunlight streaming through the doors up ahead.

His footsteps echoed behind her. She cursed, wishing he'd stayed where he was.

"So, that's it." His hand caught her elbow, stopping her with her first step outside. "You're just going to run every time I come around."

Her skin burned where his fingers touched. His scent, full of the sun and wilderness he lived by, surrounded her. For a moment, she could only stare into his hazel eyes. Stare and see glimpses of what they had once shared.

He saw it too. It was there in the softening of his gaze. The gentle tug on his lips. For a moment, they were kids again, teasing and bating each other. Searching for the next thrill or challenge raised between them.

No. She didn't want to go back there. Shaking her head, she pulled out of his hold and stepped away. "I'm not running."

"You've been running since you've been back." Anger echoed in his voice.

He risked a step forward, cursing as she took a step back. "Damn it, Cara. Is this how it's going to be? You acting as if I'm some kind of threat."

She refused to look him in the eye, averting her attention to stare into the shadows inside the barn. "It's how it is, Cade. That's all. It's better to keep my distance than try to fool myself into believing nothing has changed."

Seeing him here, inside the barn, was the last thing she wanted. The battle over her emotions was already hard enough without his presence bringing more.

"I have to go." She spun on her heels.

She was thankful when he didn't try to stop her, though the heavy press of his gaze burned into her back as she left him standing there.

Chapter Two

The ranch slowly faded behind her.

She still had time before Jackie was due to pick her up. Turning before reaching town, Cara guided her car up the twisting road cutting through the mountainside.

She shouldn't go. She knew it. But she needed to see. To remember.

How many times had she traveled this road as a teenager? Even now, she knew it by heart. The sharp curves and jutted edges caught the tires, threatening to yank her car into the tangled evergreens standing guard on both sides.

Climbing higher, the snow lingered, as it would for another month or so. The temperature dropped. Full branches hid away the sun's rays, surrounding her in shadows.

The top crest had always been the final destination. She was sure it still was for the teenagers today. Hidden from the road, nestled in a clearing, the Overlook was the place to be. Beer, music, and friends the common factors no matter who might find their way.

It was where he'd gone that night, after their fight.

*Jacob.* Her heart sighed with his name. He'd been her love through their senior year. The passion may have started to fade, the craziness ebbing, but still, she'd been sure she loved him. Was destined to spend the rest of her life with him.

Until it all went away.

She pulled over a few hundred feet away from where hard-cut boulders edged the Overlook. Hesitating, her heart pounded against her chest.

This was ridiculous. She'd been here before, back when the wounds were fresh and the pain intense. Curling her fingers around the handle, she pushed the door open and planted her feet on the hard ground.

The road was empty. The wind nothing more than a slight breeze pushing through the trees. In the stillness, there was only her and the memories she battled.

The scars along the road's edge had healed with time. No longer were there deep tire marks to be seen or broken branches littering the space between the road and cluster of oak trees climbing high into the sky.

She walked toward the trees, wondering, as she had before, what those last moments of Jacob's life had been like. Had he been afraid? Had he known the end of his life lingered only a few seconds away?

He'd been drunk so perhaps reality never had a chance to register. They'd begun celebrating soon after their graduation ceremony ended and kept it up until late into the night.

She rubbed her palm against the rough bark where his car had hit, head on, at a guessed speed of over fifty miles an hour. Here there remained evidence of the deadly impact. A large slice through the tree's flesh, too deep to fully heal.

Tears pooled in her eyes as she remembered that night. The party at the Double 'G' Ranch. Jacob's casual brush-off when she suggested he was drinking too much. And then their fight when she refused to leave with him to join the party at the Overlook.

Using the back of her hand, she swiped at the tears trailing down her cheek. She'd been mad at him. *So damn mad*. And she was sure—carried the guilt of it deep in her heart—her anger kept her from fighting harder for his keys and doing everything possible to stop him from getting behind the wheel of his car.

She *had* tried, though it didn't work. In no time, he'd discovered where she hid his keys. Had curved his large hands under her shoulders and lifted her up and away as she tried blocking the driver's door.

Watching him drive away only made her madder. Red clouded her vision as she turned, leaving behind her party.

And then there was Cade. As there always had been.

He'd wrapped a strong arm around her shaking shoulders, comforting her as he always had. They'd walked. They'd talked. Finding themselves at the river, they settled along the bank.

She couldn't say what happened from there. One minute she sat with an old friend, pouring out her heart. The next, she was in his arms, her lips captured by his, hands tangling in his whiskey-brown hair.

He ignited something deep inside she'd never felt before. She couldn't get enough. Couldn't feel, couldn't taste, to any point that satisfied her. She just needed. Wanted.

Overcome with the memory, Cara turned away from the tree, retracing her steps back to her car. A decade passed, and still she reacted to that night. Often found herself trembling in remembrance of how she'd felt.

They'd somehow made it back to his room though she had no memory of how they accomplished such a feat. Their hands roamed while their mouths savored. And everything, for that short snippet of time, felt right.

She called herself a fool whenever her thoughts drifted back to Cade's bed. Moonlight had streamed through the windows, casting a glow to surround them as their bodies met as one, sucking the breath from her lungs and searing the feel of him forever in her mind.

She'd been just a teenager. What did she know about lust? About passion? What she held in her memory was not, she was sure, anything near the truth. Her naïve mind and tender heart had created more. Created an experience that couldn't possibly exist between a heartbroken teenager and a young man on his first steps into his twenties.

Yet, at that moment, in that time, she'd felt it. Through every bone, in every breath she pulled, she took in all that was Cade.

Settling back into the warmth of the car, she closed her eyes, wishing she could chase it all away. As she turned the key, she heard the knock on the bedroom door as if she was there now, buried in Cade's arms and drawn from sleep by the pounding.

She saw it. Heard it. Cade at the door, his father on the other side. The whispered voices. The glances at her sitting up in bed, gray sheet held to her neck, fighting off embarrassment at being found in his room.

And then Cade, at her side, gathering her hand in his. She knew by the shadowed look in his hazel eyes. Took every word about Jacob's accident, his death, like a stone in the pit of her stomach.

It was the start of so much more than she could

ever imagine.

Slamming her eyes shut against the tears, she rested her forehead against the cool leather of the steering wheel. Even now, she still heard the whispers. Felt the shame mixing painfully with the heartache.

Others had seen them…her and Cade. They'd witnessed the tumble to the main house, knowing what was to come. And they talked, they gossiped, after Jacob's tragic death.

Even Jacob's parents, once so loving toward her, turned a cold shoulder on the day of his funeral, making it clear they'd heard the stories and blamed her, as she often did herself.

Flipping around in the middle of the road, she headed back for Snow Ridge. Back to the tiny apartment above her shop that she now called home. She did her best to block the dark, painful memories crawling back to the surface. Memories of the whispers that followed her. The head shakes. The pity, blame, and accusations she was sure she saw in every face she passed.

Memories she'd done her best to run from ten years ago.

Memories she struggled to chase away now that she was back.

****

It was so much like she remembered.

Jackie's arm hooked through hers, Cara took it all in, nostalgia weighing heavy, bringing back a flood of childhood memories centered around the Spring Festival. A place she once thought she'd never know again.

The salty, sweet scent of kettle corn floated in the

breeze, teasing her senses. The low hum of the Ferris wheel vibrated at her feet.

Music drifted and caught in the pines surrounding the grounds. An old-time country tune. The familiar melody pushing her along.

Making her way through the crowds, thick with laughter, she took a slow sip from her Crazy Cider. The blending flavors of apple and whiskey danced smoothly over her taste buds.

This was it. This was right. No matter how she'd argued or given a fit, she belonged here tonight.

"There." Grabbing her husband's hand while tugging on Cara's arm, Jackie pulled them through a group of teenage boys. She paid no attention to their frustrated looks as she forced them back to make room. "Madame Luwiski awaits."

Her tent remained where it always had at the edge of the game booths, tucked far enough away into a grove of chokeberry bushes to give the illusion of privacy.

"You're really going to do this?" A more recent transplant to Snow Ridge, Peter held back, reluctance clear in his bright blue eyes.

"Of course." Jackie flashed a brilliant smile. Pushing to her toes, she planted a kiss on his rough cheek. "It's a must."

She let go of his hand at the edge of the tent and tugged on Cara's arm. "We won't be long." Flattening a hand to her lips, she blew a kiss, adding a wink before turning her excitement Cara's way. "Ready?"

She was. More than she thought she'd be. Memories of past visits flashed through her mind. Two young girls, eager and ready for the best fortunes to be told.

They giggled like the children they once were. So excited. So eager.

She still felt it, though age and maturity took away some of the excitement, so much of the thrill remained.

Inside the tent, Madame Luwiski waited, violet eyes sparkling in the dim light.

She was exactly as Cara remembered. She didn't look like she'd aged or changed in all the time she'd been gone.

"Do you desire an individual or a duo reading?" Her husky voice no more than a whisper, Madame Luwiski's sharp gaze caught them both. The colorful jewels decorating her many rings danced a rainbow of color in front of her face.

"The two of us," Jackie swept a hand between them, "together."

She nodded and held out a slender hand for the money. Her lavender dress, the same one, Cara was sure, she'd worn years ago, moved smooth and light with the lift of her arm. Like a floating cloud draped around her, it glided along her in soft waves.

Jackie dug two twenty-dollar bills from her purse, paid for them both before Cara had a chance to agree or argue.

Without a word, she took the money, tucking it away in a zippered pouch she quickly hid beneath the table.

"Follow me." She stood and held out an arm toward the rear of the tent. "We'll gather in the reading room."

The reading room. Cara knew it well. She and Jackie both did. It was exactly as it had been, so familiar and comforting.

The music and laughter faded as Madame Luwiski secured the nylon flap into place then invited them to take a seat along one of the many overstuffed floor pillows scattering the pebble and dirt littered ground.

"This was a hell of a lot easier when I wasn't exploding with pregnancy." Jackie curled her fingers around Cara's arm, gently easing her way down.

Waiting until she was sure her friend was settled, Cara claimed the pillow beside her. Tucking her legs beneath her, she collected Jackie's hand into her own.

Just as it had always been. The two of them together, holding on and eagerly awaiting their futures to be read.

They weren't disappointed. Within seconds, Madame Luwiski claimed one of the large pillows across from them. Settling in, the folds of her lavender dress falling softly over her knees, she shook her full head of auburn hair and sent it falling in a delicate cascade over her shoulders.

She reached for Jackie first, folding long, slender fingers around her hands. Holding them up and staring at them, she talked about the pregnancy. Predicted a boy and promised a long, conflict-filled but loving marriage with Peter.

It was, in the reality of things, nothing spectacular. Which, Cara admitted, was normal for their visits. Still, it didn't change their yearly need to see her and hear her predictions.

Some things just couldn't be explained.

She turned to Cara then, reaching for her hands. Warmth, odd in the strength of it, spread up her arms as Madame Luwiski's fingers wrapped firmly around hers.

"Ah yes, I thought I'd remembered." She gave a soft smile. "It's been a good lot of time since you've last come to see me."

Her violet eyes softened as they passed over her. "You've been in pain for some time. Pain you have reached the right to let go of."

Okay. That was too close. Cara resisted the urge to pull free, reminding herself it was all part of the tradition and nothing more.

Seeing Madame Luwiski was about the fun. There was nothing serious to take away from it.

She turned Cara's hands over, palm side up. Letting go of the right, she trailed a soft finger along the lines stretching over her left palm. Forehead creased, deep wrinkles burrowing above her dark full brows, she raised a troubled gaze. "I sense a darkness."

Where Cara wished to laugh it off, Madame Luwiski's probing violet eyes stopped her. There was something there. Something shooting an icy chill up her spine.

Jackie sensed it too. She nudged Cara, offering the chance to escape. To stand up and walk away before any more was said.

But she couldn't do it. Something kept her there. Stopped her from yanking her palm free, turning her back, and running from whatever the darkness was.

"There is so much fear. So much—"

The press of her finger against the lines tracing Cara's palm increased. "Danger. I see it. The dark cloud of danger, hanging heavy around you. Your future faces trouble. Your fate shows such despair. Such—"

"Time to go." Refusing to stay a second longer, Jackie circled a firm hand around Cara's elbow, urging her to her feet.

Always, Madame Luwiski had been fun, entertaining. That's what they expected. What kept them coming back year after year.

But this…it was too much.

There was no argument or resistance, from Cara. She stood, her palm falling free from Madame Luwiski's grasp as she backed away from the pillows.

Before she could get away, Madame Luwiski reached for her, grabbing the tips of her fingers. "Be cautious, dear one." Her troubled gaze held tight, hitting in the core of her heart as it raised her pulse to a frantic level. "With many, I don't always see clearly what I share. But with you, the knowledge is strong, almost painful. You must hear me. Danger will be yours soon. Protect yourself."

"Come on." Jackie's arms twisted tighter through hers as she came close to dragging her from the tent.

The sounds and scents of the festival surrounded Cara as she took her first step outside. A game had just been won, the bell ringing high in the distance. She concentrated on that, on the invasion of the breaking sound, drawing away from the eerie crawl of her nerves.

Jackie led them toward Peter, frustration quickening her steps. "I sure as hell hope you didn't take a single thing she said as truth." Stopping at her husband's side, shoving Cara in front of her, she stared hard and fierce. Hands on her hips, disgust flickered in her brown eyes. "I don't know what got into her tonight, but it's a bunch of bull."

Cara believed that. At least she wanted to.

There was fear, though, sparked to life by Madame

Luwiski's dark premonitions.

No. It was crazy. Getting older didn't mean getting dumber.

She'd always known, never questioned, the entertainment value offered by Madame Luwiski. Throughout her younger years, there was never a doubt to how serious she took the predictions and foretelling of her future.

She refused to make it more than it was now.

"How did it go?" Peter threw an arm around Jackie's shoulders.

"I think," Jackie looked at Cara, at her husband, "it calls for a drink. And not that Crazy Cider crap, but the real stuff."

Cara, still a bit lost and frightened by the whole thing, nodded. If there was a time she fully agreed with her friend, this was it.

"Yes. A drink is exactly what I need."

\*\*\*\*

He watched her.

Through the colorful balloons attached to the corner of old Sanderson's booth, he kept his gaze glued to her every move as Cara and Jackie stumbled out of crazy Madame Luwiski's tent.

He'd hoped she'd be here. Was distracted to all else but his search for her.

Then she was suddenly just there. Her silky fall of ebony hair standing out against the drab surrounding her. His heart jolted. His limbs tightened at the sight of her. Just as they had all those years ago when he'd first reached Snow Ridge and discovered the beauty hidden within.

She'd been there, so beautiful, at this same festival,

reminding him of *Her*. Of all those old feelings he'd buried, only to be attacked again as Cara's sweet blue eyes met his, jerking forward all he'd sworn he would forget.

But who could forget such perfection? Such beauty?

It was as if God offered him a second chance.

God, who had taken so much for so long, finally offered him the prize he deserved. Who had left him weak and vulnerable to the hands of *Her* punishment. The one whose memory Cara brought back to life.

Then Cara had moved away and the torture he'd sworn he would escape tumbled back after him. How cruel was God to tease him so? Offering her up, a symbol of all he deserved from his sacrifices, only to punish again. To hurt. Taking her away almost as soon as he had given.

She moved past, close enough for her intoxicating scent to take over, suffocating him in all it promised.

Ah yes, he'd mourned her departure. Mourned until he'd realized the greater message hidden in it all. Heard God's message coming through, promising the best he deserved if only he practiced patience and sacrificed himself in the way demanded.

Stepping out from the protection of the balloons, he followed, checking his watch, knowing his time was limited.

Soon, he'd have to pretend to be one of them again. Another foolish, ignorant part of this town they blindly loved. Never knowing or understanding that all parts of this Earth were evil. A part of the Hell he'd been shown and lived through during the years when Saint Pedro's was the wall keeping him prisoner. Holding him in for the torture of a young sinner, kept away from society as he learned the punishment his sins brought upon him.

Patience had paid. The chance came, opportunity staring him in the face, and he'd taken it, starting the steps bringing Cara back to him. Back to where she belonged to fulfill the destiny they had in store—two souls that would come together to make one whole.

The temptation was great to take her now. But he had to hold control. For her, there must be perfection. Nothing less would do.

Practice was needed first. He knew that, had already prepared for it.

She waited for him, the one who resembled Cara but could never match her beauty or perfection. He would use her. Use as many as needed until he was ready. Until there was no doubt his every skill was honed, perfected for the one who most deserved it.

But he had plans that still included her. Plans that would let Cara know her time was coming.

## Chapter Three

It was the sleek ebony tumble of hair that caught his attention as he raised a plastic cup to his mouth and took a slow sip from the rich, deep stout.

Flanked by his older brothers, Cade watched Cara's slim, seductive shape grow closer. Her head fell back in laughter, the soft melody so familiar to his ears. Her neck arched, smooth, silky skin his for the taking.

He figured she would show up. Though he pissed her off just by being near, his brothers were exempt from her fiery temper. Of course, they hadn't destroyed her trust. Hadn't been foolish enough to destroy a lifelong friendship.

He'd seen the proof of it back at the barn where she'd left him standing alone like the fool he was. The anger had been there, as strong as it was before she left. And the guilt. It was clear to see she still held on to it. Even after all these years, she continued to allow Jacob's death to control her in so many ways. A guilt he'd once struggled with himself.

"Now there's a sight for sore eyes." The oldest of the Grady brothers, Luke pushed away from the booth, tossing his cup in the trash before turning for Cara.

Arms locked with Jackie, the two practically dragged her husband along. Poor Peter was learning what the rest of them already knew. Cade couldn't help but smile. There was no keeping up with them. Many had tried and failed. They were an entity to their own. One a simple male like Cade never could understand.

In a few easy strides, Luke reached her. Folding his big arms around her, he swung her up and off her feet. As he turned, she caught Cade's gaze over Luke's shoulder. Her smile, beaming only seconds before, quickly faded.

She recovered, he would give her credit for that. By the time Luke had her back on her feet, his eyes meeting hers, the brilliant smile had returned as if it had never faltered.

Only they knew better. Just like only the two of them knew so much they never shared with the others. It was easier that way. Simpler.

"She looks damn good, doesn't she?" Cara heading their way, Jake shot a look over his shoulder, requesting, without words, another beer from those working behind the booth.

An answer wasn't expected. Cade knew it, but still he agreed. What had attracted him a decade ago now screamed, demanding his attention.

Cara approached. Jake left him, grabbing her in a hug of his own. "You look amazing."

"Why, thank you." She pushed up to brush a soft kiss across his cheek. "You don't look too darn bad, yourself."

She turned just right so he had only her back to see. Cade caught the slight of it. Felt it in his heart. Anything that had once been between them was gone. And she had no problem reminding him of that.

****

She felt Cade's eyes on her. Had felt them since Luke grabbed her. Still, Cara ignored him, knowing she stayed stronger the longer she avoided meeting his gaze and seeing what smoldered there.

Luke swept around her, taking a spot between Cade and Jake.

And there they were…the Grady Brothers.

Their family history was deep in Snow Ridge, going back generations to Dominic Grady, one of the founders of the town. He'd helped bring in the ranching and the horse trade, breathing life into this tiny part of the Rocky Mountains.

Graced with rugged good looks from their Irish ancestors, they had a reputation for catching the hearts of many and breaking a few along the way. They were rowdy, mischievous. Loving and loyal. So much alike yet so different in their own way.

While they shared the rich hazel eyes from those before them, Cade and Jake took their fairer-coloring from their mother. Their whiskey-brown hair, deep in color, contrasted against Luke's thick black hair, a direct match to his father's. It was cut short and proper for a man in his position as Snow Ridge's Chief of Police.

They were a unique, interesting trio unmatched by anyone else in Cara's life. They'd been the whole of her childhood. Her friends. Protectors. For as long as she could remember, they'd always been there, arms outstretched, ready to catch her if she fell.

Which was part of the problem she never saw, never realized, until she'd ventured out on her own. She'd needed to fall. Even just once. Needed the chance to learn the consequences and fight the battles to bring her up again.

She shook the thoughts from her head. This wasn't

the night for it. Not during the festival. Smiling, she accepted the beer Jake held out and lifted it to her mouth, savoring the strong brew.

She looked up at the careful carving in the wooden sign centering the simple booth. *Grady's Pub*. Jake's dream when she'd left Snow Ridge and now his reality.

It sat a block down from her store, hitched on the edge of the mountain. Dark, weather-beaten wood proof of its age, it was visible all along Main Street.

It had once been the old firehouse during a time when stables graced the backside of the building. Home to the magnificent horses who pulled the fire engines toward the threatening flames.

By the time she'd left Snow Ridge, it was nothing more than old, crumbling wood. An eyesore on the far side of town.

It was clear, even from the outside, Jake had worked hard, bringing it new life. He kept the look and history of it. Using love and care, he brought back what was forgotten and neglected for so long.

Soon, very soon, she'd venture inside and discover the other miracles he'd achieved in creating his dream.

"Jackie. Peter. What can I get you?"

"I've been craving your famous wings for a week." Jackie groaned, curling an arm around her bulging stomach. "I already feel like I'm going to burst, but I must have some."

"Wings it is. Peter?"

"Just a beer. Same as Cara."

Turning to those working behind the booth, Jake placed the orders, coming back with them in his hands only minutes later.

"Handing out free booze, Grady?"

The voice, breaking out behind Cara, held a familiar tone. She turned and tried to place the face looking back at her.

"Not for the likes of you, Marshall." Jake stepped forward and held out his hand.

*Colin Marshall.* She remembered. He'd arrived in Snow Ridge a couple years before she'd left. The pampered son caught between two wealthy, placid parents who'd divorced after his birth. At eighteen, he'd left the pomp and privilege of Beverly Hills, giving it a go with his father—owner of one of the most prestigious, popular ski resorts in the area.

He looked the California type, she thought as he and Jake exchanged the age-old firm, smacking handshake of males greeting one another. Sun-kissed blond hair, just long enough to be considered rebellious, hung recklessly over piercing blue eyes. Blessed with classic, handsome looks, he drew the attention of most everyone around.

He looked over Jake, catching her in his stunning gaze. "You..." He moved closer. "I remember you. You're old Joe's daughter, aren't you?" He was smooth and precise in his approach, knowing how close to get and how to lower his lids to be flirtatious without being obnoxious.

"I am," she confirmed, ignoring Jackie's poking, urging her closer.

"Sorry about him." He shoved a hand through his hair, tossing long strands carelessly over his forehead. "I can't imagine it's been easy going through what he has."

She flashed back, saw her dad as he'd been back at the house, angry and discouraged. "It's not. But it's getting easier," she lied, preferring that to telling the truth that her father's injuries were sucking the life from him. The man she knew and loved vanishing into someone she didn't know. Couldn't help, no matter how hard she tried.

"Joe's a fighter." Jake slung a friendly arm over her shoulders, pulling her close. "He'll make it through. I don't doubt it for a second."

She had believed that too, in the beginning. Now…she didn't know.

Giving up on the idea of free beer, Colin stepped up to the booth, ordering and paying for his drink. Wrapping a large, firm hand around the plastic, he turned back with another one of his brilliant smiles. "I hear the old band has the stage tonight. How about heading over, giving them a listen?"

She wasn't sure if the invitation was for her or for all.

Cade spared her from having to find out, moving between her and Colin. Brushing close, he reached over, grabbed her beer, and took a sip for himself. "Sounds like a good idea to me. We just have to convince Jake his booth will survive without him in charge."

He placed the cup back in her hand, the look on his face hard to read. Was he playing with her or with Colin? She couldn't be sure.

"I'm up for it." There wasn't any hesitation in Jake's voice. "It's been awhile since I've heard the guys play. How about the rest of you?"

Jackie shook her head as she slid her hand through Peter's. "Sorry. I can't do it. Junior and I," she curved a loving arm around her stomach, "are worn out. The problem is, we're Cara's ride home."

"We'll get her home." Luke looked Cara's way and winked. "I've got a squad car I can throw her in the back of."

Though she'd wanted to hear the band, Cara wondered at the fact she hadn't agreed or disagreed before it was decided for her.

Didn't matter, she figured as she finished off her beer and tossed the empty cup in the overloaded trashcan. Either way, she was going.

****

The stage sat in the same place it always had—at the far corner of the festival, just out of the way of the Ferris wheel. Tucked inside a dense growth of pines, old and beautiful along the mountainside, the platform provided a wealth of scenery as well as talent.

Picnic tables, worn and beaten from weather and age, were scattered around the temporary stage erected each year at this time. Only to be taken down and stored the next day, waiting for spring all over again.

For Cara, sitting with the brothers at a picnic table beside the stage, it felt like a warm blanket settling over her shoulders. The comfort was one she savored, enjoyed. Experiencing it again as if she'd never lost it.

The band was one the town had always known, made up of ranch hands from the many dotting the landscape outside of town, using their other talents to entertain those gathered to listen and sing along with the familiar tunes. Though the members may have changed over the years, the band, aptly named, *The Hands*, remained loyal to what it was, had always been.

She couldn't be sure if it was plan or coincidence when Colin claimed his place beside her, Cade doing the same on the opposite side. Sandwiched between them, pricks of uncertainty crawled up her spine. Made her consider joining Luke and Jake on the other side.

And how obvious would that be?

Uncomfortable, uncertain, she stayed where she was.

The musicians moved onto the stage, lugging their instruments, equipment, and microphones behind them. She caught the look of one, gazing at them over the long curve of his guitar. A quick smile spread across his youth-kissed face a moment before he flattened a hand on the edge of the stage. Swinging over, his feet hit firmly on the ground.

She recognized him. Knew him.

*Jimmy Richards.* He'd come to the Double 'G' Ranch the year before she'd left. She could still hear her dad's rough voice, grumbling about the "green" they'd hired. Complaining the young pup knew nothing of the ranching business.

It was true. He hadn't. He'd come from his mother's home in New Mexico. Barely out of high school, he was seeking adventure he'd sworn he could never find in the small border town he'd grown up in and known his entire life.

Yet he'd proven himself in a short amount of time, earning the reluctant respect of not only her father but all who worked the Double 'G.' He worked hard, was eager to learn and found no problem settling in with the others.

"Was wondering if you guys would make it." Jimmy stuck out a hand.

He worked around the table, reaching her last. "Hi, Cara. It's good to see you again."

She held out her hand, meeting his. "Thank you."

"We've got a good set tonight." He swept his clear emerald gaze over the table. "You guys should enjoy it." Turning back to the stage, he lifted one last hand in a wave before rejoining his fellow band members.

He was right, Cara decided as they got underway. The music was good, lively and quick. Encouraging sing-alongs and swaying in your seats.

There wasn't much for the country music she'd grown up with back in Denver. She could travel some, find herself at one of the most well-known country bars across the nation with a quick jaunt down the interstate.

But for where she was, where the nightlife existed, there wasn't anything like this. And until tonight, she hadn't realized how much she'd craved hearing the distinctive tones again while singing along to familiar words sweeping in and out of the sometimes moody, sometimes excited music erupting from the stage.

They'd enjoyed a good hour of the fun when Luke's phone jangled at his hip. Excusing himself, he flattened it to his ear as he stepped out of the way of the table.

Cara watched him, knew the minute he went from the Luke Grady she knew and loved to the Chief of Snow Ridge Police, respected and trusted by many.

"I've got to go." He returned to the table as he set his phone back to his waist. "We've got a missing person's report I need to take care of."

"Who?" Concern darkened the questioning look in Jake's eyes.

"Gina Simms. Frank and Ruth's daughter. Seems she never made it home last night."

Cara didn't recognize the name, but her heart

Cassandra Bella

tightened with concern. She couldn't imagine such fear.

Luke bent beside her to drop a kiss on her temple. "Don't be a stranger, do you hear me. I expect to see you soon."

Before she could respond, he was off, a distracted wave left behind.

The band continued with their final songs but, for Cara, the mood had dimmed. She thought of the poor missing girl and her parents. She couldn't imagine what they were going through. Couldn't even begin to know such worry.

She hoped for good news from Luke the next time she saw him. Prayed they'd be reunited by morning.

Applause exploded as the last note fell. She stood with the others. Hands pounding hard together, she shook off the troubling thought of a missing person in such a quiet, simple town like Snow Ridge.

"I should get back to the booth." Jake shot a wave in Jimmy's direction as he came around the table to join the others. "Boss or not, I have my fair share to do before everything winds down for the night."

"You ready to head home?" Cade fell into step beside her. "Or do you want to stay a bit longer?"

A ride home from Cade was the last thing she wanted. Reason settled, though, as they neared the booth. Luke was gone, tending to more important business than her lack of transportation. Jake still had the night to spend at his booth. Hours would pass before he could leave.

That left…Cade.

Groaning silently, she did her best to hide the dread growing inside. "I'm ready." It was the truth. It had been a long day.

And getting a ride from Cade wasn't exactly the end of the world. She'd known much worse. And she was as a grownup now, able to handle whatever she needed to.

Even if he tested every ounce of her control.

\*\*\*\*

Since he'd taken over for his father and the operation of Double 'G' Ranch had fallen on his shoulders, Cade had been through many tests of his patience. Had survived situations pushing him to act even when he knew it was foolish.

But nothing tempted or teased him as much as having Cara close. Bundled in beside him, her delicate scent surrounded him, called to him.

With ease, he guided his truck down and away from the festival, heading for the heart of town. Urges battled in his head. So much he wanted to know, understand. But wisdom warned now was not the time to throw questions or seek the answers he'd desired for many years.

But sometimes, even the wisest man couldn't control himself. "So, you're staying in Snow Ridge. No running again?"

"I never ran." They both knew she lied but he decided it was best not to push it.

"Sure seemed like running to me." Cade spared her a glance, both hands wrapped tight around the steering wheel. "The question is, were you running from Jacob's death or from what happened between us?"

"What happened a decade ago hardly matters now."

"Sure it does." Stopped at the light, he turned his head, catching her hesitant gaze with his. With just a look, he challenged her, daring her to delve into an area he knew she'd rather forget.

She sucked in a deep breath. "We had sex, Cade." Her voice and her gaze were flat, no emotion to be seen or heard. "And Jacob died. That's it."

"And I pushed you away when you needed me most. You beat yourself up with guilt. And then you fled town as quickly as you possibly could." Self-disgust tore through him.

She looked at him, studying the deep lines creasing his forehead. "You did push, and I did feel guilty. But whether I knew then or not, I needed to go. I needed to leave Snow Ridge and find a life different from what I'd always known."

He eased into an empty spot in front of Precious Gems. "Why?"

She struggled to explain. He saw the proof of it pull tight through her expression.

"I don't want to claim I was weak. It feels like an unnecessary insult. But I wasn't strong, either. I never had the chance to be."

Inside the warm comfort of the truck, she stared out the window at the darkness surrounding them. "All I'd ever known, ever lived, was the protection of so many. It was such a part of me, I never realized the exaggerated extent of it until finally venturing out on my own."

"Hell." She shoved a hand through her hair. "I didn't even know I was being suffocated until I was away. Till that moment when I had my first true breath of freedom. And the first time I fell, in the early weeks of my new life, and had to pick myself up instead of relying on others to do it for me."

He watched her drift back to memories he didn't share. An odd reality he wasn't sure he cared for.

"My entire childhood was about being protected from anything and everything that could go wrong in my life. I couldn't even climb a tree for the first time without you, Jake, and Luke huddling nervous underneath, ready to catch me if I fell."

"And I had my dad, your dad, every hand that worked for them, hovering."

Cade shifted so he faced her, elbow resting on the steering wheel. His worn, beaten boot edged close, lingering below her knee. "You were the only girl. What did you expect?"

"I expected nothing. I knew nothing. I never once, in all my years on the ranch, realized how much I craved some independence. I did, though. I just wasn't wise enough then to see it."

She looked at him, a need for understanding in her eyes. "I know I was damn lucky to have you and your brothers. To grow up on the ranch."

"But…" She looked away, closing off the emotions she'd given him a hint to. "I was also suffocated and way too dependent on you. I needed to learn to survive on my own. To know life on my terms and my rules."

"And I realize, had I known that thirst for independence sooner, what happened between us never would have. We could have been spared all that came with it."

"And, *what exactly*, came with it?" Anger simmered hot within Cade's words.

Surprised, she looked back. "This." She spread her arms out. "All of this. Even sitting here now, carrying on as we are. It came from that night. From everything that happened because of it."

"So, sex with me made it all bad for you?" There was frustration, tinged with a hint of hurt, raging through.

"Sex with you was great." There was truth in her voice. "But what led to it and what came after it…wasn't. It's my truth, Cade. The way I see it."

And that was the core of it. The strength Cara knew she'd have to cling to when she made the choice to come back here. Back to where she'd run from long ago.

Her truth was hers. And it was one she couldn't forget, no matter the temptation. She had to remember the girl she was. Know it was someone she didn't want to be again.

She cringed every time Cade came near because he was the threat to taking her back. But it was ridiculous. She was stronger than she'd been. Wiser and older. She knew her way, her place. She would never be foolish enough again to depend on others or allow them to dictate for her.

Not even Cade.

"Thanks for the ride home." She bent a hand around the door handle, eager to escape. She didn't want to give them more time for argument. They used to be good at that. But she didn't have the time or patience anymore to repeat it.

Cade swung his door open as she did her own. "I'll make sure you get in safely."

She paused, her foot hovering above the curb while denial lingered on her tongue. She wanted to tell him not to bother. Wanted distance between them. But a glance over her left shoulder at the determination darkening his heavy stare reminded her there were some things not worth fighting over.

His need to make sure she made it to her place safe and sound was one of them.

"Fine." She pushed out of the truck. Stepping onto the empty sidewalk in front of Precious Gems, she gave the door a good push, so it slammed closed.

Reaching into her purse, she dug for her keys, bumping against something hard and firm as her fingers curled around the cool gold ring.

Stumbling back, she looked up expecting to find Cade, but the eyes looking back at her weren't rich hazel. They were, instead, a pale blue, glimmering underneath the dim streetlight a few feet away.

"Easy there." Large, firm hands wrapped around her arms, keeping her in place.

He was...she recognized him. Knew the face. Dark and daring, he went beyond handsome. The fine lines etching his sharp features hinted at strength and confidence. His easy smile was smooth, seductive.

*Seth Mandy.*

She barely knew him, but she remembered him.

Remembered the irritation and dread when he'd come around. The desperate need to turn and get away as fast as possible whenever she saw him coming.

Only a few months before she'd left Snow Ridge, he'd appeared, settling with his aunt and uncle on Moonshine Ranch. Nobody knew the story of what happened to his parents or what brought him from Chicago to the large, sprawling ranch butting up against Double 'G' land.

Recognition lit in his eyes as Cade stepped up beside her. Hooking an arm through hers, he gently eased her back, out of Seth's hold.

She would have objected except, in this case, she was thankful. Seth had been one who refused to take the word no. He kept pushing, in the time she was dating Jacob, for a date—dinner, movie, park and some necking. It never mattered to him. He kept asking, and she kept saying no.

"Good to see you, Cara. I'd heard you were back in town." He took another step back as if reading her need for space. An act he'd never known in the past.

Perhaps age and maturity had changed him. She could only hope. "Thank you." She accepted the hand he offered, dropped it quickly, remaining firmly at Cade's side.

He smiled, a simple, quick lift to the corners of his mouth. "I won't keep you. I'm sure I'll be seeing you around." He edged his way past and continued down the sidewalk.

He was nothing like what she remembered. Relieved, she moved away from Cade and headed for the skinny cut between Precious Gems and the coffee shop next door.

"I'm glad to know he's not the same old Seth," she tossed over her shoulder. Cade followed a step behind as they walked single file through the tiny opening toward the back of her store.

"Uh-huh."

Caught by the strange tone rumbling through his deep voice, she stopped to look back at him in the dim light sneaking through.

"What?"

He moved in closer, his warmth surrounding her, reminding her of things better left forgotten. "Can't help but wonder…" He glanced over his shoulder as if making sure they were alone. "Why was he hanging out around here at this time of night? Most of the town is at the festival. Nothing is open tonight. Yet Seth happens to be lingering around your place. There for you to conveniently run into."

"You think he meant to be here?" The thought sent a chill up her spine.

"No way to know for sure. But the Seth I know hasn't changed all that much. That I can tell you."

Dread from years before returned at the thought. She didn't want to believe that even a decade later she'd still be facing the constant push of Seth and his desires.

"No reason to worry about it tonight." Cade gave her a little push.

She agreed. It had been a great night and she didn't want to darken it with such worries. Spinning on her heels, she continued the last few steps, breaking out into the alley, dark and shadowed.

Cade remained right behind her, following her step for step as she made her way past the back door leading into the storage room and up the skinny metal stairs heading for the apartment settled quaintly above the store.

At the top of the stairs she stopped, keys dangling from one hand, the other curled around the silver worn doorknob. "I'm good from here."

She wasn't ready to let him inside her personal space. He'd already invaded more than she'd intended tonight. He'd reached his limit. And she had definitely reached hers.

She didn't see it coming, didn't have a chance to

prepare. Under the faded glow of the light pouring through the window behind her, he bent down, touching his warm lips to her cheek. He lingered a moment before pulling back, his eyes capturing hers, holding on as she struggled for a breath.

"Goodnight, Cara." He turned, was already halfway down the stairs before she realized she stood frozen in place, watching his retreating back.

Cursing him, cursing her, she shoved the key into the lock, pushing the door open with more force than necessary.

Damn him and her traitorous reaction to nothing more than a quick kiss on the cheek.

She knew better, had learned better. And from this point on she wasn't going to forget it, no matter how much Cade tempted her or reminded her of what she'd had. What she still dreamed about.

She wasn't traveling that road again. She would do good to remember that.

Chapter Four

She had the headache from hell.

Fighting against the pain ripping through her temples, Gina forced an eye open only to slam it closed as bright white light blinded her.

Where was she? What in the hell was going on?

She forced her mind to go back. To remember.

She'd had a date…with Keith. Flashes of his car sprang through her mind. His roaming hands everywhere, seeking what she wasn't willing to give.

Her thoughts sprang to the Double 'G' Ranch. The truck.

Yes. That was it. She'd been walking down the road by the ranch, and the truck had come. *He* had come.

Fear tightened around her heart, twisting painfully.

"You're with me again, aren't you, Gina?" His voice drifted, in and out, like a fleeting echo.

She forced her eyes open, saw the face hovering above. He smiled, evil tightening the lines around his mouth, darkening his gaze. "So beautiful." He hummed as he ran the brush of his fingers against the bare skin along her arms.

"Yet, you aren't her. You will never be her."

She tried concentrating on his words. But it was hard. So hard. Every thought in her mind was sluggish, almost painful as they drifted.

She tried pushing up, seeking some stability but found she was held down. At her arms. Her legs.

This had to be a nightmare. Some sick twisted game in her mind she would soon wake up from and be relieved to find herself at home, warm and safe in bed.

"It's useless to fight what waits for you." His face hovered above hers, hot breath sliding over her. He pinched her chin hard between his fingers, tilting her head to the left, the right.

"If only you were Cara. This would be right. Fated."

*Who in the hell was Cara?*

Nothing made sense. Nothing but the fear crawling through her veins, pounding ruthlessly in her heart.

He lifted, his face suddenly gone from her sight.

Seconds later, shots of pain registered through the fog holding her captive. Whimpering, the most she could do, she shifted, trying to escape, knowing it was useless.

The pain was wet and hot. It burned over the inside of her thighs, the sensitive circle around her nipples. The tuft of curls between her legs.

She hadn't even realized, hadn't known, she was naked until the pain started and refused to stop.

She wanted to go home.

"You aren't pure, but you will be cleansed." He was back in her sight, holding a small silver bowl, balanced in the palm of his left hand. "Through the boiling of holy water, I will redeem you."

He dipped his fingers into the bowl and then let them hover above her cheek as water dripped, burning her face. "I shall save you. Sanctify you. As is God's way. As is his will."

Raising his arms and holding the bowl above him, he stared down at her. Eyes flashing madly. Face tinted a bright red. "You are my step toward Cara. My gift. Her gift. Offered so all will be right when the time comes."

In a half daze, she watched as he tilted the bowl, water sliding over the smooth edge. Falling…falling.

She screamed as her scalp burned, yanking on the restraints at her wrists and ankles. Desperately fighting to be free from the pain spreading like wildfire through the roots of her hair.

"Be baptized." He speared long, skinny fingers through her hair. "Find redemption."

*Why?* The single word raced through her mind, echoing as he again disappeared out of sight. None of this made any sense. She didn't know. Didn't understand.

And then he was back, light dancing along the slick surface of the knife he held. He ran the blade, soft but threatening, along the column of her neck.

Even in her lost state, she felt the quick slice of blade into tender skin as he shifted closer. The warm drip of blood hitting still burning flesh.

He straddled her, holding the knife against her neck, bending low until his face was only inches from hers. "You will be mine. As it should be."

Cringing, she averted her eyes away. Staring off into a world of nothing, she forced better thoughts forward to fight against the knowledge of what was happening. Of the pressure against her neck, between her legs.

Instead of the horror weighing down on her, she saw and lived in the images of a better place. One full of sunflowers with bees hovering at their full centers. Rainbows gleaming in a cloudless sky. Birds singing a glorious tune.

She drifted far from the horror he created. Fell away until the pain he inflicted was nothing but a brief realization. A flash of knowledge that couldn't compete against the fantasy she'd created.

A fantasy that stayed with her until her final breath.

****

*Well, hell.* Cade kicked at the hard ground, dust spiraling up and around him.

He'd had a good few hours to labor it off, just as he'd planned. But it hadn't worked.

His night had been hell for sleep, thoughts circling, without relief, around Cara and her words. The way she looked. The urges he'd had.

He'd thought the morning chores would wear away such struggles, bring him back to the balance he needed. But it only proved to bring more questions and more confusion.

The damn woman was barely back in town and already she was driving him crazy.

Just as she had before she ever left.

And that was the hell of it. Cade stopped at the training arena to watch as Jimmy worked with young Karlie atop Maple, one of their most beloved geldings.

Ten years she'd been gone. And he would have sworn to anybody that asked he'd found his way free from any memories, any bad feelings, that might still linger after what happened between them.

But then she came back, all that wonder and flourish, always a part of her. And all he believed and counted on was swept away from the mere sight of her.

Kicking him hard with the reminder of the old feelings and frustrations he'd known.

"*Take care of her, boy.*"

His father's voice drifted back from years ago. As a young boy, he'd understood his responsibility, his duty was to look out for Cara, to protect her. Closest to her age, it fell heaviest on his shoulders. He knew it. Never doubted it.

Confident Jimmy had a good, stable hand with their newest riding student, he turned to the main house.

He'd done as he was told. He was there, always there, for the injuries and the losses. If she hurt, he did his best to fix it. If she struggled, he tried to help.

Just as he'd done the night of Jacob's death. The night he'd lost control of what had teased him for months before. Tempted him relentlessly no matter how desperately he fought it.

But damn. Cade hit the front door with more force than necessary, passing from cool morning sun to the cozy warmth spreading through the big house. Guilt had twisted him. Attacked from every angle. Especially knowing, as he loved and adored every inch of Cara's beautiful body, Jacob had suffered before slipping into death.

And how the hell does a decent man live with such knowledge?

But his guilt, over the years, had faded. And yet his passion and desire for Cara obviously never did. He wanted her just as much when he saw her standing there, in the breeding barn, as he had all those years ago.

And that was the problem.

Following the familiar rise and fall of voices, he

tried again to shove down the constant thoughts, working his way to the back of the house.

The crisp, sharp scents of bacon and fresh-brewed coffee drew him in. The kitchen, bright with morning sun, simmered in the usual morning routine.

"Things all good?" Asking the same question he'd asked since Cade had taken over operations of the ranch, Patrick Grady looked up from the newspaper spread in front of him.

"They are," he reassured his dad. Cutting between his brothers, carrying plates overflowing with scrambled eggs and crisp bacon, he found his way to the coffeepot. "We've got some fence needing to be fixed on the west end, but that's about it."

His dad nodded before flipping to the next page. "Good."

He would be out there after breakfast, Cade knew, checking the fence for himself. His heart attack might have given him the reason needed to pass on the responsibility of the ranch. But it didn't keep down the need to be part of what he'd known and worked his entire life.

"Here." Hattie shoved a full plate in his hands. "Sit."

She waved a spatula toward the table where the rest had settled before turning back to the stove. After almost four decades caring for and tending to the Grady family, she didn't waste time with unnecessary words. She said what needed to be done and others listened.

She was one of them...family. Young and foolish in love, she'd followed an American soldier from Ireland to the East Coast. They'd married quick and settled in Snow Ridge for work. Then he was gone.

Killed in a mining accident.

She'd come to them after that. Brokenhearted. Tears stinging her eyes. Come to them and found a different love. One of family. Of little ones to tend. A big rambling house to look after.

She'd come, found her place, and built her life.

Cade settled beside Jake, across from his dad still flipping through the newspaper. "Any news on the missing girl?" He picked up a slice of bacon, savoring the first bite.

"Not yet." Luke lifted his coffee cup and took a sip. "Frank seems to think Gina could be making a point, staying gone to prove she's an adult now who has no need for parental interference."

"Wouldn't be the first time one acted so foolish." Frying pan in hand, Hattie stepped up to the table, dumping the rest of the eggs on their plates. "Better that than the idea of someone being abducted around here. That doesn't sit well."

It didn't. They could all agree with that. Snow Ridge held a reputation for being safe, even in the chaos of the tourists during ski season. To think something bad might have happened to one of their own wasn't an easy thing to accept.

Cade looked at his older brother. He sure as hell didn't want to be in Luke's shoes if something happened to Gina. As chief, he would hear the worst of it.

"I've got my men making the calls to her friends." Luke scooped up the last of his eggs. "If we're lucky, we'll have her found and home by dinner."

And if they weren't...it wasn't a thought any one of them wanted to ponder.

\*\*\*\*

Mornings had never been her friend.

Shoving a hand through the tangles gripping her hair, Cara stumbled down the short hall toward the kitchen. Blurry eyed, still half in her dreams, she grabbed a cup from above the coffeepot, the promise of caffeine calling to her as she poured.

After rifling through the small pantry by the back door, she pulled out a power bar. Not her breakfast of choice, but it would do. It would get her going past the sleep still pulling her down and tempting her back to bed.

She ripped open the foil and tossed it in the trash, then took a nibble before she sipped. Slowly, achingly slow, she came to life as she headed back down the hall toward her bathroom and the shower calling her name.

Thirty minutes later, fed, caffeinated, and clean, she emerged from her room more of the woman she was. Making a mental list, checking off what had to be done, she poured a second cup of coffee and headed for the interior staircase leading down and dropping her off in the heart of the storage room for Precious Gems.

Only a few more weeks until opening day.

Looking around at the boxes overflowing the main floor of the store, she wasn't sure she'd make it. There was still so much to do, to unpack and display. So many treasures she had to take care of before officially opening her doors.

Heading for the front of the store and the wall of windows facing out to the street, she decided to start there and work her way in. If she kept going, refusing to stop, she might make it in time.

Setting her coffee cup on the floor beside her, she

knelt and grabbed the corner of a large, heavy box stuffed between shelves lining the walls of the store. She shifted, getting a good hold on it as her gaze passed over a thin beige envelope lying a few feet away.

*What in the world?*

Slid through the mail slot at the bottom of the door, it rested there alone, delivered separately from her regular mail.

Curling her fingers around the corner and turning it, she found nothing. No address or return address. Just a blank envelope, not even sealed at the top.

Pushing through the flap, she cautiously reached inside, pulling out a picture of the Double 'G' Ranch.

It took her a moment to realize what else she saw. Transfixed, like a shadow drifting over the original photo, the face of a young woman, naked and bound, looked back at her.

Horror chilling her to the bone, she dropped the picture and stumbled back.

It landed face up, the horrible look of it taunting her.

Was this some kind of sick joke? Who would do such a thing?

Leaving the photo where it was, she headed back for the counter and the telephone she'd had installed two days earlier. She should call 911, get somebody there as soon as possible.

But was it an emergency? She had no clue. It was a picture—a disturbing one—but did it merit calling out the cops and getting them involved?

The memory of the face looking back at her gnawed at her insides, pushing her to press the buttons. It could be nothing more than a cruel joke. But if it wasn't, that poor woman was suffering. She had to be. And it was up to Cara to do something to help.

She'd call Luke. It wasn't 911, but it was still the cops. Whether it was a joke or something much darker and real, he would know what to do.

Her hand shook as her fingers fell, from memory, against the numbers for the ranch. He had to be there. She desperately needed him to be since she had no other way of reaching him other than, as she first debated, calling 911.

"Double 'G,'" Cade's familiar voice broke through the line. Her knees weakened at the sound, threatening to give in.

"Cade, it's Cara." Her words, she knew, escaped much too quick. "Is Luke there?"

"Are you okay?" Concern poured thick through his voice.

"Yes." She looked again at the picture face up on the floor. "No...I don't know. I need to talk to Luke. Is he there?"

He hesitated, and she bit back her impatience. "He's here. Just a second."

There was shuffling, whispers, then Luke's familiar voice. "Cara. What's wrong?"

"Somebody delivered something to my shop." She refused to look at the picture. It was too much. "Something I think you need to see. I can't...I didn't know what to do except call you."

"Okay. Hang tight. I'm on my way."

Relief swelled. That's what she needed to hear.

Hanging up the phone, keeping her eyes away from the disturbing picture staring up in all its horror, she grabbed her coffee cup.

She sipped on it while she waited for Luke, praying her worst fears were far from the truth.

Chapter Five

She heard the truck. Peering out the window, she watched Luke, Cade, and Jake climb out and hit the sidewalk together as one.

She wasn't surprised they had all come. After all these years, she expected it.

Reaching the door as they did, Cara pushed it open and stepped aside so they could enter. Cade came through first, dark gaze intent on her face, searching for answers.

"What's going on?" He grabbed her hands, holding tight. The warmth from his touch helped chase away some of the chill.

She pulled free to point around him. "Somebody left that. It was inside the envelope, pushed underneath the door when I came down. It could have come last night or this morning. I don't know for sure."

"Hell." Luke's angry voice erupted through the store.

Cade turned, following his brother's gaze to the picture clasped hard between his fingers. He inched only far enough away to get a look at the horrifying image, cursing low under his breath.

Sensing his need to reach for her when his attention came back, Cara wrapped her arms tight around her middle and moved around Cade. Finding a safer place by Luke's side, she turned away from the picture in his hand.

"That's Gina, isn't it?" Jake moved closer, taking his own look at the picture.

"Gina." Her heart pounded against her ribs. "The one who's missing?" Her head began to spin. How was that possible? Why would anyone send her such a terrible photo of the missing woman?

"What the hell does this mean?" Cade grabbed the photo from Luke's hand, carefully keeping it away from her sight. "Sending this to Cara?"

Luke shoved an angry hand through the black tumble of his hair. "I don't know. But I don't like it." He unclipped his phone from his belt. "Not the tie with Cara or the ranch. None of it's good."

Frustration and impatience clear in his movements, he jabbed quickly at the numbers before stepping away from the others.

"How are you doing?" Jake grabbed Cara's hand, cradling it between his. He swept at a tendril of ebony hair tumbling down her cheek, tucking it behind her ear.

Though taller and skinnier than his brothers, his hold held the same strength and power of all the Grady men. The warmth of his hands helped ease the chill settling in her bones.

"I'm getting better." She exhaled deeply, chasing away some of the fear. She couldn't get the image of the bound woman out of her head. Especially now since knowing her name made her all the more real.

Who would do such a thing? Be so evil?

In full chief mode, Luke clipped his phone back to his belt. "I don't like this." Scowling, he bent down, retrieving the envelope at his feet. After shoving the picture inside, he held it up. "I'll take this and see if my officers can lift any prints."

He reached for Cara's hand. "I have someone on the way. They'll stay with you while we head back to the ranch and organize a search party."

"I don't need anybody to stay with me. If you're planning on searching the ranch, I'm going with you. I know that land as well as all of you."

All three heads shook. Biting back an angry growl, she stared hard at the stubborn, overprotective men towering over her. "You need every able body you can get. It would be foolish not to let me help when I know the area so well."

"Foolish or not, I'm not willing to risk your safety." Luke's voice was firm, holding no room for argument. "Whoever sent this," he shook the envelope, "made a calculated point to include you. I'm not about to set you out there in his reach."

"You aren't. I am." She steeled her spine, preparing to fight if that's what it took. She wasn't the same girl from ten years ago. She knew how to take care of herself and make her own decisions. "I'm putting myself out there. I'm choosing to risk my own safety if that's what it is. I'm all grown up now, Luke. I can make my own decisions."

"Damn it, Cara. Something isn't right here." Cade grabbed her by the elbow, spinning her around to face him. Frustration and fear darkened the gold rims of his hazel eyes, pulled tight the lines around his mouth. "You've just come back to town. Whoever sent this knows you—has known you. He's aware of your connection to the Double 'G.' The last thing you need to do is walk right into whatever trap he might have set up for you."

She held on to her patience, knowing it was all she had working in her favor. "I'll be safer on the ranch than here with somebody hovering over me. And I won't be searching alone, so the risk isn't as big as you think."

Silence hit, lingered.

"She's right." Jake finally spoke up when his brothers continued to say nothing.

Stunned, Cara turned his way, gratitude softening her expression. She wanted to throw her arms around him and hug him tight.

"Even your best officer," he dared a glance in Luke's direction, "won't be able to keep her as safe as she'd be on the ranch with us. We can keep her close and make sure she's never alone."

"And we can't even be certain I'm in any danger," she added for emphasis. "That photo wasn't about me. It was about Gina. About the ranch."

"Hell, I don't have time to fight with you." Luke threw up his arms. "Lock up and let's go."

"Thank you." Pushing to her toes, she brushed a soft kiss against the stubble darkening his cheek.

He reached out, curled strong hands around her shoulders, and pushed her out to arm's length. For several long seconds, he said nothing, only stared. "I don't like this. But if you're insisting on being part of the search, one of us will be with you at all times. That, I'm not willing to negotiate."

"Okay," she agreed without hesitation. "Give me a few minutes, and I'll have everything locked and ready to go." She headed for the back of the store and the stairway leading upstairs.

Cade followed, close on her heels. "I'm coming with you."

She looked back. For a moment, she was tempted to argue but decided against it, continuing on.

She knew he didn't like the thought of her going along. Would protest more if he thought he had a chance. It didn't matter to her. Like she had told Luke, she was all grown up now and able to make her own decisions.

Even when those decisions were not ones Cade agreed with.

****

Cara hadn't been inside the main house since that fateful night with Cade. Once a place that felt like her own home, she'd found only reluctance at the thought of returning.

Standing there, looking up at it, she remembered the love and comfort she'd always found inside. Before she'd allowed one night to change everything and turn her away from so much she cared about.

It was a house of character. Of many generations adding their own touch. From the simple homestead Dominic Grady built for his young bride to the many additions added on as the years passed, there remained grace in the style and build.

Bright sunlight bounced off the crisp white shutters accenting the deep emerald color of the house as she fell into step between Jake and Cade headed up the gray stone walk. Soon, she knew, as spring set in more firmly, the low-lying planters lining the edge would bloom in a wondrous myriad of flowers, creating a colorful explosion of beauty and life.

The lush lawn would turn a vibrant green. Trees,

full of leaves, would give the perfect shade for a lazy summer afternoon.

Oh, the memories such thoughts brought. Sitting under the big oak, back resting against the thick trunk, sipping Hattie's lemonade while wasting the day with Cade in whatever way they could find. Climbing the sturdy branches. Always in a race with one of the brothers. To be quicker, climb higher.

The sounds and sights she'd always known as a child came back as if she'd never missed them. Never walked away from her life here.

Aged, yet sturdy wood sighed as they stepped onto the wide porch circling the house. Ahead of them, Luke shoved open the front door, his heavy, determined steps against the gray tile floor echoing back.

It felt right to be here. In the large front room with its old red-brick fireplace, through the wood-paneled dining room, to the bright, cheery kitchen, Cara took it all in. All that had changed and stayed the same. For all the house had grown, there remained a comfortable coziness. A welcoming warmth wrapping around all who entered.

"My Lord, she does exist." Sliding a towering stack of Styrofoam coffee cups onto the kitchen table, Hattie then swept Cara into a hug full of tenderness and love. "*A stór*. I've missed you."

As it always had, her Irish accent thickened with her endearments. Stepping back, she held Cara out for a good look. "So beautiful. And so grown up." She nodded, approving. Reaching up, she tucked a strand of hair behind her ear and let her finger rest against Cara's cheek. "You are a good tug on this old woman's heart."

Dropping a kiss where her finger rested, Hattie

smiled softly before turning back for the coffee brewing on the counter behind her.

Oh, how Cara had missed her. Under her wing, she'd held close the four young ones who'd lost their mothers too soon. She'd given to Cara, to Luke, Jake and Cade the love and care they had needed while always being sure to keep their mothers' memories alive.

"My love is not to take your mother's place," she'd told them often. "It is to cherish you as she would. Keep her alive so you'll always know how much you were treasured."

And she had. Always.

"You okay?" Jake slung an arm through hers as he flashed his bright, friendly smile.

She nodded, pulling back from the memories and concentrating on what surrounded her.

So many had already gathered.

Some faces she recognized. Others she didn't. They collected around the table and hovered at the back door, voices tumbling over one another. Anticipation and desperation rose in a thick cloud around them.

As she expected, hands from the Double 'G' Ranch, from those surrounding it, gathered in the kitchen. She saw Jimmy, Seth standing beside him, both engaged in conversation with a uniformed officer. Head bent, voice low, he dispensed orders for the search.

Surprise rose as her eyes passed over Colin, leaning casually against the counter edge, part of yet another group being briefed by an officer.

It wasn't what she expected from her memories of him. Digging in, becoming a part of the search didn't fit the image of the man she'd known before she'd left Snow Ridge.

Of course, people changed.

"You are a great sight to see in all this craziness." Patrick Grady slung a loving arm around her shoulders and pulled her tight. He dropped a soft kiss on her forehead, his hazel eyes twinkling, as they always had.

Like her own father, he'd aged with the decade. Gray finding more and more room around his temples, peppering through black hair, an exact match to Luke's.

"You're not too bad yourself." She leaned in, enjoying the comfort he offered. She loved him. He'd always been there, looking out for her. Spoiling her. Making sure she was treated as another member of the Grady family.

For as much as she knew her coming back to the ranch, even her return to the main house wasn't under the best of circumstances, there was the realization that there was good in it, too. Good in the reminder that, no matter how much she might push back in her fight to keep the independence she had found, the ranch would always be her home and the Gradys would always be her family.

Through the good and bad, nothing would ever change that for her.

****

Luke pushed his way through the many bodies gathered, waving a hand at Cade. "We're covering all the ground we can. But I want to concentrate on the ranch, considering the picture delivered to Cara. I'll place one of my officers with you. Take the horses with Cara and search every acre of this land. I'll get you a good group to help."

Cade nodded. "We'll get them saddled up."

He looked at Cara, caught in his father's hold, and saw the determination continuing to spark in her deep blue eyes. Much as he wished he could, there was no hope of changing her mind. So, she'd go with him. He'd keep an eye on her. And hopefully, everything would end on a good note.

Luke's firm voice vibrated through the kitchen as he called out those joining them on horseback. Cade was thankful he threw both Jimmy and Seth in. Good riders were what they needed. And the fact they knew the land only added to the benefit.

He continued, pulling out Carl from the hardware store. Old Mr. Lancaster who knew these parts better than most. So many from Snow Ridge gathered, ready and willing to search for one of their own.

He cringed as Colin was the last Luke chose to join them. He was more than a fair hand with the horses, he'd admit that. But his quick steps to settle at Cara's side were enough reason for Cade to have no desire for him.

It had nothing to do with the deep-set need to protect her. Or the fact it just plain and simple set his teeth on edge watching Colin's pathetic act to get Cara's attention.

No. That wasn't why he dreaded Colin being a part of their search.

It had to do with his older brother unwisely settling him with both Seth and Colin. Two who had a serious problem keeping their wayward thoughts off Cara. One he could handle keeping an eye on. But both...damn. His brother would owe him in the end.

"Take these." Hattie shoved a large thermos and

Styrofoam cups at him as he broke a path through the crowded kitchen, leading the way outside.

On the back porch, he stopped and waited for the others to collect. Cara came through the door last. He saw it the minute she stepped out onto the porch, knew she was distracted.

And, following the direction of her intent gaze, he knew why.

He moved through the others, wrapping a hand around her slender arm. "Go." He jerked his head toward her childhood home. "See your dad. Make sure he's okay. Then meet us at the main barn when you're done."

She turned her tempting deep blue eyes on him, kicking him in the gut. "Just for a minute." She looked back to the house she grew up in. "So he knows what's going on."

"Go." He pushed gently at her back. "It will take some time to get the horses saddled and everyone ready to start out."

She looked at him, her gaze softening for the first time since she'd been back. "Thank you." She sidestepped around Jimmy and Colin standing in front of her. "I won't be long."

Cade watched her go, down the steps and across the gray stone path leading between the main house and the much more modest foreman's house. A path he'd traveled often. Always for Cara.

Yeah. It had always been for Cara. And until she'd come back, he'd almost had himself fooled otherwise.

## Chapter Six

"I haven't told him anything."

Standing on the front porch, Penny looked through the screen door then back to Cara beside her. "I heard enough, though. That poor woman missing. The picture someone left you." She shook her head, fear and disgust clashing in her green eyes.

"He doesn't need to know about the picture." Cara pulled open the screen door and found her dad in his usual place in front of the television.

Penny shot her a doubtful look but said nothing, joining her in the front room.

"Hi, Dad." Cara dropped a kiss on his cheek. He barely spared her a glance, his attention drawn quickly back to the news program flashing over the screen.

"Thought you were busy with that store of yours today."

Frustrated, she moved in front of him, forcing him to look at her instead of the chunky weatherman predicting calm before a spring storm moved in. "I'd planned to be, but something came up."

"And what would that be?" Though he scowled, he made no attempt to move around her. He remained still in his wheelchair, the same disgusted, discouraged look in his eyes he'd carried since his accident.

"Gina Simms is missing. Cade and I are going out with a group on horseback to search the ranch."

A flicker of concern flashed in his gaze. "Think that's wise? Been awhile since you've sat in a saddle."

"Just like riding a bike, right?" Offering a small smile, she moved out of his way, giving him back his view of the television. "Besides, I had an amazing instructor."

She'd hoped for a return smile. A nod. Something acknowledging the memories of the two of them together on their favorite horses. Girdy had been hers. A smaller, yet feisty as hell, black-spotted mare. Good old Red had been her dad's. A sweet chestnut who he spoiled like his own child.

Nothing came, though. He turned back to the television as if the memories didn't exist.

Her heart fell. Disappointed tears bit at the corners of her eyes.

"You be careful." Penny stepped into the silence, folding a soothing hand around Cara's arm.

"I will be," she promised, swallowing hard. She bent low to kiss her father goodbye. "I'll check in later if I'm able to."

She turned for the door, her slow walk, soft silence, saying much more than words ever could.

****

Penny's heart broke as she watched her go, wishing for something she could do to make it better. The screen door slammed closed. Her steps echoed on the porch and then she was gone.

"You're a damn old fool." She turned on Joe, yanking the remote from the arm of his wheelchair. Anger and frustration battling inside, she jabbed a hard finger against the power button.

The images on the screen disappeared. "What the

hell?" His angry voice boomed through the room. He reached out, trying for the remote.

She quickly, effortlessly moved out of the way. Crossing her arms firmly across her middle, she stared hard at her patient who had finally pushed her to the limit.

"Turn the damn thing back on."

"For what? So you can continue to use it to ignore the life around you?"

"It's my house...my choice." He narrowed his gaze as he spun his wheelchair around, facing her. "Give me the damn remote and leave me the hell alone."

"I can't. Not when you're so blinded by your self-pity, you can't even see clear enough to know your daughter needs you."

He inched his wheelchair closer, looking tempted to roll her over with it. "No one needs someone in my worthless condition."

"Enough." Penny's voice exploded around them. "Cara does need you. More than you know."

"What the hell do you mean by that?"

Sucking in a deep breath, she calmed her anger and fear for what she knew. What Joe needed to know as well. "That woman who is missing—Gina—whoever has her also has Cara in their sights."

Before he could argue, which his expression showed he was prepared to do, she pushed forward. "Somebody left her a picture this morning, of Gina bound and restrained. They left it at her store, specifically for her to find."

Confusion, concern, and disbelief battled in his deep blue eyes. "That makes no sense. What the hell would Cara have to do with it? She's been gone. Hasn't even stepped foot in this town for ten years."

"I don't know." Deflated, she surrendered the remote and settled on the edge of the chair.

He wrapped his long fingers around it but didn't turn back to the television. "Patrick and his boys will see she's safe." He rubbed an agitated hand against the stubble darkening his chin.

"Is that what you want," she challenged, praying she'd reach the man, the father, he used to be. "To leave your daughter's safety up to others?"

"What other choice do I have?" He slammed his palm against the thick foam armrest of his wheelchair. "Nothing I can do from here."

She wanted to argue, wanted to tell him he had the ability to change his circumstances and become a force there for his daughter. But she saw it, watched as he shut down again. With one final scowl, he hit the power button on the remote and turned back to the television.

He had to want to be there for Cara. She couldn't make him. All she could do was hope and pray his love for her would be enough to pull him through and give him reason to change. To fight for her. Protect her. Just as he had when she was his little girl in pigtails, crawling on his lap, finding the comfort only a dad could offer.

A comfort Cara desperately needed.

\*\*\*\*

In all the time she'd been back in Snow Ridge, nothing felt like home as much as guiding a horse over the rise and fall of Grady land.

She hadn't forgotten all the lessons, the time she'd spent in the saddle. At Cade's side, Cara guided her buckskin mare through a thick grove of evergreens and over an outcropping of steel gray boulders rising from the mountainside bordering the west side of the ranch.

Mischief was her horse's name. From the start, they had proven to be the perfect match. Leaning forward, she ran a gentle hand down her long, sleek neck, staying steady with Cade and his black-spotted stallion, Midas, as they led the group forward. Searching. Hoping to find Gina in time.

The morning sun slipped away as they came over the crest, edging around the sides of a modern log home tucked away in a mix of aspen and spruce trees.

Luke's place, she knew. The construction had started the summer she'd left, setting him far enough away for privacy yet close enough to be quick and handy if the moment arose.

*Like it did today.*

"I want to head deeper in." Cade looked over his shoulder, verifying the officer assigned to their group heard him. At his nod, Cade tugged gently on the reins, guiding Midas toward the river slicing through the heart of the ranch to the open land stretching on behind it.

She knew where he was headed. Toward the outer boundaries of the ranch that was rarely used. At one time, the rugged, potted land had been part of the livestock transfer between ranches. Back when the railroad was the primary source for moving cattle and horses, there had been a designated path connecting the ranches, bringing and taking their stock.

It was now, for most of the ranches, forgotten land. Terrain too harsh to be used for much else than hiding away broken and outdated machinery and equipment, aged and rusted.

It was also the perfect place for privacy if one was

hoping to kidnap and torture a woman.

Cara cringed. The horrifying picture surged back, chasing chills down her arms.

As if sensing the sudden dark turn of her thoughts, Cade turned. "You okay?"

She hated he could still do that. Still held some strange, irritating sixth sense telling him when she was troubled.

"I'm fine." She knew her response was short. Testy.

He raised his dark brows, doubt lingering in his eyes. He said nothing, though, turning his attention back to the long stretch of land ahead.

She was thankful he asked nothing more. As the day inched into late afternoon, the wind picking up the chill of the cold front pushing its way over the mountaintops, frustration began setting in.

They had found nothing. The other search groups had found nothing. No sign or clue of where Gina might be or of the evil mind that took such a horrifying picture of her.

An old, rotting cabin greeted them on the last bend before the fence line. It was where the ranch hands stayed in the days of the livestock transfers. When time was measured in days, sometimes weeks, rather than the modern-day conveniences of hours.

Cade pulled Midas to a stop a few feet away from the sagging front door and swung his leg up and over, dismounting in one smooth motion. "Doubt there's anything here to find. But we still need to search and be sure."

Cara and the others followed his way, tethering their horses to the evergreens edging the front of the cabin. An eerie silence settled. The cabin being so far removed from life there was nothing, no sound or sight hinting at the living, breathing reality existing on the other side.

They spread out, inside the cabin and around the land surrounding it, seeking any sign that Gina might be near.

"Stay close." Cade wrapped a firm hand around her elbow before she had a chance to step away from the group of tied horses. He looked down at her, his hazel gaze so intense she felt it all the way to the tips of her toes.

Remembering her earlier promise, she knew it was best not to argue. "I'll be right here. In clear view of the others."

He looked carefully at her, searching for truth. Satisfied with what he saw, he nodded and let go. "If we don't find anything, it'll be time to head back. We don't want to be this far out when night falls."

It was dangerous for even the most seasoned, with the lay of the land, to be caught at dark this far away from the heart of the ranch. Though the stars offered some light, they didn't give much against the thick, inky blackness that fell around these parts.

This truly was the far edge of civilization. Even the bravest were wise enough not to take unnecessary chances.

She didn't follow Cade inside, choosing instead to stay with those searching the surrounding ground and groves of aspen growing thick and heavy. The low-lying shrubbery spiraled long tendrils over abandoned paths and forgotten clearings.

She started off following Colin spearing west,

away from the cabin and toward the thickest of the growth. She saw it then as he continued forward—a slight indention on the hard ground. It was hard to know if it was anything. If it was a new carving or an old one.

Still, she followed it, turning off between two large stones edging what was once a well-traveled route between the transfers and the cabin.

Keeping to her promise, she kept to the wider clearings, making sure she could be seen. Could see the others as she moved deeper along the path, closer to the fence line.

She was almost ready to turn back, knowing much farther and she'd be out of range of the others. But there was something odd glimmering in the setting sun.

A reflection bounced off a thick group of aspens, not yet budding for the season. Branches, long and bare, reached up in a cold, empty show of the winter that had passed.

She wasn't sure what it was. Wasn't sure she wanted to know. Yet she pushed forward, old leaves and twigs breaking under her hesitant steps. The wind picked up, whistling through empty branches.

She came to a clearing, thick overgrowth at her feet, and looked up.

Her heart stopped. A chill swept over her, freezing her in place.

There, just a few feet away, hung Gina's body.

There was no life. No hint of the soul that once existed. Naked and bared, she was pinned to one of the larger trees, dried blood shocking against pale skin.

She'd been left crucifixion style. Her head and feet bolted to the thick trunk. Arms stretched out tight were bound to smaller branches. Her eyes were open, death clear in the thick sheen, staring out at the world she would never know again.

Shock held Cara motionless, speechless. Her mind barely worked, trying to make sense of what she saw. As realization kicked in, her heart raced as fear clawed through.

And in that instant, with a horror she had never known, never wanted to know again, she screamed with all the ugly show of death staring her down.

**\*\*\*\***

Cara's scream pierced through the rotting cabin walls, punching deep in Cade's gut.

"What the hell?" He shoved past Jimmy, moving entirely too slow toward the door. He broke out into a string of shadows growing thicker and deeper with the setting sun. His feet fell hard and frantic against the hard ground. His heart beat a terrified tempo against his chest.

Others moved as well toward Cara's scream. Cade caught them, passed them, unable to focus on or think of anything but the desperate fear ripping through her high-pitched voice. A sound he was sure he'd never heard before in all the years they had grown together.

He reached her first. She stood frozen in place, her back to him, head tilted back, staring up. He followed her gaze, his blood-chilling to the core. "Damn."

Pushing past the shock of the horror he saw, he reached for her, pulling her toward him and away from the gruesome sight of Gina hanging lifeless from a tree. He turned her into his chest, folding his arms around her and holding on with all he had as she began to shake.

"Who—"

A violent sob ripped through. She buried her head into the crook of his shoulder and clasped her hands around him, holding on with all she could.

"Who would do this?" Her breathing was fast. Too fast. "I don't understand."

He eased her away, others coming in around them, gasps of disbelief echoing through the bare branches. With one arm still firm around her delicate waist, he pulled his phone from his pocket. Using the pad of his thumb, he awkwardly punched out the numbers for Luke.

"Chief Grady." The relative calm of his voice was proof he hadn't yet heard the news.

"We found Gina. She's dead." Cara shivered at his words. He moved her farther away, into a small clearing where they would be out of the way while avoiding any sight of the gruesome murder scene. "We're up by the old transfer cabin."

"Damn. I'm on my way."

He clicked off without another word. Cade knew he would be calling the officer assigned to their group, getting more details while shooting off orders to keep the scene secure till he arrived.

After stuffing the phone back into his pocket, he wrapped gentle hands around her slender shoulders and held her out from him, needing to look at her.

Her pale face stuck out in the gathering darkness, eyes red-rimmed and swollen. She shook under his hold, chilled skin seeping through her clothes. She opened her mouth, closed it, and shook her head as tears began to fall again.

He pulled her back to the comfort of his warm

chest. Holding her, he curved a hand around the back of her head, another around her waist.

"How—"

He listened closely as she struggled to speak. "How could someone be so evil, Cade? How could they do something so horrible?"

"I don't know. I just don't know."

There were no answers. No explanations for something so horrific, so unbelievably cruel.

He wished he could do something to chase away what she had seen. Erase the memory he feared would haunt her for the rest of her life.

****

He couldn't react. Couldn't show a trace of excitement or satisfaction at his masterpiece.

Standing there with the others, he expressed the right amount of shock and horror at the sight of Gina's body hanging in beautiful glory for all to see. Her own crucifixion, saving her from her sins…the sins of others.

It was perfect. Right and fitting for what his fate had led him to. And to have Cara be the one to find her. It was more than a sign. It was words from above speaking to him. Holding him up in his acts of worthiness that would someday include Cara herself.

He looked over his shoulder to where Cade had rushed her away.

It was unfortunate he had not been the one to reach her first. He would have loved to fold her trembling body into his arms and hold her close, knowing soon the frantic beat of her heart would be all for him. For the power he'd possess over her.

For now, though, he would take what he was

blessed with. The perfection of Gina. The triumph of Cara finding her and being the first to set eyes on his offering to her.

Part of him itched to take her now and satisfy every desire.

But he knew better. Knew not to let his pride haze over what must still be done.

It wasn't her time yet. Just as he had forced himself to wait for *Her* all those years ago, he'd do the same for Cara.

For now, he'd simply let her know he was anticipating her. That her time would come. Would be glorious. For it had already been destined many years ago when she was first brought into his sights.

A destiny that would bring a perfect, harmonious end for them both.

## Chapter Seven

Cara hadn't felt this exhausted, this worn, since the night of Jacob's horrible death.

Cade wanted to take her back to the main house, came dangerously close to demanding it. But she couldn't go. Couldn't leave until she knew Gina's body was safely removed from its grotesque position on the tree and given some dignity for a young life ended in the worst of ways.

She felt connected. Responsible for her.

It was the picture. The image of her bound and helpless. As if she had somehow been tied to Gina from the start though she'd never known her. Never saw her before her terrified face gazed up at Cara, reaching out to her in the worst of fear.

"They're getting ready to take her body down." Cade, always at her side since she'd found Gina, nudged his head toward the action taking place a few feet away.

The night had settled full and thick. But where they were, you couldn't tell. Bright, intrusive floodlights surrounded the area, lighting every inch along the ground and in the thick of trees surrounding them.

A large white canopy centered the clearing with tables spread out underneath. Equipment, phones, water bottles, and crime tape cluttered the tops.

Luke worked quick, pulling in all the resources and

manpower he could from the sheriff's office and state police.

This was not a case to allow pride to get in the way. He'd known it from the start, using every power he had to bring in as much help as possible.

And the result was more uniformed officers, more controlled chaos than Cara had ever seen confined to one place. They worked quick, buzzing around Cade, Cara, and Jake—the only civilians allowed to remain—like a swarm of bees.

She didn't want to, but she forced herself to watch as four uniformed officers carefully lowered Gina's body from the tree.

Cade tried shielding her from the sight, but she moved around him. She couldn't explain to him, couldn't even explain to herself, why it was important she watched. But it mattered. And because it did, she remained firmly where she was. Refused to turn away, no matter how hard her gut wrenched until they had Gina's fragile body lowered and rested on the gurney waiting below.

Luke stepped up, draping a white cloth over her. She saw the horror, sadness, and disbelief in his gaze. Knew not even the hardest cop could sit comfortably with the hell looking back at him.

"Are you ready now?" Cade curled long fingers around her elbow, Jake coming up on the other side. At her nod, they led her away from the ugliness she would never forget.

The horses long ago taken back to the main barn, Jake's bright red truck sat surrounded by white sedans and oversized four-wheel drives with emblems from the local law enforcements etched on their sides. Lights flashed an eerie spectrum of red and blue reflecting in the dark night.

Jake started the big truck and turned on the heater to full blast, fighting against the chill settling as soon as the sun set. "We need to stop by the house and talk to Dad." He put the gear in reverse, carefully working his way free. "But, after that, I think we've earned a couple stiff drinks over at the pub."

Cara thought to argue but decided against it. The thought of going home alone with the frightening memory of Gina's body hanging from the tree was less than tempting.

A couple drinks might prove to be just what she needed. At least for now, when chasing away reality sat at the top of her list. As it probably would for some time.

****

It was odd, life as usual continued to tick on inside Grady's Pub.

Warmth and comfort greeted them the minute they walked through the heavy, wooden doors. With his brother Jake on one side, Cade stayed close to Cara's side, afraid moving away would leave her struggling on her own two feet.

A traditional peat fire crackled in the gray stone hearth centered on the far wall. The distinct scent drifted through the crowded pub, offering a coziness that blanketed over the many gathered around old whiskey barrel tables and the worn but elegant mahogany bar.

Greeted by many as he moved them through, Jake led the way to a table tucked away between the fire and the musician's stage.

Knowing Cara was still shaky, Cade helped her into the high-backed chair closest to the fire, hoping the pleasing warmth would chase away some of the bite.

He settled beside her, looking her over from head to toe. "Are you sure you're up to this?"

"Yes. I need this. I need normal."

"And I can deliver it." Jake wrapped a soft hand around her shoulder and squeezed. "I'll get us some beers and order up some food."

Cade watched his brother work through the crowds, taking the time to greet his patrons. He showed no signs of the horror and stress they had faced such a short time ago. One had to look close to notice the tense lines cornering his eyes and mouth. The shadows haunting his gaze.

"Damn." Cara rubbed rough hands over her eyes, sucking in a long, harsh breath. "It's all so unreal. These things don't happen. They don't."

He couldn't argue with her. Couldn't find any words to try and make life seem normal at the moment. Across from them, a couple was huddled close, laughing. Loud jokes rose from the young men grouped at the edge of the bar. It felt so odd, so surreal, after everything that had happened.

Grabbing her icy fingers, he rubbed them between his palms, hoping to bring some warmth back. He didn't have words for her. Nothing to take away the shock and horror of what she saw.

All he had was guilt and anger at himself for failing to protect her. He should have kept her at his side. Should have made sure he knew exactly where she was and what she was doing.

They were looking for a missing woman, after all.

One who'd been bound and restrained. It only went to figure finding her could be a dark and frightening sight. One nobody should have had to stumble on. Especially not Cara.

He knew the self-disgust quickly growing. Had experienced it before—a decade ago when an early summer night with Cara wrapped in his arms ended on the knowledge of Jacob's death.

He'd failed her twice then. Guilt and anger pushed him away, forcing him to hide when she needed him most. Leaving her, for the first time in their lives, alone to face the hell of her boyfriend's tragic death. The shame and blame that followed.

He wouldn't make the same mistake again.

****

"A healthy dose of normal, just for you." Returning to the table, three thick beer mugs frothing at the top caught carefully in his hands, Jake set them on the table and slid one at Cara.

He rested long fingers around the high back chair at her side. "Irish stew is on its way." He settled at the table. Grabbing for his own mug, he pushed the other toward Cade on the opposite side.

Cara hadn't eaten since the power bar that morning. The suggestion of food should have been tempting. Instead, the thought of eating had little appeal.

She curved her hands around the sides of the mug, taking a long sip from the rich stout. Beer she could do. With any hope, it would chase away the images she couldn't get out of her head.

"News is starting to spread. My bartender had questions when I fetched our beers." Jake tilted his head toward the crowded bar. "Won't be long before the whole town knows what happened."

"Luke's gonna have a hell of a time with this one." Letting go of her hand, Cade reached for his own beer. His eyes passed slowly over the customers crowding the pub. "Hard to believe we have someone that evil around here."

Cara looked up in shock. "You think whoever did this lives in Snow Ridge?"

The fire doing nothing to stop the chill racing over her, she looked out over those sitting around the tables and gathered at the bar. It was all so…normal. Everyday, ordinary people enjoying the night together. Conversation heavy. Laughter thick in the air.

She couldn't imagine anyone in these parts with a heart so cold.

"Here you go." A pretty brunette slid up to the table, the black and green dress of the pub employees hugging her slender curves. She rested a full tray on the edge and pulled off, one by one, overflowing bowls of Irish stew along with a wicker basket holding half a dozen crusty rolls.

Amazing scents drifted up from the stew. It was enough to make even the most reluctant take a bite. Yet, Cara's stomach turned in response.

Even though she'd asked for this, desired normal in all the ugliness of the day, it felt strange sitting there, safe and warm inside the pub…alive.

*Unlike Gina.*

The horrifying images burst forth without warning, chilling her to the bone. Would she ever be able to forget?

"You need to eat something." Cade pushed her

bowl closer. "I promise it's the best around. It's Hattie's recipe." He scooped a large spoonful from his own bowl and took a long, savoring bite.

Sandwiched between two overprotective men, she knew arguing would only create a headache. Following Cade's advice, she scooped a small amount on her spoon, delicious flavors exploding against her tongue. A wonderful reminder of snowy winter nights around the blazing fire in the main house, warming up after a day of play on Hattie's famous stew.

The brighter memories helped chase away some of the darker images battling in her head. After forcing the first bite down, she grabbed one of the crusty rolls, pulled off a small part of the corner, and dared another bite.

"Hattie should have your room set up when we get back to the ranch." Cade dropped his spoon into his bowl then picked up his beer.

"Excuse me. What?" She pushed her own bowl out of the way, glaring over the curve of her shoulder at Cade enjoying a long, slow sip of his beer. "Why would Hattie be setting a room up for me at the ranch? I have a place…here…in town. Just a block away, in fact."

He set his mug on the table, looking at her over the thick rim. "In case you've forgotten, the person who murdered Gina also knows you have a place here in town. He visited you, remember, in the form of a picture shoved under your door."

She let out a long, heavy breath. This was it. This was why they would always clash. Why letting her guard down, in any way, around Cade would only prove to take her back to that sad, dependent girl she once was.

His first kick-gut reaction would always be to protect her, whether she wanted it or not. He didn't know different, she understood that. But she wanted different. Had learned to live with different. Getting close to Cade again, allowing him to take her backward, was not a fate she desired.

"I'm not a fool. I have locks. And an alarm I'll be sure to set."

"That's your answer?" Cade grabbed his mug, wrapping tight fingers around the handle she figured he'd rather be wrapping around her neck. "You'll be safe from a homicidal maniac with a few flimsy locks and a mediocre alarm?"

There was no missing his frustration with her. It waved over her, hotter than the fire she sat beside.

"Don't be stupid." His harsh words jolted through her. "Now is not the time to play Miss Independent. You need to protect yourself better than that."

Turning on him, she did her best not to let anger take over. "Not agreeing with you, making my own decisions, does not make me stupid. I'm all grown up, Cade. And, believe it or not, I've succeeded in surviving safely for the past ten years, without your help. I'll decide where I need to be. What's the best option for my safety."

Picking up her mug, she drained nearly half of it with one frustrated gulp. Beside her, Jake wisely remained quiet, looking off toward his customers gathered around the bar.

She was sure Cade was tempted to toss her in his truck and give her no choice but to go back to the ranch with him. But instead, he pulled several harsh breaths through his lungs, forcing his frustration down. "You're going to dare to claim that you feel safe going back to your place...alone?"

"I'm saying..." She exhaled slow, measuring her words carefully. "I'm old enough and wise enough to know to be more cautious. But I'm not willing to give up my life, as I want to live it, for a worry we can't even prove is real."

"Damn it, Cara." His open palm hit hard against the wood table, drawing the attention of those around them.

Aware he was creating a scene, he sucked in a breath, bringing his temper down a notch. "There is no reason for you to take this risk. The ranch always has been, still is, your home. Staying there isn't forcing you to give up anything."

He would never understand. Sadly, she knew it was a truth she had to accept. "I'm going home, Cade. To my place, not the ranch."

The temptation to continue the argument was evident in the tight lines around his mouth and the sparks of anger flashing through his hazel gaze.

Knowing, understanding, she'd been the one to change the ground rules their relationship had always existed on, she reached out to curve a gentle hand around the dark stubble darkening his cheek.

"I'm not her, Cade." Her voice was soft, almost a whisper as she caught his gaze with hers. "I'm not the Cara you knew. I've spent ten years learning to depend on myself and only myself. I can't, and won't, go back."

He wanted to argue. She saw it, felt it.

Relief settled when he didn't.

\*\*\*\*

The clock clicked close to midnight by the time they found their way out of the pub.

"I'm walking," Cara repeated for the fifth time, Cade close at her side as she pushed open the door between the warm pub and chilly night.

Part of her felt bad, understanding how drastically she was pushing his limits. But it wasn't enough to keep her from giving up on her own wants. One of which included walking to her place rather than allowing Cade to drive her.

"You've always been so damn stubborn," he grumbled, frustration rolling off him in hot waves. He shoved his hands deep into his coat pockets and kept pace with her along the sidewalk.

All was quiet and still around them. Windows dark. Street empty. Other than her and Cade, there was no life to be found. An eerie ending to a tragic day.

Cold came in with the wind rustling through the trees lining the street's edge. Fighting back a shiver, she hunched deeper into her coat. A storm was definitely on its way.

"I don't like this, Cara." They reached the front of her shop which was dark and locked up tight. For a moment, the memory of what she'd found under the door had her doubting her decision to stay.

She chased the uncertainty away. It was nothing more than letting Cade's worry get the best of her.

"If you refuse to come back to the ranch then maybe I should insist on sleeping on your couch." Moving through the small space between the two buildings, Cade's broad chest brushed against her back as he stayed close, too close, to every step she took.

"The problem with that is," she stepped into the

alley, putting space between them, "I haven't, and won't, give you permission to stay at my place tonight. Sorry, but I like my privacy too much."

She smiled, softening the denial before heading up the stairs, aware of him fuming behind her. Frustrated steps pounded against the thin metal leading up to her door as he followed.

"Damn it." On the top landing, he grabbed her elbow, spinning her around to face him. Anger darkened his hazel eyes and pulled lines tight around his full mouth. "This is serious, Cara. Not some kind of joke. A murderer is out there. One who targeted you with that picture of Gina."

He moved in close, crowding her until her back pressed into the railing. She stretched her neck back, staring up at him, refusing to give an inch. No matter how much he tried intimidating her. "I'm fully aware none of this is a joke."

She shifted around him to thrust her key in the door. Turning the knob, she threw it open with more force than necessary. "But I refuse to change anything under the fear of maybes and what ifs."

"And if he comes after you? When you're here…alone?" Stopping her from disappearing inside, he wrapped two firm hands around her arms and pulled her tight against him. Hard sculpted muscle rubbed against softer curves.

He was beginning to test what was left of her patience. She tried pulling free but failed. His hold on her arms was tight, demanding. "I'll be okay. I'll be sure to set my alarm and keep my phone close by."

"That's it." He pushed her farther into her apartment, trapping her between him and the small stretch of wall between the door and kitchen countertops.

She hadn't yet been ready to invite him into her private space but he'd effectively taken the choice from her. The thought stroked at the flicker of anger growing inside.

"Yes. That's it." She glared at him, sparks racing through her. "And if you'll excuse me, it's been a long day. I want to go to bed."

She tried pulling free only to find him holding on tighter.

He said nothing. He only looked down at her, hazel eyes dragging her in, trapping her when she desperately wanted to flee. His fingers dug into her arms. Angered heat rolled off him, burning her in place.

"You're so damn stubborn." Cade felt her firm breasts push against his chest as Cara sucked in a deep breath, preparing for another comeback.

She'd argue until the end. Never quitting. Driving him out of his mind as she'd always been good at doing. Her constant refusal of his protection cut painfully. Worked up a rage full of frustration and fear.

"I don't care. I want—"

Cutting her off, he yanked on her arms, pulling her to her toes and capturing her full, soft lips under his. He took without asking, unable to stop the hard flow of anger and frustration rushing through. Pushing him to drive her as crazy as she was driving him.

She gasped, eyes widening in surprise, deep blue catching him and pulling him under. He knew he should pull away. Stop before it was too late to turn back.

But he couldn't do it. The taste of her. The feel of her against him, soft and delicate under his demanding hold. It was a potent mix of temptation he couldn't fight against. Exciting him and angering him in one giant wave.

He took again, hands sliding down her arms, catching her slender fingers in his and pushing her firmly against the wall at her back. Trapping her against him.

She froze and, for a moment, he was afraid she'd push him away. A flash of uncertainty darkened the blue of her eyes before she moaned, low and fierce, opening to him and deepening the kiss.

A swift fire erupted as he sought more, needed more. Releasing her hands, he speared his fingers through her hair, cupping the back of her head and holding her still as his mouth ravished hers. Taking all he wanted without caution or care.

This. It was everything he'd missed. Everything he'd sworn he would forget the minute she turned her back on the ranch—on him and what they had shared. He had to have more. Was lost to the desire pumping through his veins.

"God, Cara." Fisting his hand in the long, silky strands of her ebony hair, he pulled her head back, baring her long, slender neck. Her frantic pulse beat against her skin, drawing him in. Her exotic scent surrounded him. Her slender shape melted into him. Every curve fitting perfectly, becoming a part of his own rougher edges.

He wanted. Needed.

Dropping his lips to the throbbing vein, he tasted all that was sweet and tempting. He was desperate for her…in bed…under him. Holding tight as he filled her and brought them both to the explosive release they had once known.

He didn't know where her bedroom was. Didn't care. He wanted her. Wanted her now. He'd stumble and find his way. It would be worth it in the end.

As she shivered in his hold, he eased her around, never taking his lips or hands from her body. "Cara...where?" His lips passed over the gentle slope of her neck, the slender curve of her chin, finding and capturing her lips again.

He couldn't think straight, couldn't find the ability to speak in anything that made sense. Not when his mind was a mess with wanting her.

Cara slid her hands up, over the hard lines trailing his chest and shoulders. Hooking her hands behind his neck, she brought his mouth back to hers. Needing the connection.

Needing him.

He eased her away from the wall, never allowing the heated contact to fade. She held on tight, desperate for more.

And he would give more. She knew it, craved it.

He'd bring every inch of her body to a burning fire she couldn't control. He'd take every need she had, satisfy it until she could take no more. He would give her all until she was nothing more than a weak puddle clinging to him.

She knew because he had. She knew because—

Because she'd already been here with him. Desperate in his arms. Needing more. Craving all that he could give.

And it had ended in loss. In pain. In a thick cloud of shame.

The memory washed over her, taming the desire

burning in her blood. She couldn't do this. Not again.

"No. This can't happen." She stepped back, breaking the hold between them.

His heated gaze clouded over as he struggled for understanding. She waited, knowing it would come to him. Saw when it finally registered.

"What?" He drew in a harsh, long breath and shook his head.

"I can't do this." She took another protective step back, fearing she'd lose all will if he reached for her again. "You and I. It isn't right."

She watched the battle shift over him. Knew when full understanding finally hit. He shoved an angry hand through the careless tumble of his whiskey-brown hair. Looked at her with a mix of cooling desire and building frustration.

"When it comes to you and me, nothing's ever been right, has it?" She knew he was itching for a fight, eager to redirect his heated emotions toward another outlet for release. Whatever it took to ease the tension vibrating inside.

Sadness took over, chasing away all other emotions. "Go home. Please."

Though she knew he wanted to, he didn't argue. She felt helpless, standing there, arms crossed defensively over her middle. She knew, if he reached for her again, she'd be lost and all that held her up and gave her the strength to say no would disappear under his tempting touch.

It was a risk she feared. One she hoped he wouldn't bring.

Thankfully, he didn't say a word. With one final look at her, he turned on his heels. She watched him head for the door, pausing for only a moment to look back at her over his shoulder before slipping out the door and quietly closing it behind him.

Still, she waited until she heard his footsteps on the metal stairs. She crossed the kitchen and flipped the deadbolt on the door before punching in her security code on the panel next to it.

Relief flooded through her, weakening her bones till she felt like she could dissolve into a useless puddle in the middle of the worn, linoleum floor.

Only the thought of her warm, comfortable bed kept her upright. The day had been too much.

Too much fear. Too much horror. Too many memories.

She needed sleep. Needed time to recover and regain her senses and her strength.

Tomorrow was a new day. A day she would face with the same determination she'd held the moment she'd stepped foot back into Snow Ridge.

To be successful, independent and never again slip back into the needy, young woman she'd been all those years ago when she'd said goodbye.

Chapter Eight

She was a frustrated whirlwind bursting through the door of the shop.

Dropping her purse on the counter, Jackie turned accusing eyes on Cara. "As one best friend to another, I want you to know, I'm officially pissed as hell."

Her brown eyes shooting daggers, she crossed her arms over her pregnant stomach and shook her head in disgust. "Not a call. A visit. A word. Nothing. I was reduced to hearing it through the grapevine."

"*The grapevine, Cara.*" Her voice rose an octave, anger clashing with hurt. "Do you have any idea how wrong that is?"

Guilt set in, stopping Cara from emptying yet another box. "I'm sorry." She rested a gentle hand on Jackie's arm. "Everything happened so fast. I barely had time to think."

The memories came tumbling back, reminding her of the race of emotions taking over from the minute she'd found the picture slid under the door.

"I was going to tell you. Today. As soon as you got here. But, by then, you already knew."

"Everybody knows," Jackie tossed back. Sucking in a long, deep breath, she settled her temper. "This is Snow Ridge, after all. Secrets aren't allowed."

Oh, how Cara knew that. She'd learned the hard way the night Jacob died. Even when you thought you were alone, the gossip still came.

"I'm sorry," she offered again.

"I know." Jackie covered her hand with her own, tangling their fingers together and linking them as they'd always been. "I won't hold it against you...for too long." She smiled, easing the mood.

"The day sucked." Cara leaned a hip against the glass edge of the counter, looking out over the mix of merchandise and half-packed boxes. "From the moment I found the picture shoved under the door to Cade's kiss when he walked me home, everything about it was wrong."

"Wait." Jackie straightened, brown eyes intent and curious. "What? Nothing in the grapevine mentioned a kiss."

Cara looked up and shook her head, clearing her mind. Reminding herself, even in Snow Ridge, some things weren't known, at least not right away.

"We—"

"No." Jackie held up her hand. "Not here."

Grabbing her purse and swinging it over her shoulder, she slung an arm through Cara's and led her toward the door. "We need a real, spill-your-guts moment."

She pushed them both onto the sidewalk, stopping long enough to lock the door behind them. "And since I'm craving the pub's famous wings, I can't think of a better place for us to do just that."

There wasn't a chance to answer. To agree or disagree. By the time Cara mentally caught up with her friend, they were already down the sidewalk, leaving Precious Gems behind.

\*\*\*\*

"You and Cade are a product of each other." Jackie wrapped her lips around her straw and took a long, slow sip from her iced tea.

At the front of the pub, the scent of the peat fire drifted strong, offering comfort to those who dined inside as clouds gathered outside in threat of the upcoming storm.

Cara took a drink from her own tea. "What does that mean?" She stared cautiously over the rim of her tall ice-filled glass, sure she wasn't going to like where the conversation headed.

As she always had, she'd told Jackie everything. From the moment Cade's lips found hers to watching him walk out the door.

Some things, though, she couldn't make sense of, even for her best friend. Things she struggled with herself, centering on the feelings Cade sparked. So much of what she'd been sure she'd moved past and forgotten.

Until last night. Until his lips captured hers. Reminded her of the fire that had burned between them their one night together. A fire that had obviously never been thoroughly doused.

Jackie smiled softly, resting her hand over Cara's. "Since I've known you both, Cade's entire focus has been on protecting you and keeping you safe. I don't think he knows any other way of coping with whatever friendship or relationship you two have."

Their waitress, barely looking old enough to work the pub with her bright red hair and innocent green eyes, stopped at the table to place their food in front of them.

"It used to work." Jackie grabbed a wing and tore

off a bite. "Before Cade failed you, before you went out to build your own life, all that protection never bothered you. It was what you knew. Accepted."

"That doesn't make it a good thing." Cara picked up the cut half of her Rueben. Her thoughts flashed back to those years when she was a child. So protected. Suffocated in everything she did or dared to try.

That first month on her own, it had felt like taking a large draw of breath for the first time in her life. She'd run because of shame but stayed away because of freedom. "I never knew how much I was being held back from discovering my own strength. My own courage."

"Finally having the chance to fail and thrive on my own terms changed everything, including my drive to make something of my paintings." The tantalizing flavors of her sandwich danced against her tongue, stirring back the appetite she'd lost the night before. "Depending only on myself gave me the ambition to push on, no matter the barriers."

"Leaving Snow Ridge changed you," Jackie stated the obvious. "For the better, if you ask me. But it also put you and Cade on differing sides for the first time in your lives."

She nodded at their waitress, approaching with a pitcher of iced tea, and held up her glass for a refill. "All Cade has ever known is everything you don't want again. It's a battle, for both of you."

"Maybe." Cara shrugged, not entirely convinced. It didn't matter anyhow. When it came to her and Cade, it was best to have very little between them. It was better that way. The more time they spent apart, the less chance they'd have to battle.

Which wasn't going to be easy in a small town like Snow Ridge. Not when the ranch was as much a part of her life as it was his. And not when, she groaned silently, watching the door swing open, she visited his older brother's pub.

Bringing a rush of cold air with them, the Grady brothers entered. They were, always had been, a sight to see. There was no mistaking the blood between them. No question of their Irish heritage in their rich hazel eyes and the faint hint of freckles along the bridge of their noses.

Luke noticed her first. His smile held the proof of how deeply Gina's murder affected him. It barely peaked at the corners, never reaching his eyes as it usually did.

He turned their way, Jake and Cade following.

Much as she hated to, Cara focused on Cade, the memory of their kiss returning with full force. She saw him, pinning her to the wall, capturing her mouth with his. And she reacted…again. Her body coming to life as heated shivers raced through her limbs.

And that was the problem.

Cursing the unwanted reaction, she made a point to distract herself, concentrating instead on what was left of her sandwich.

Jake grabbed an empty chair from the table beside them, legs scraping against the wood floor as he added it to the two sitting on the opposite side of her and Jackie.

"Hello, ladies." He grinned, his boyish charm shining through. Of the three, his concerns and worries seemed to weigh less on his shoulders. His smile was genuine, reaching his eyes with a mischievous spark.

They settled in the chairs, Cade claiming the one beside her. His broad thigh rubbed against her, sending a shock of awareness through her blood.

*Damn.* It had been hard enough dealing with her awareness of him when she'd first returned to Snow Ridge. Now, every look, every touch, hit harder. She wasn't sure she had the strength to deal with it.

Unlike the night before, Jake waited for the waitress to approach the table rather than going to the bar himself. She took their drink orders, added an extra smile for her boss, then left.

"Is there anything new?" Cara, looking to Luke for the answer, moved as close to Jackie as she could. Putting space between her and Cade, she hoped to chase off her growing awareness.

"Not really." Luke rubbed a hand over the rough dark hairs poking through his chin. "We've been working it nonstop since you found her. But there's not much to go on."

Their waitress returned, her smile bright under the shock of red hair. She pushed a large frosty beer mug in front of Jake and Cade, a glass of iced water for Luke.

While his younger brothers enjoyed their beers, Luke, still on duty from early the day before, settled for his water. He lifted it to his lips for a long, slow drink. "We're assuming the killer is local."

His intense gaze settled on Cara. "He has to have knowledge of Snow Ridge, of the surrounding ranches, to know to leave you that picture."

Though she tried not to, she shivered at the reminder.

Cade caught it and looked at Cara. He wanted to reach for her and comfort her. But he knew, any touch from him wouldn't be welcome.

"I'm worried about you." Luke reached for her and, for him, she allowed the touch. "For whatever reason, this killer has you in his sights, and I don't like it."

Neither did Cade. The thought of it kicked at his temper, left him wanting to strangle somebody, anybody, who dared to put her at risk.

"But we don't know why he left me that picture," Cara countered. "It could be nothing more than leaving it for me so the ranch would be searched."

Though she did her best to put on a strong front, Cade caught the slight shake to her hand as she pulled free from Luke's hold.

He wanted to reassure her but knew there was nothing he could say that would do so. The truth was, she needed to be a bit frightened, a little scared. It would help keep her more alert for any dangers that might come.

Of course, if she weren't so damn stubborn, she wouldn't have to face such fears. At the ranch, she'd be safe. He wouldn't have to worry about anyone getting to her.

"And if it is more?" Cade pushed. "What if he has more planned than a picture shoved under the door?"

She shot an angry glare his way. "Then I'll find a way to deal with it." She shoved her plate out of the way and pushed to her feet. "I don't have the time to argue with you again. I need to get back to setting up the store."

She pulled a twenty out of her wallet, dropping it on the table. "This should cover lunch." Before Jake could object to her paying for her food, she was at the door with Jackie close behind.

Cade watched her go. His emotions a tangle between frustration, fear…attraction.

It wasn't a good combination. Groaning silently, he raised his mug to his mouth, finishing off what was left with one large swallow.

"She's definitely grown into that stubborn streak of hers." Luke took a sip from his water. "And just like when we were kids, you seem damn good at testing the limits of it."

"We're damn good at testing each other's limits." Cade ran hard fingers over the throbbing in his temples before signaling their waitress for another beer. Midday or not, he needed it.

"Do you think she's in danger?" Jake looked briefly at his older brother before turning back to their waitress approaching, ordering another beer and a platter of Irish Nachos to share.

Luke's worried gaze said it all. "There's no evidence it's anything more than Cara suggested, using her to make sure we searched the ranch. But my gut tells me there's more. That Cara is purposely being brought into this as someone's sick, twisted game."

It was exactly what Cade feared. What he wished Cara would understand.

It was beyond what was or wasn't between them. It was about an evil mind who had already killed once. Who had Cara in his sights and could easily be looking to her for his next victim.

****

Joe sat in his wheelchair, staring at the television without seeing a thing.

He knew what he had to do. But he hated having to

do it. Asking for help ate at him. Made him feel like nothing more than a worthless old fool, better off put to pasture then cause trouble for others.

But he had no choice. A once quick walk between his place and the main house was a nearly impossible chore stuck in this damn wheelchair. He would need Penny's help. Dreading it, hating it as he did, there was no other way to get to Patrick. To get the truth.

He'd heard them this morning.

Hattie had been at the door barely after the sun had risen, carrying a large plate overflowing with her homemade cinnamon rolls. "I made a big batch so there'd be plenty to share."

The sweet, tantalizing scent filled the house as Penny ushered her to the kitchen. She returned, a cup of coffee and two rolls arranged on a plate for him. Made sure he had all he needed before disappearing again.

He would have been satisfied sitting there, savoring her cinnamon rolls and watching his news programs. But the quiet got to him, stirring his curiosity.

Two ladies, usually so loud in their laughter and conversation when they visited, carried on in hushed tones, mere whispers drifting back from the kitchen.

He wouldn't have given it a second thought. But Penny's words about Cara worked their way back to his mind.

Words that he'd had a hard time fighting off when he'd first heard them and couldn't forget as their lowered, cautious voices reached his ears, pushing worry for his daughter back to the surface.

Knowing better than to lower the volume on the television, a true way to get Penny's attention and end whatever they discussed, he eased to the archway between the front room and kitchen, straining to hear what he could.

Cara's name was there. And the missing woman's. He picked up on bits and pieces. None of it he liked. He understood the mention of death and Cara being near it.

But even in the words filtering in and out, making little sense, he heard something else—clear and undeniable fear, dark and potent in their voices.

Fear that pushed from the kitchen to surround him where he sat and listened.

It lingered still, hours later. Long after Hattie said her goodbyes and Penny started her daily chores. Around him, in his heart and mind, that fear stayed, refusing to be chased away.

There was something—something no one thought to tell him, even when it involved his daughter. He needed answers. Knew only one would give him the direct truth. Only one would treat him as he always had.

*Patrick Grady.*

His old friend wouldn't sugar coat, wouldn't try hiding the facts simply because he was now rendered useless in the damn wheelchair. All Joe needed to do was ask, and he'd get the answers he wanted.

But first, he had to get there.

Reminded of the restrictions weighing on him, he faced the temptation to slip back into not giving a damn. To turn back to his news program and lose himself in others worries and problems so he wouldn't have to concentrate on his own.

He fought it. He couldn't give in this time. Not with Cara involved.

And so, he prepared to do what he despised and

expose his weakness by asking for help.

"I need to get to the main house." His harsh tone caught Penny by surprise as she came out of the bathroom, hands weighed down by a basket of dirty laundry. "Today. As soon as possible."

She looked at him, green eyes wide and questioning. "Okay." She didn't ask for any information though he saw, in her gaze, the need to do so. "Let me get this last load started, and we'll head over."

He nodded, satisfied.

She headed for the laundry room at the back of the house as he turned back to the television to wait.

Soon, he'd know what the hushed voices were hiding.

Soon, he'd know the truth about what was happening with his little girl.

Chapter Nine

Back turned, Patrick dropped three ice cubes into two small glasses then half-filled them with his treasured Irish whiskey.

Inside the subdued comfort of his office, where their past had brought them together many times, Joe took the drink from his old friend and watched while he settled in the gray leather recliner across from him.

Their decades-old friendship was more than one working for the other. More than a shared love for the ranch, the land, and the horses.

They also found strength and loyalty in the loss they had suffered. They mourned, in the same year, the deaths of their wives. Only two months after Patrick's wife lost her battle with cancer, the knock came on Joe's door. Two State Patrol Officers, hats in their hands, told him the horrific truth. A semi lost control on the interstate, his wife's car was one of three he struck. There were no survivors.

Many nights they'd come together. A drink in their hands, sitting in silence. Needing no words, only companionship of two men suffering horrible holes in their hearts. Understanding the hell the other struggled through.

"Penny will have my hide if she learns I'm drinking this." He raised his glass in a toast and savored a long sip of the amber liquid. It had been so long—too long—since he'd sat inside the welcoming warmth of Patrick's office, enjoying a drink with him.

And he had only himself to blame. The realization hit hard. Since his accident, he'd done all he could to cut Patrick, along with all others, from his life.

Even now, he wouldn't be here, would have never taken this step, if worry for Cara hadn't driven him to do so.

"What she doesn't know won't hurt her." Patrick took his own sip then cradled his glass on the arm of his chair. "How you doing, Joe?"

He shrugged, not wanting to share such details. "I'd be better if I knew what the hell was going on with my daughter."

"What do you know?"

"Not enough." Frustration tightened his hold around his glass. "Only so much I can pick up with all the damn whispering going on. I know about the picture sent to her. About finding the missing woman and Cara being part of it."

"She's the one who found her." Patrick's words were slow and cautious. "Out by the south fence line. She was—" His gaze troubled, he took another long, slow drink from his whiskey. "She was hung, naked, crucifixion style from a tree. My boys say it was a horrible, gruesome sight."

"Damn." Joe smacked his hand hard against the arm of his wheelchair, vibration shooting painfully up his arm. "How the hell did Cara end up the one to find her?"

"No." He shook his head as Patrick opened his mouth to respond. "Don't answer that. I already know."

She was stubborn as hell. A lethal mix she

inherited from both him and her mother. And she'd grown up surrounded by the rough tumble of ranch life. Spent her childhood with three rambunctious boys who ran reckless over the land.

Fear wasn't something she was good at accepting or admitting to. "The one who sent her the picture, he's the one who killed that woman and hung her from the tree?"

"Luke believes it is." Concern danced in the shadows darkening Patrick's expression. "Too much connection to think otherwise."

It was what Joe knew but didn't want to hear. He glanced out the window at the evening growing dark, his thoughts on the one threatening his daughter. "She can't be out there alone. It's not safe."

Patrick's answering look was cautious. "She won't accept anything different. She's insisting on staying alone at her place in town. Hattie had her room ready for her. She turned it down."

Though the truth terrified Joe, it didn't surprise him. He'd watched his girl since she'd left Snow Ridge behind, seen the changes, understood the experiences she'd found.

None of it mattered. Not when her life might be in danger. "She's a good girl. Knows how to take care of herself. Still, I don't like it. Don't like the thought of her alone while some crazed killer is on the loose."

In the months he'd been bound to his wheelchair, he'd never felt as helpless as he did then. He wanted back the man he was. The one who had the ability to climb in his truck, toss his daughter over his shoulder and bring her back here. To the ranch. To the one place he knew she would be protected from harm.

"Luke's got a patrol passing by her house. Jake's place is a block away." Patrick finished off what was left of his whiskey. "And Cade's barely let her out of his sight. She's not alone. Not really."

It helped to know but still came short of easing his fears. Only having Cara in front of him, safe and sound, would do that. And with as stubborn as she was, as helpless as he was, it wasn't something he put much faith into happening.

****

Living alone for a decade, Cara was used to silence, enjoyed it more times than not. But tonight, the quiet rubbed wrong and brought a hint of worry to the surface.

She curled her fingers around the slender top of the wine bottle she'd fetched from her apartment and poured a hefty share into the wine glass sitting on the glass countertop inside the store. She needed it, not just to take a layer off the worry but to help her get through the mind-numbing paperwork she continued to put off.

Opening day was coming quick. She'd filed for all the necessary licenses and was waiting for them. But inventory still needed to be logged and accounts created. For her creative mind, such things took their toll.

She'd push through though, taking care of what needed to be done. And tonight was the perfect time to do it.

After a long afternoon, unpacking and organizing stock, Jackie had headed home, reminding her to lock up behind her.

Fat flakes of snow began falling soon after, confirming what she'd already planned, staying inside in the warmth instead of venturing out in the cold. It was her, a bottle of her favorite Chardonnay, and piles of paperwork.

The sudden knock on the front door vibrated through the shop. Lost in the rows of numbers dancing before her eyes, she jumped. Wine swirled in her glass and came close to spilling over the rim.

Sucking in a deep breath, willing her heart to slow, she set her wine on the counter and turned for the door. Unease set in as she strained to make out the dark figure looming on the other side of the glass.

Dark images of the picture left, Gina's naked body hanging from a tree, flashed through her mind, slowing her steps. Streetlights cut shadows through the thick snow, casting a strange glow on whoever waited at the door.

For a moment, she was tempted to turn around and call the police. Would have if she didn't catch the hand lift, waving at her. The flash of white teeth behind the friendly smile.

A few feet away from the door, she paused. Slowly, through the white flakes, she saw the familiar face.

Shocking blue eyes. Careless tumble of blond hair.

*Colin Marshall.* He stood in the wet, mountain cold, peering through the door of her store, looking about as pathetic as she ever remembered seeing him.

Fear draining, she covered the last few steps with quick, long strides. "Are you crazy?" She swung the door open, standing to the side to allow him in. "It's freezing cold out there."

"It's not too bad." He shook snow from his coat as he moved farther in, taking in the wide variety of

119

merchandise already unpacked and displayed for purchase. "Wow. Look at this."

He offered a quick smile as he moved between the various displays. Cara watched him from where she stood by the door, the cold he brought in lingering. "Jackie and I only have about half unpacked. By opening, there'll be much more to see."

He returned to her side, his bright blue eyes continuing to stroll through the store. "I'm impressed. You've done well."

"Thank you."

She waited for him to say more, curious why he'd come and eager to get back to the half-finished glass of wine she'd left on the counter.

Though she didn't fear him, unease took root as he stood silent, staring at her. "Sorry for coming by so late." His deep voice broke through the quiet. "I was leaving the market and saw the store lit up."

His blue eyes caught hers and held firm. "I didn't get your number the other night at the festival, so I figured I'd see if you were around. See if you wanted to head over to Jackson's Steakhouse Friday night for dinner. His place is still the best around for prime rib."

She thought for a minute of accepting. To have a reason to take a break and enjoy a single night out on an innocent date, something she hadn't done in way too long.

But, even as she considered it, she knew she wouldn't be going. "I'm sorry, Colin. I have so much to take care of. I can't commit to anything right now."

A flash of anger darkened his gaze, but he chased it away and forced a smile. "Seems to me, with all this work, you deserve a break."

"Maybe. But I can't afford to take one right now."

He looked tempted to argue more, obviously not used to being turned down.

She didn't want to hear what he had to say, knowing there was no chance of being persuaded to answer differently. "And right now, I really need to get back to work." She turned for the door and waited until he followed.

Anger flashed again in his blue gaze as he paused at the door, hand resting on the smooth silver handle.

She waited for him to try again, relieved when he said nothing. Yanking on the door, he stepped into the snow falling even harder than it had before.

Releasing a thankful sigh, she flipped the lock and went back to the work waiting for her.

Colin was handsome. She had no problem admitting that. And from the time she'd spent with him, she knew he was a smooth character, fitting into just about any situation and easy to get along with.

A date with him, a break from all that had happened, would have been nice. She didn't doubt it for a minute. She wouldn't have regretted dinner with him. Would have said yes except—

*He wasn't Cade.*

Damn it. She grabbed her wine glass and took a long, slow sip. She wasn't going to go there. It was useless territory to roam.

All she needed to concentrate on was getting Precious Gems up and going and setting the foundation for the future she had planned.

A future that did not include Cade. One that left the past far behind, where it belonged.

\*\*\*\*

Had he been asked if he was a jealous man, Cade would have answered no, without question.

But then Cara sauntered back into town and turned around everything he thought he knew. Believed he had dealt with.

Both arms wrapped around the top curve of the steering wheel, he watched Colin come out of Cara's place. He paused on the snow-slick sidewalk before turning and walking off in the opposite direction from where Cade sat inside his idling truck.

He'd been there long enough to watch Colin knock before disappearing inside. He'd wanted to barge in and put an end to whatever he had in mind. And he had something in mind. That much Cade knew.

But he didn't figure Colin presented any threat. At least not at the moment. And since that was his excuse for sitting a few spaces away from Precious Gems, watching closely all that might happen, he couldn't justify following Colin through the door. Though every part of him demanded he do exactly that. Storm in and stop whatever encouraged Colin to visit Cara at such an odd time.

And sitting there now, snow falling in heavy, thick flakes around him, he knew he still had no good reason to go in.

Cara would be pissed. Oh, how she would be pissed. His hovering outside her place, watching her without her permission, would send her off on another one of her tyrants. The ones that always included how independent she was now. How much she didn't need him looking out for her or protecting her.

*Yeah.* Hattie had taught him well from her beliefs for respectful Irish lads. It wasn't as if he had old, sexist views when it came to his need to look out for Cara.

He didn't want to suffocate her. Didn't want to control or dictate what was or wasn't good for her. He just wanted to do what he'd always known. What was as much a part of him as every breath he took.

Look out for her. Protect her, as best as he could, from any pain or harm that might come her way.

Still, the urges were hard to fight. Just one sight of her, one chance to take in her delicate, innocent beauty before facing a long, cold night parked in front of her store, was more tempting than any wrath she might send his way.

And maybe, if he was lucky, he would find out what exactly Colin wanted from her at such a time of night.

Decision made, he turned the key in the ignition, killing the engine and the hot air blowing through the vents, fighting off the chill of the storm.

He would check in, say a quick hello, and then be gone again. No harm done.

Even as he thought it, he knew better. There was nothing quick and simple when it came to Cara, nothing at all.

Reaching the glass door fronting her shop, he knocked, waited. With the glare of light shining on the other side, he saw her perfectly. The caution in her moves as she set down her wine glass. The hesitation in her eyes as she drew closer and peered hard through the glass, searching to recognize the face looking back at her.

He knew the minute she did. Every emotion sparking in her deep blue gaze turned to a mixture of dread and suspicion. There was nothing happy about her as she reached the door and clicked the lock open.

"What are you doing here?" She cracked it open wide enough to stick her head through. Small enough to ensure he couldn't get through unless he wanted to run her over in the process.

"I was at the pub." It wasn't a lie. *He'd been there.* Stopped in when he'd first reached town. "I saw Colin coming out. Thought I would check in and make sure everything's okay."

The look in her eyes was doubtful. "It's fine." She didn't budge—didn't open the door any wider. "He just stopped by to ask me to dinner Friday night."

Cade bit back his angry retort, knowing it wouldn't go over well. Snow fell around him. Cold penetrated through his worn leather coat. Restricted to the sidewalk in the frosty night while Colin was allowed inside didn't sit well at all.

He knew it was wrong, but at that point, he didn't care. Knowing she couldn't stop him, he pushed in closer, wedging his body between her and the door until she had no choice but to step back and allow him inside.

"I'm busy, Cade." She glared at him. "I don't have time for whatever it is you want."

He saw the temptation to shove him right back through the door he'd forced his way through. If she'd thought she had even the slightest chance of being successful, he was sure she would have tried.

"Go back to what you were doing. Don't let me stop you." He shrugged and took a firm stance, letting her know he didn't plan to go anywhere. She fisted her hand and he was sure she wished she could land it in his gut.

Blowing out a harsh breath, she turned her back on him and made a direct line for her wine. "What do you want?" She wrapped tight fingers around the slender stem and took a stabilizing drink.

"I told you." He came at her, hitching a hip against the corner of the counter. "I wanted to make sure everything was okay."

He hovered close, knowing it would bother her.

The wine in her glass swayed. Cursing, she set her Chardonnay on the counter behind her. "And I told you, everything is fine. So, obviously, there's no reason for you to stick around."

He noticed the tremble, the passionate darkening of her deep blue eyes. The red stain growing over her high cheekbones. Only a sick man would enjoy her suffering the way he was.

But who could blame him? She pushed hard and ran often. Gave preference to those like Colin who did nothing for her, he was sure, only to leave him suffering in the cold with his need for her. For all she promised in the sexy, frustrating, intriguing woman she was.

She wanted him as badly as he wanted her. She just preferred to be annoyingly stubborn and do all she could to deny the heat sparking between them. Deny what was true and passionate between them.

"I can think of many reasons to stick around." He pressed in closer, forcing her to arch her neck, bare the lovely ivory skin for his taking.

He pressed two fingers against the pulse line beating along the delicate curve. "This," he looked hard into her eyes as he flattened his hold firmly against the desperate rhythm, "is enough to know there's something worth staying for."

Her eyes widened, but she didn't protest. Taking advantage of her momentary lack of response, he grabbed her arm and spun her around until her firm, beautiful breasts pressed against his chest. Teased him. Tempted him with all that ran hot and desperate through his blood.

He wanted her. Oh, how he wanted her. Every bone in his body cried out for the treasure of her pinned underneath him, gasping in unrelenting frenzy. Falling, again and again, against her, driving them higher, crazier than they had ever been.

"Please, Cade. Just go." She flattened her hands below his shoulders, a weak push doing nothing to move him. She turned her eyes away, staring at the shelves over her right shoulder.

Hooking a demanding finger under her delicate chin, he forced her gaze back to his. "Why are you so desperate for me to go?" Leaning low, he dragged his lips over the pulsing line gracing the curve of her neck to the delicate slope of her shoulder. "Because you want to deny this?"

His rough hands traveled over the slender grooves of her waist to tease the sides of her breasts. "Because you want to keep pretending there is nothing between us?"

He caught her deep blue gaze, building the desire raging hot and needy around them, before he lowered his head, catching her supple lips in a kiss exploding with all that battled inside, demanding release.

She sighed, soft and sweet, under his hold. It was all he could do not to push for more. Head them in the right direction, satisfying what they both wanted so desperately.

But this wasn't the night for that. This was the night to show Cara, to prove to her, how hot her blood burned for him. How deep their desire ran. Fusing them together in a flame of need so great there was no fighting it.

As he took control of her mouth, his hands roamed, feeling every curve, every line. Seeking the round sweetness of her breasts, he rubbed his thumb over the hardened nipple.

"Oh, God...Cade."

Cara's heart pounded painfully against her chest. Her blood ran hot, turning everything inside to a desperate, needy rush she couldn't control. Couldn't stop.

Her hands sought, needing the strength of him. She trailed gentle fingers over corded muscles and pushed up over his broad shoulders, holding on as if her life depended on it.

His hungry mouth strayed, trailing a line down the slope of her chin, the curve of her neck, finding the low-cut center of her shirt. He dipped lower, finding and lavishing the sensitive groove between her breasts, teasing, torturing. His tongue grazed against the curve of her breast, promising more without ever following through.

She needed—

So much. Too much. There was no connection with reality. With sensible thought. There was only Cade and her. Together in the reminder of all they had known. What they could have again.

He backed her up, trapping her between the counter at her back and the firm, deep-cut shape of him pressing seductively against her.

"This, Cara…" His mouth found and claimed hers again. "This is what we are. What is good between us." He buried long fingers in the soft fall of her hair, holding her captive, refusing to let go.

"You can try, but you will never be able to deny this. Deny us." Tightening his hold in her hair, he nipped at her bottom lip.

She moaned, low and desperate, swaying into him. Surrounded by the heat of him, she could only give in to what he offered. Taking it. Needing it. His scent—full of earth and sun—teased her. Drawing her to want more, knowing she would never fully be satisfied.

Cursing, he stepped away, leaving the chill of separation to jolt her back to awareness.

She looked at him, confusion running through her as she shook her head.

"I'm going to go." He brushed the pad of his thumb over her lips, swollen from his kiss. "Just as you asked."

He reached behind her, picking up her wine glass. "But, when you're ready to accept what's between us I'll be here." He gathered her shaking hand into his and pushed her Chardonnay into her hesitant grasp. "Ready for you. For everything that could be so good between us."

Not bothering to wait for an answer, he spun on the heels of his boots, never looking back as he headed for the door.

She said nothing, made not a sound, as he stepped outside onto the slippery sidewalk quickly growing thick with snow.

It took several seconds to regain her composure enough to follow his path to the door, flipping the lock into place.

She caught sight of him outside the door, waiting there on the sidewalk, and knew he stayed to make sure she locked up behind him. Because that was Cade. That would be who he always was.

## Chapter Ten

*Sweet Gina.*

She'd been so perfect. In the timing. In the chance to pick her up on the side of the road, desperate for a ride. He'd barely learned of Cara's return when she'd presented herself, given him the opportunity he prayed for.

But she'd been a risk. He'd known that from the minute he took her. She was part of the town, known and missed by many. It was too close. Too risky.

There was no way he could expect his good fortune to carry through a second time.

Needing the practice that he did was not equal to placing himself in such risky situations. He could do all he needed, give himself to becoming the perfect pursuer for Cara, without bringing such uncertainty his way.

There were many. Many who would do, offering exactly what he needed to find perfection. Taking another from Snow Ridge would be foolish.

He could do better. *Would do better.*

His truck idling behind the stretch of pines lining the busy gas station, he watched and waited. Here, right off the interstate, there was so much to offer. So many opportunities.

They came, one after another, exiting for gas, bathroom breaks, and food. All the regular needs for those traveling the long stretch of interstate.

He saw, calculated so many.

There was the one, in her pretty red convertible, so like *Her*. Tempting him to grab her, use her as his personal validation for all he struggled and fought to prove and become.

But…no. It would never work. That was Cara. She was the one so close to *Her*. The one who would give him the redemption he'd sought for so long.

So, he waited…watched.

He didn't fear being noticed, even so close to the heart of town. It was Sunday. It was snowing. Snow Ridge either sat properly in their pews or kept themselves warmly tucked away in their homes.

Only the travelers, facing the constant change of weather along this stretch, were out to be seen and noticed by him.

Even the clerk, who he knew well, had no idea he hovered outside her sight. Watching. Waiting for the chance to become better. Perfect all he was meant to be. So Cara would know and understand how important she was. How much he had worked and given to become the one worthy of her ultimate sacrifice.

The chilly morning stretched into afternoon then into early evening. Still, he waited in the falling snow. Knowing she was out there, waiting for him.

A soft blue compact with Nevada plates pulled in, cigarette smoke and the latest pop hits spiraling through the crack in the driver's side window.

He watched, caught by the sight of her and the soft black curls tumbling down her back as she crawled out of the confines of her car. Still, he wasn't sure. Didn't know if she was the one.

Until he saw it—the delicate golden cross falling

between her ample breasts. Its simple shape, the reminder of all it stood for, called out. Grabbed and pulled him in.

It was another sign. One he'd come to expect. Telling him he was doing right, following the proper path from those who ruled above.

She was the next fated to be his. And as she popped the cover for gas on the side of her car, paying no attention to those around her, he approached.

She was his. And with a few swift moves, he made it clear that everything she'd known had drastically changed with what he had in store for her. With what he would carry out by the direction of those who guided him as they had for so long. For the many, many years he'd suffered under the belief of absolute law. The evil truth coming with it.

****

Cade was beyond tired. Exhaustion gripped him from head to toe. Left him desperately needing a warm, comfortable bed to collapse into and sleep for a good week or more.

"Killing yourself isn't going to do you or Cara any good." From across the kitchen table, Patrick shook his head.

"Stupid, stubborn woman," Cade grumbled into his half-full cup of coffee, earning a smack against the back of the head as Hattie entered the kitchen.

She turned on him, hands on her ample hips. "Seems to me you're the stubborn one. Cara's gone and made her decision to stay at her place. You're the one refusing to accept it. Camping outside her store and refusing to believe she's capable of taking care of herself."

"In normal situations, I'm sure she's fine at taking care of herself." Cade chased away his answering scowl as she narrowed her eyes. He knew that look too well. Only a fool would ignore it. "But it's far from normal when some sick monster is out there murdering innocent women."

"I don't like it either." Hattie turned away to grab the coffee pot. "I'd rather she be here with us." She filled his cup then set the pot on the table within easy reach.

"But I also respect the fact she's chosen not to run in fear. You should try doing that, too."

Cade grabbed his cup and lifted it to his mouth, hiding his returning scowl behind the rim. It wasn't a lack of respect for Cara's choice…was it?

He hadn't tried forcing her to the ranch. Had backed off from pushing her in that direction. He'd simply decided to take matters into his own hands to keep an eye on her. It was fear driving him, not a lack of respect.

*Hell.* He ran a rough, frustrated hand through his hair. Why did women always have to be so complicated? Men he understood, never having to question his response or actions.

But women, especially one in particular, left him frustrated and confused, trying to figure out what exactly they wanted. What was right and what wasn't when it came to understanding their needs. Their wants.

"Joe's got her coming by tonight," Patrick told Cade, recognizing the confusion mixing with fear shadowing his face. It was one most men understood when it came to finding their way through the unknown territory of a woman who'd firmly found her way into your heart.

Not that his son had figured out that Cara had indeed found her way to his heart. Such a realization still needed time. "He's hoping he can get her to see she'd be safest here on the ranch."

"Good luck with that," Cade grumbled, earning a stern look from Hattie.

"I know…I know." He held up a hand before she repeated her lecture. "No matter what happens, it has to be her choice."

He grabbed the coffeepot, refilling his cup to the rim. "I'm going to take a long hot shower before meeting Luke over at the south fence line. They're clearing the scene today."

Hattie watched him go, clucking her tongue as she turned back to Patrick sitting at the table. "*A stór*…he's got himself a struggle."

"That he does." Patrick grabbed the corner of the newspaper, pulling it in front of him. His boy had some things to figure out. Fortunately, he was a Grady. His heart and his courage were great. It wasn't going to be an easy road, but Cade would make it. Just as all Grady men before him had made it when it came to the uncertain battle of falling in love.

\*\*\*\*

Cara pulled up in front of her dad's house and sat for a minute, letting the engine idle.

This was the first time since she'd moved back that he'd invited her over. Actually, Penny had been the one to extend the invitation, but she'd been adamant the idea was her dad's.

She prayed it was a good sign. Proof the anger and resentment weighing over him were finally beginning to clear.

She killed the engine and stepped out of the car, her boots falling into the soft snow lining the drive. The storm may have passed, but it would take a few days before the temperatures climbed high enough to cause any real melting.

Such was the way of mountain life. Back in Denver, snow came and melted quickly. She'd always known the winter wonderland she viewed out her window wouldn't last long.

But here in the Rockies, it was different. The thaw took longer. Snow lingered. And in this time before summer, nature created a beautiful dance of cold and warmth. Coming together in memory of what was leaving. A promise of what was to come.

Somebody, a ranch hand she guessed, had shoveled a path up the porch steps to the front door. It opened before she had a chance to knock, Penny's smiling face greeting her.

"Oh. It's cold." She wrapped her arms around her middle. "Come in before you freeze to death."

Cara didn't argue, quickly entering the cozy warmth inside. Slipping her snow-covered boots off at the door, she paused, surprised at what she heard. Or rather, what she didn't hear.

The television. The constant drone of those reporting the news.

"Hasn't had it on all day," Penny supplied to her startled look. She slipped an arm around Cara's shoulders and led her through the pleasingly quiet front room. "He's in the kitchen, enjoying the one before dinner beer I'm willing to allow."

Oh, the memories that brought rushing back. Her

dad coming through the back door after a long day working with the horses. Pulling off his boots, he'd leave them in a careless pile on the kitchen floor before tossing his hat on the hook by the laundry room on his way to the refrigerator.

He always grabbed a beer, popping the top and enjoying a long, slow drink before tending to what waited inside the house. Sometimes, she'd already had dinner prepared. Others, they worked together, side by side inside the small, comfortable kitchen, preparing a meal while Cara told her dad about her day. Or she listened to his latest news from the breeding barn and around the ranch.

The one beer before dinner.

Her heart tightened. Tears threatened the corners of her eyes.

She hadn't realized one escaped and trailed down her cheek until Penny's arm tightened around her shoulders. "You okay?"

She swiped at the single tear and nodded. "I'm okay. Just an old memory coming back."

Penny smiled, understanding full in her gaze. "Come on." She moved again toward the kitchen. "We leave your dad in there too long and he'll decide to go after all that food for himself."

"Plus," her green eyes sparked as they entered the kitchen, "I did better than beer for the two of us. I sent Jimmy to the liquor store. Had him get us a good bottle of wine to share."

"Now that I like." Cara smiled. She turned from Penny walking away toward the counter and found her dad at the table, beer in hand.

"Hi, Dad." She came up beside him, dropping a

kiss on his rough cheek. "Enjoying that?" She nudged her head at the half-finished bottle.

"I have to since she rarely lets me have one." He shot a frustrated look at Penny, busy filling two slender wine glasses with Chardonnay.

A smile graced her delicate features as she grabbed the stems and approached the table. "I told you. I'll give more when you give more." She handed a glass to Cara.

Other than an answering scowl, he ignored her. "Here." He backed up his wheelchair, motioning Cara toward the wooden chair closest to him. "Sit."

"I should probably help Penny with dinner first."

"Don't you dare." Penny waved a long, perfectly manicured finger her way. "You sit. I'll serve. You'll only be in my way, otherwise."

The determined look on her face made it clear arguing was useless. Grabbing the back of the chair, Cara pulled it out from the table and sat down as her dad suggested.

There was a change in him. Subtle enough to be hard to find, but still there. She was sure of it.

"You doing okay?" The hard press of his gaze reminded her of her younger days. Her teenage years. When he used such a look to get the truth out of her.

"I'm fine." She kept her voice steady, looking him in the eye without so much as a flinch. For the first time since his accident, the relationship between them hinted at a shift back to her dad being the caretaker, looking out for her.

"I know what happened." Slow, much too slow, he lifted the bottle to his lips and took a drink. "I know you were the one to find her...that woman who went missing. And I know exactly how you found her, too."

Horror ran up her spine at the reminder. She chased it away, refusing to go back and travel through that dark memory again. "It wasn't—"

She swallowed hard over the knot forming in her throat. "It wasn't anything I care to repeat in my lifetime." She lifted her wine glass to her lips. "But I'm okay now that everything is settling back to normal."

Normal. That wasn't exactly correct. She hadn't known normal since returning to Snow Ridge.

"I can't imagine it." Penny pushed up behind her, placing a large ceramic platter, overflowing with her homemade spaghetti and meatballs, in the center of the table. "Finding that poor girl like that."

"Thankfully, it's over now." Cara wished desperately for a change of subject. The memories still haunted her, kept her awake at night. The last thing she wanted was to relive them.

"You sure about that?" Her dad leaned forward in his wheelchair.

She looked at him, wondering how much he knew as Penny pushed a plate of garlic bread and a bowl of salad into the center of the table before sitting down across from her.

"Of course I am." She made a point of helping Penny dish up the food, avoiding her dad's prying eyes. "Why wouldn't I be?"

He pushed closer to the table, setting his beer next to the plate she set in front of him. "Perhaps because nobody else is so sure. The way I hear it, the one who murdered that girl might also have you in his sights."

Well, damn. So much for keeping the worst from him. He'd apparently learned all there was to know. All she had hoped he would never find out. "There's no way of knowing what he wanted when he shoved that picture through the door. Just because certain people are thinking the worst doesn't make it true."

*People like Cade.*

Groaning silently, she picked up her fork and speared it through the spaghetti filling her plate. She'd promised herself she wasn't going to waste a second thinking about him. Especially not after the stunt he'd pulled the other night.

He was better off forgotten.

"Listen." Her dad leaned close, folding one hand over the other along the edge of the table. "I get it. You're strong, spirited and stubborn, just like your mom. I wouldn't expect any less."

He picked up his garlic bread, letting it hover above his plate. "But there are times when you can't possibly face and do everything on your own."

He glanced down at his wheelchair as if registering his own advice. "The ranch is your home." He looked back at her, the love he'd once held in his gaze returning, bringing back the father she'd missed. "We can keep you safe here."

And there, in that moment, she wanted to give in and agree to what he asked. Because there he was, the man she'd missed so much since his accident. Over a plate of spaghetti, he looked at her with the affection and love she'd once taken for granted. Had missed more than she'd known was possible.

But she couldn't. Wouldn't.

"I promise," she reached over, resting a hand over his, "I won't be dumb. If I start to feel threatened, I'll come stay at the ranch."

Doubt deepened the blue in his eyes. "I don't like

it. You should be here. Where you belong." He grabbed his beer, never looking away as he took a swallow.

"You swear, no foolishness? None of this being stubborn for the sake of it. Anything more happens, you're coming back here where I don't have to spend my time worrying about you."

Anything was a bit broader than she liked. Still, she chose not to argue. "I swear," she promised with a gentle smile.

Pushing up from her chair, she took the steps needed to reach her dad and dropped a kiss on his cheek. "Thank you."

"For what?" He watched her curiously as she sat back down and picked up her fork.

"For being my dad again." She didn't look at him, instead concentrating on twisting long spaghetti noodles around her fork. "I've missed you."

He grumbled under his breath. Daring a peek his way, she caught the slight smile stretching his lips. The touch of tenderness in his gaze.

It was all she needed to see. Enough to calm the fears he would be lost forever. Allow the hope she'd been terrified to claim.

There was a chance the man he'd become was losing hold. A hint that she might get her dad back, after all.

****

"You know, you keep poking at her and, sooner or later, she's going to strike back." Luke shook his head at Cade leaning against the front bumper of Cara's car.

Snow kicked out behind the heels of his boots as he came up the lane between the main house and Joe's place. Reaching the car, he hitched a hip against the fender at Cade's side. "How long do you plan to wait for her?"

"As long as it takes. I need to hear Joe convinced her to stay at the ranch."

"You think it's possible?" Luke glanced at the large front window.

"With that woman," Cade shoved a frustrated hand through his hair, "who knows? She's about as irritating as one can get."

His brother's answering smile was too knowing for Cade's comfort. "But, I figure, if anyone can convince her she's safest here, it will be her dad. Hopefully, he can talk some sense into her." Shoving his hands into the front pockets of his jeans, he ignored the repeat of Hattie's voice rambling inside his head. Fear beat respect every time. Especially when it came to Cara.

And it had nothing to do with not respecting her, anyhow. He refused to believe different.

"She's tough, you know. We made her that way." Luke turned as movement through the front window caught his attention. A minute later, the front door opened. "I'm betting she's damn good at taking care of herself."

Without waiting for his response, Luke pushed away from the car, making his way through the snow as Cara and Penny stepped out together.

Both looked at him as he placed a boot on the porch step. Penny reacted first, her smile wide and welcoming. "Why, hello, Luke. I didn't expect to see you here."

Cara glanced up, catching his gaze with her deep blue eyes.

"Just passing by. Had some things to tie up before

heading back to my place." His response drifted back to Cade and he knew his brother was deliberately being vague. The things he'd had to tie up involved the site where Gina's body had been found. Not something, Cade knew, he wanted to go into detail about.

"You doing okay?" Luke stepped onto the porch, wrapping his arms around Cara.

"I am." She stepped back from his embrace, giving a genuine smile. "Every day gets a little—"

Cara's smile faded away as she stared over Luke's shoulder. "Better."

She turned her back on Cade leaning against her car. Ignored the extra beat her heart took at the sight of him. The heat tingling the back of her neck as his eyes bore into her.

Penny looked down where Cade stood then turned back with a gentle smile tugging at her lips. "I should get back inside with your dad. Make sure he doesn't follow through with his threat to grab another beer."

She pulled Cara close to catch her in a tight hug. "Don't be too hard on him." She kept her voice low, for Cara's ears only. "He's worried about you. Just like the rest of us."

If only Penny knew. She returned the hug, choosing not to say anything else.

How could she explain it anyhow? How did one make sense of something that was so hard to grasp? Cade's worry was one thing. Something she'd grown up with and knew how to handle.

It was the other problems he created. The ones leaving her gasping for breath like a lovesick teenager. Kept her up at night as she imagined sharing his bed and finding the passion that once exploded between them.

She wished his worry for her was the worst of it. But that didn't even touch the tip of it. It was the temptation to break every precaution, every rule, she'd set in place. To give in to what her body begged for every time he was near.

Luke stayed at her side as she left the porch before waving goodbye halfway to her car and leaving her alone with Cade. A situation she'd been caught in way too often lately.

"So." Cade pushed away from the car as she approached. "Should I let Hattie know to expect you tonight?"

"No. Why would you do that?" She made a wide curve around him, doing all she could to keep a safe distance between them.

Cade watched but didn't follow as she reached the driver's side, leaving the safety of the hood between them. "Because I can't imagine even you are stubborn enough to continue fighting against staying here when your own dad agrees it's the best place for you."

"What's between my dad and I is our business." Unease filled Cara as he came around the front bumper, hazel eyes heated with a look she'd come to know all too well.

She opened the car door, using it as a shield between them. "I need to go. I've already stayed longer than I planned." She didn't want this—whatever it was between them. It was too complicated. Too much to deal with on top of everything else going on in her life.

She'd already taken this path and failed miserably. She didn't have it in her to repeat the mistake.

"You're still insisting on staying in town." Surprise

filled his voice. He stopped, leaving only the door between them. His distinctive, alluring scent curled around her.

She fought against the tease, wishing he'd turn around and go back to the main house. Leave her and her traitorous reaction to him alone. "I am. There's no reason not to."

He frowned, looking ready to argue further.

"Goodbye, Cade." She cut him off before he had a chance. Climbing into her car, she closed the door with more force than necessary.

He stepped back as the engine roared to life. Through her rearview mirror, she watched him. He stayed rooted where he was, staring after her as she disappeared down the drive.

For a moment, she wondered what it would be like, coming toward him instead of always desperate to leave him. Finding the comfort of his hold and the heated passion in his kiss.

Only for a moment though before reality kicked in, reminding her she'd gained so much while out on her own. Came far enough that she wasn't willing to give it away for anyone. Not even Cade.

## Chapter Eleven

He watched Cara leave.

He'd been tempted to approach and exchange friendly hellos without her knowing any different. But he decided against it. He had better ways to make his presence known.

He glanced again at the delicate cross resting in his palm. He'd known, the minute he'd taken it from her delicate, slender neck, where it belonged.

He thought of her—the one he'd taken. The one waiting for him in bare beauty. Waiting alone in silence, facing her worst fears. Never knowing, soon she'd be redeemed as Gina had been.

So many were foolish, never seeing what was right in front of them.

He'd learned that long ago and had used it to his advantage.

Anyone watching wouldn't have cared to believe anything other than the fact they watched him walk up to the beauty at the gas tank and gather her into a hug before helping her into the passenger seat of her car.

He'd even been kind enough to finish filling her tank before climbing into the driver's seat. Happy to see the quick prick to her arm had done the job, knocking her out cold.

From there it had been easy. A quick trip past the ranches stretching the long stretch of highway to the

145

small hunting cabin he'd bought years ago. To the bunker carved inside the mountain, hidden by decades of growth.

She'd been so supple, so soft, in his hold. He'd almost hated to leave her. Wished for the time to enjoy her, giving her a hint of the glory coming her way.

But it was too risky. Time too short.

He started his truck, pulling away from where he'd watched Cara.

The cross slipped from his palm, dangling from its chain around his wrist. It would soon be Cara's. A gift from him, letting her know he was there, watching her. Waiting for her.

Soon, what was meant to be, fated a decade ago, would come to reality. Giving them both the glorious joy they deserved.

****

Where were they?

Cara dug through the unpacked boxes piled in the spare room of her apartment.

She'd been so busy, so taken over by everything that had happened since she'd returned to Snow Ridge, she hadn't yet unpacked her painting supplies.

But she needed them tonight…now.

Sitting on the carpet, she grabbed the corner of another box and pulled it to her. As happened so often, once her emotions raced, so did her creativity.

Everything inside called out for her to create. To use all the feelings pushing at her to bring life to canvas. She needed it. Craved it.

Reaching in, her fingers swept across the familiar texture of her brushes. Eager, she pulled them out, setting them on the carpet beside her.

Back to the box, she soon had a pile at her side. She carried everything to the front room and dumped it on the couch. Retracing her steps, she moved through the maze of unpacked boxes, pulled her easel and blank canvases from their resting spot on the wall and added them to the supplies waiting in the front room.

Oh yes. Excitement drummed. This was what she needed. A chance to forget and lose herself in her painting. In the blank canvas begging for life.

Stuffing her iPod into its dock, classical music filled the tiny apartment as she headed into the kitchen to fetch a bottle of Chardonnay from the fridge and a wine glass from the cupboard.

She was ready. It might not be the studio she'd put so much time into creating back in Denver, but it would still do. Still offer what she needed most.

The release of all her emotions into a colorful explosion of art.

She grabbed a brush and realized she'd hadn't held one in her hand since her dad's accident. It had been too long. Too much held inside, needing a release.

The rousing rhythm of Vivaldi's Spring exploded around her, pushing her, inspiring her.

And she was lost. Gone was her apartment. The ups and downs of the past weeks. The fear and confusion.

Only her brush and the paints existed, bringing life to the canvas. Drawing from everything inside, she created a release that spoke better than words ever could.

She had no idea of time. Hours passed, one after another, as she stood there in the middle of the front room, creating and losing herself in the way she did best.

It all came through. Her heartache after her dad's accident. The fear circling around Gina's tragic death. And Cade.

*Always Cade.*

She'd never known life without him. Even in the decade away, he still existed. In her thoughts. Her memories.

Dipping her brush in the thinner and sweeping it through the thick oil paint collected on her palette, she brushed dark red over the canvas. Her heart dictated the strokes, guiding her as conflicting emotions surfaced, bringing out what she couldn't admit, not even to herself.

Grabbing the bottle of Chardonnay, she tipped it over her empty wine glass only to find a few drops left. The realization she'd finished it off pulled her back. A glance at the clock hanging on the far wall told her she'd been at it for a good four hours.

Midnight had come and gone long ago. The early morning hours hovered, reminding her of the six a.m. alarm that would explode through her bedroom way too soon.

Sleep teasing, she gave in. Collecting her brushes, she left the canvas to dry. Thoughts of Cade lingered as she headed for the sink and set the faucet to warm.

She wished there was an easy answer. A simple solution. But she knew there wasn't, never would be.

She would deal with what she had to. Find the best way to work through it while satisfying the expectations she had for herself and her life.

Of course, it was always easier said than done.

Exhaustion catching up with her, she fumbled

through the tasks waiting for her, the thought of her comfortable bed becoming more and more appealing.

Brushes cleaned, she laid them carefully on a soft linen towel at the foot of the easel. Grabbing the empty wine bottle with her glass, she tossed the bottle in her recyclables. She rinsed the glass and propped it carefully on the top rack of her dishwasher.

Suddenly more tired than she realized, she stumbled to the back door. Flipping the lock, she made her way through the front room, doing the same with the one between her apartment and shop.

There. Now she could sleep. At least for the few hours she had left.

Her bed welcomed her. Even thoughts of Cade disappeared as she stumbled forward, collapsing on the pile of pillows. Pulling the thick comforter to her chin, she closed her eyes and found sleep in a matter of minutes.

\*\*\*\*

Patience kept him there, waiting until the lights in her apartment finally went dark.

The night temperatures had dipped to freezing, but he barely noticed. Adrenaline pushed heat through his veins as he stood behind the bank of cedars crowding the corner down from Cara's shop.

The perfect place to watch not only Cara but Cade as well—back in the same place he had been for nights. Truck idling as he sat and watched.

It was noble, really, the lengths he was going to in order to look out for her safety. Not that it would do any good. He knew too much. Had his own hold around Snow Ridge and the ranches surrounding it.

He knew where to be. Who to watch out for.

When the time came to make Cara his, there would be no stopping him. No chance of anyone coming between them or what was meant to be.

And tonight would only serve as proof Cade's guard was useless when coming up against what he desired.

He stuck his hand in the front pocket of his coat, fingers closing around the smooth gold cross inside. He could still see it, even now, the cross hanging around *Her* neck, similar to the one he held.

Closing his eyes, taking a moment before carrying out what had to be done, he brought *Her* back. Saw the cross swinging from her neck. Felt its impression pressed against his bare skin, leaving its mark.

She'd never taken it off. Not even as she stood naked in front of him. She wore it always, a reminder of who she served even in the torrid punishment she carried out day after day.

Oh yes. It was proper, the reminder of *Her* becoming a part of Cara.

Slow, cautious, he came out from the shelter of the trees, careful under the cover of shadows and far from the streetlights illuminating the sidewalk around Precious Gems.

He patted his other pocket, made sure he'd grabbed the tools he needed as he slid, unnoticed, between the buildings.

He was confident Cade hadn't seen him. The dark was heavy enough to keep him cloaked from prying eyes. Silent, he made his way up the stairs to the outer door leading to her place.

Though he knew it was a risk, he paused there, holding a hand against the grooves carved into the wood. This was the most intimate he'd been with Cara. Never had he been granted a chance to be so near. So involved in all she was. All she offered.

Pulling the tools from his pocket, he worked swiftly on the lock. Minutes later, he closed his hand around the knob, carefully and quietly pushing the door open.

He waited on the threshold. Listened. No sound. No hint of anyone up and moving, giving him the freedom to enter the dark kitchen and quietly close the door behind him.

Yanking free the small thumb-light from his tools, careful to keep it pointing down and away from the windows, he took in his surroundings. The modest kitchen led into the main room, red-brick fireplace claiming a corner. Soft dark green couches stretched along the opposite walls.

Centering the room, a painting rested on an easel with recently scrubbed brushes drying on a towel at the base. Her work, beautiful and powerful, just as she was.

He glanced at what she'd created during the late hours. The gold and greens clashing through slashes of red could very well be her final work of art. Her farewell painting, treasured in the art world.

And he, the one destined to take her life, was the first to view its breathtaking beauty.

Yes. This was meant to be. Just as he'd known all those years ago. Nothing could change what was coming. All the signs led to that moment when he would finally know the glory of Cara.

Knowing he was wasting precious time. Understanding the risks he faced every second he lingered inside, he turned away from the painting, finding his way to the skinny hall cutting through the back half of the apartment.

He only planned on leaving the cross then getting out as quickly as possible. But he needed to see. Needed to be close to where she slept. Where she was the most real, tempting in the intimacy of her private space.

In seconds, he found her. Standing in the open door of her bedroom, he watched her sleep. A deep blue comforter was gathered at her waist, her face buried in a thick pile of pillows.

The sight of her, so beautiful with ebony hair contrasting against the white of the pillowcase and slender shoulders rising and falling with each breath, left him hard with wanting. Eager to satisfy the need burning through his veins.

He could take her now. Show her what was theirs. A few steps and he'd be there, at her side, close enough to touch, to smell. Surrounded by everything that was her.

He took a step, then stopped himself. *No.* This was not the time. He had to have patience. Had to hold on to his self-control.

For Cara, he demanded perfection. No less would be worthy of her. And perfection came with practice.

Practice waiting for him back in the bunker, offering another chance to learn and know what fate called for him to do. To complete another step before paying full tribute to *Her* memory through Cara.

Shoving his hand into his pocket, he dug out the cross and held it tight in his palm. He thought of leaving it here, in her bedroom, her most private space.

But it wasn't the right place. He felt it. Knew, at

that moment, where to leave his gift.

With one last look at her curled peacefully in sleep, he retraced his steps through the hallway. Back to her painting in the center of the front room.

This was the most primal part of her. A creation straight from her soul. He could get no closer without actual physical contact.

It was the perfect place to leave proof of her destiny.

He rubbed a rough thumb over the smooth, cool surface of the cross. Lifting his palm, he dropped a kiss where the chain looped through the top, and then carefully draped it over the edge of the canvas.

It rested against the bold red she'd used in her painting—proper and fitting in so many ways.

He took a moment, admiring the cross one final time. Satisfaction warming his insides, he turned for the kitchen and the back door.

The night had been good. Very good. Closing the door behind him, the thought of the sweet beauty he was leaving behind tangled with the reminder of the luscious body waiting for him back at his cabin.

At that moment, in that second, it was the best of all things. He'd suffered. He'd hurt. But this made it worth it. Gave him reasons for the redemption he'd sought, agonized through.

It was time. His blessing was on the horizon. A bit of patience and he would finally have all he desired…deserved.

Chapter Twelve

Her brain was thick with sleep.

For a moment, Cara laid there, warm under her comforter, letting her senses come back to her. It was dark, silent. A quick glance at the clock centering her bedside table told her sunrise still lingered a couple hours away.

Something woke her. Though she couldn't figure out what it was.

She glanced around her room, making out the familiar shadows of her dresser against the opposite wall and the wooden rocker tucked into the corner.

Had she heard something? She couldn't be sure. But an unease settled. A sense that something wasn't right.

Images of Gina's body hanging from the tree rushed forward. She shoved them back, refusing to go there.

It was probably nothing. Just a reaction to all the worry surrounding her. The fear she'd battled and seen in the eyes of those around her.

It would only make sense her imagination was on overdrive, causing her to worry about things that never existed.

She would check out the apartment and assure herself everything was fine. Then maybe she could sneak in a couple more hours of sleep.

Decision made, she flipped her comforter aside, fighting off the answering chill. Her feet hit the floor and, for a moment, she debated crawling back into bed, burying her head in the pillows, and forgetting about it all.

But she couldn't. She'd never get back to sleep until she made sure all was as it should be inside her place.

Flipping lights on her way, she stepped out of her bedroom and into the hallway. Pausing to listen, she heard nothing.

She turned to the spare room, her soon to be studio, finding nothing but the mess she'd left earlier when she'd hunted down her painting supplies.

Her steps muffled by the thick gray carpet she'd had installed before moving in, she headed for the front room. Though she'd yet to find anything out of place or any reason to worry, the unease refused to go away. It urged her on, eager to turn on the floor lamp at the end of the hall to chase away the lingering shadows.

Like the spare room, the front room was just as she had left it. Pillows tossed carelessly on the couch. The magazine she'd been reading a couple days ago left on the dark oak coffee table.

And her easel and recent painting in the center of it.

It was close to complete. Just a few touch-ups she would take care of in the morning.

Stepping up for a quick look, she caught a strange glimmer from the corner of her eye. Slow and hesitant, she turned her head, her gaze falling on a slender chain draped over the edge of her painting. A delicate gold cross dangled from it.

"What the—"

She stumbled back. It was—

It couldn't—

She forced a breath through her lungs, slamming her eyes closed against the sight of the cross hanging there. Taunting her.

She'd been here. She'd painted. She'd gone to bed.

And after that—

Her heart beat painfully against her ribs. Every breath became a struggle, threatening to strangle her under her fear. Somebody had been inside her apartment. Left the cross.

No. She shook her head. It couldn't be. It was too terrifying to imagine somebody roaming through her private space while she slept, unknowing.

Who would do such a thing?

Even as she wondered, she knew.

Leaving the cross untouched, she half stumbled, half ran, back to her bedroom. She grabbed her phone with shaking fingers, dropped it, and picked it up again.

This wasn't…it couldn't be real. Never had she felt so violated or frightened by the thought of someone moving around freely while she slept unsuspecting, unknowing of their presence.

She felt sick. Dizzy with disbelief. Willing her fingers to obey, she awkwardly punched out 911 and pressed the phone hard to her ear, waiting for an answering voice on the other end.

\*\*\*\*

"Where are you?" Luke's voice burst through Cade's phone.

"In my truck. In front of Cara's place. Why?"

"You're there. At Cara's. And you saw nothing?"

The unsettled timber in his voice set Cade's instincts to overdrive. "What's going on?" He glanced up at the lights reflecting in her windows. They'd burned into the late hours, went out for a little while over an hour ago then returned.

He'd assumed she'd had a hard night of sleep. Who would blame her with everything she'd gone through?

"She called 911. Said somebody had been inside her apartment while she slept." Frustration and fear battled in Luke's words. "I have officers on the way, but if you can, get up there."

Cade was already grabbing the thin silver handle at his side, shoving the truck door open. "How the hell?" His feet hit the ground only a second before he took off in a run. "I've watched her place all night. I didn't see a damn thing."

He started for the front door of Precious Gems then thought twice about it. Better to go up the back side.

Which, damn, was more than likely the same route the intruder had taken.

Why hadn't her alarm gone off?

"I'm on my way." He ran through the small space between the buildings, his feet a hollow echo in the still night.

Images of Cara tortured him. Alone. Sleeping. Unaware of someone moving around in her place.

He didn't have to think twice who it was. He already knew.

The one who'd abducted and killed Gina and sent the pictures to Cara was the one who returned tonight. Proved again his connection to her was more than some random passing.

"I'll call Jake, get him over there." Luke's voice

barely registered as fear and anger clashed inside Cade. "My officers should be there any minute. I'll be right behind them."

Cade grumbled a goodbye and dropped the phone in his pocket. His feet pounding against the metal steps, he knew only one thing would calm his growing worry—setting his eyes on Cara. Seeing for himself she was safe and unharmed by the lunatic targeting her.

His fist hit hard against the door, vibrating it inside its frame. He twisted the knob, cursing when he found it unlocked.

"Cara." His voice echoed in the silence. Stepping into the kitchen, he tried tempering down his anger, but it did no good.

He was mad. The hot, blinding mad making clear thought damn near impossible. Mad at himself. At Cara. At the danger threatening her, invading her life.

Why was her door unlocked? Why had her alarm not gone off, warning him of the danger happening right under his nose?

Damn. He'd screwed that one up. Didn't do much good to watch over her when he never even had a clue someone was lurking around inside.

"Cara, where are you?"

He hurried through the kitchen, the front room, and down the hall. She came out of her bedroom, dressed in nothing more than an oversized shirt and thin cotton shorts. Her face was pale, deep blue eyes haunted and damp with unshed tears.

In two large strides, he reached her, wrapping his hands around her slender arms. She was warm...alive. "Are you okay?"

She trembled under his fierce hold. Opening her

mouth to respond, she swallowed hard over the knot lodged in her throat, nodding instead of fighting to form words.

Relief swelled, clashing dangerously with the fear and anger tearing through. Forming a clear, rational thought was impossible. All that mattered, swelled around him, was the feel and sight of Cara, unharmed.

Tightening his hold, he pulled her closer, molding her slender shape to his chest. Her eyes widened as he stared down at her. Every fear, the force of his anger, reflected back at him.

Cara gasped as his demanding mouth captured hers. The hold of Cade's large, powerful hands around her arms became almost painful. The forceful possession of his kiss left her struggling for stability, sucking her under a dark cloud of fevered desperation.

Wrapping her trembling arms around his sides, she responded in the only way she could. Opening to him. Giving back the same desperation, need, and passion he executed over her.

For that moment, in the heat of his embrace, the fear she'd known since finding the cross disappeared. Left her feeling, knowing, only the seductive pull of his lips taking hers. His arms molding her into every solid curve and line of his body.

"Damn it, Cara." Ripping his mouth away, he speared long fingers through her hair, holding her gaze captive with his.

She saw so much in his hazel eyes. So much she didn't want to accept and struggled to deny. Yet, the strength of his emotions, the anger and relief boiling over, caught her. Left her unable to turn away and ignore the tremors vibrating between them.

"I can't—"

He groaned. A low, frustrated sound pushed up from deep inside. Cupping his hands behind her head, he pulled her mouth back to his to catch her in another heated kiss.

He held her there, trapped under his hold, taking all he desired.

She melted into him, molding her body with his until they were one. No space, no breath, between them. Every desire bared, seeking satisfaction in the most intimate of ways.

"Cade. Cara." Jake's voice drifted from the kitchen.

Cursing, Cade lingered for a moment more before pulling away. "We're here." He didn't let go, holding her close as he stared hard into her eyes.

"You okay?" Jake rushed down the hallway, pulled her from Cade's arms, and curled his own around her. "Luke said someone broke in while you were sleeping."

The reminder sent a chill down her spine. "They left a cross. On the painting I was working on." A horrific addition to her own creation. The thought of ever again touching that painting made her sick to her stomach.

"A cross?" Jake held her out at arm's length as the echo of sirens broke through the distance.

She nodded and pointed down the hallway. "It's in the front room. You can see for yourself."

Jake let go, turned on his heels, and headed back the way he had come.

She stood frozen where she was, watching his retreating back.

"Why don't you go brew a pot of coffee?" Cade

returned to her side, grabbing her chilled hand between his, offering the warmth she desperately needed. "In a few minutes, this place will be overrun by uniforms. Caffeine will be sure to keep them happy."

Yes. Coffee was good. It kept her in the kitchen, away from the sight of the cross hanging on the corner of her painting.

Keeping her attention away from the front room, she veered off in the opposite direction as Cade turned to join Jake.

Her head spun. She felt off balance. Unsteady.

Grabbing the edge of the counter, she pulled a long breath through her lungs, willing her nerves to settle.

She could fall apart later. And she planned on doing just that. But for now, this moment, she had coffee to make.

****

Cara watched Cade wade through the many bodies crammed into her small apartment, following his brothers into the kitchen.

"How you holding up?" Luke reached her first, swinging a gentle arm around her shoulders as she prepared a second pot of coffee.

Looking up at him, the truth was there, in the shadows haunting his gaze and the lines pulling heavy on his mouth. "I'm okay." She pushed the brew button. Stepping away from the counter, she slipped out from under Luke's arm. "Ready for the night to be over."

"Technically, it is." Jake pointed out the small window above the sink, the first hints of dawn shimmering in the distance.

She shook her head, biting back the frustrated response lingering on her tongue. She wanted to go back to her bedroom, bury her head under the covers and forget any of this had happened.

"Sit down." Luke grabbed her elbow, leading her toward the worn kitchen table pushed up against the wall. Pulling out a high-backed chair, he waited until she fell into it before taking a seat beside her.

Cade claimed the chair on the other side. Jake remained standing, hovering at the edge of the table where he had a clear view of both the kitchen and the front room.

"Tell me again what happened." Luke's voice was gentle. Still, it did nothing to ease the wave of nausea rising in her gut at the thought of retelling such a frightening ordeal.

She inhaled deeply, doing her best to keep her voice steady as she repeated what had happened after she'd been pulled from sleep.

"What about the alarm?" Cade dropped a warm, steady hand over her trembling fingers. She looked down, his dark skin covering hers, thankful for the touch, needing it more than she knew. "Was it set before you went to bed?"

Had she set it? She went back over the night and what she remembered. What she didn't. She'd come home, searched for her painting supplies and lost herself in her art. She recalled finishing and cleaning up. But there were no memories of actually punching in the code for her alarm.

"I don't think so. I was—"

She sucked in a long, troubled breath. "I was lost in my painting for most of the night. By the time I was done, all I cared about was sleep. I must have forgotten to set the alarm before heading back to my bedroom."

"I pretty much invited him in." She shook her head in disgust.

"Enough of that." Luke pushed against her shoulder, pulling her away from the self-blaming path she ventured down. "You had the place locked up tight and still he knew how to get through. There's nothing to say he wouldn't have been able to do the same with the alarm set."

The thought terrified her. Who in the hell was he? What did he want with her? None of it made sense.

As if reading her thoughts, Luke grabbed her free hand and squeezed. "We'll find him, whoever he is. I promise you that."

Through the corner of her eye, she watched Jake leave his place. Coming around behind her, he dropped firm hands over her shoulders. "Don't you worry." He pressed a soft kiss on the top of her head. "You've got the three of us. Only a fool would try getting to you with the Gradys standing in the way."

Surrounded by them. The three who had always been there, through every up and down of her life, a hint of peace found its place within all the worry and fear holding her hostage.

And she realized where she needed to be, for now, while the horror facing her was more than any one person should ever have to face alone.

She needed to go back to the ranch. To her first home. Her safety. Her comfort.

As much as she had fought the idea, she knew the time had come.

Chapter Thirteen

She was so tired.

Sitting on the back porch of the main house, cradling a steaming cup of coffee between her hands, one of Hattie's handmade quilts draped over her, Cara watched the ranch slowly wake up and come to life.

No matter how hard she tried, she couldn't clear the image of the cross from her mind. It haunted her as she was bundled into Cade's truck to head for the ranch. On the phone with Jackie, reassuring her she was okay. With Penny, making sure her father knew where she was.

"You're going to get yourself sick out here." Coffee pot in hand, Hattie stepped out onto the porch and filled her cup to the rim.

"I'm okay. Really." She offered the best, convincing smile she could.

"Hmmpphh." Hattie fussed with the corners of the quilt, pulling the warmth closer to Cara's chin. "I'm no more of a fool now than I was when you were nothing but a child. You couldn't trick me then. You can't trick me now."

She curled warm palms around Cara's cheeks, holding her gaze even with her own intent stare. "I know. I understand what you desire for yourself and your life." She dropped a tender kiss on her forehead. "Being here doesn't take away from that. It only proves your wisdom in knowing when it's time to surround yourself with the help of those who love you."

For a moment, Cara couldn't respond. Swallowing hard over the knot forming in her throat, she took a long, slow sip of coffee, stalling the best she could. "I know. On some deep level, I know that. It's just hard not to feel like some weak victim. Like I'm taking a giant step back to that needy girl I used to be."

She stared out over the ranch she knew so well, finding comfort in all that was familiar. In the solace it brought. "But I can't do different now. I need help. Only a fool would claim otherwise after all that has happened."

"A smart girl you have always been." Hattie straightened, a sincere smile stretching over her lips and sparking in her caring eyes. "That's why Cade loves you so."

"Hattie." Cara's eyes widened even as she shook her head in denial.

With a look only she could do, leaving no doubt arguing was useless, Hattie placed a soft finger over Cara's lips, stopping the disagreeing words lingering there. "Finish your coffee. Straighten your thoughts. When you come in, your room will be ready."

And then she was gone before Cara had a chance to utter a single word.

Which was for the best since the only response she could come up with was weak and pitiful.

It was, really, too much. Her dad's accident. Coming back to Snow Ridge with all the memories living here. Facing the threats surrounding her on top of the constant pull Cade left on her heart.

When did she have the right to say enough was

enough and walk away from it all?

"You doing okay?" The rich timber of Cade's voice reached her before he did. Turning away from the ranch spreading out ahead of her, she caught him in her gaze, her heart skipping a beat at the sight of him.

He was…everything. All she wanted, yet denied. There was something so strong and powerful about him. There always had been. That's why she'd found comfort and reassurance in his arms, sought it when life had become hard. Just being him. Just being Cade. He offered it without hesitation. In his arms, she'd always felt safe, treasured…loved.

"That seems to be the question of the day." She attempted what she could of a smile.

"And what's the answer?" Cade skimmed a finger against her cheek. Needing to touch her, reassure himself she was okay.

When he thought of someone inside her apartment, moving around freely while she slept—the anger and fear were too much to handle. Left him with an urge to hit the streets and search as long as it took for the one who dared to pull her into such a nightmare.

"Honestly." Terror lingered in the deep blue depths of her eyes. "I don't know. I feel safer here. *I know I'm safer here*. But I'm still terrified. And I don't have a clue what to do or think about it. I hate it. Hate feeling so helpless when it comes to my own life."

"You aren't helpless." He wished he could chase the doubt from her eyes. Fight away the fear holding her hostage. "Hell woman, you're far from it. You fought me. Argued with me. Refused to give in when I wanted you to stay here."

Frustration returned at the memory of it. "A

helpless woman would have given in long ago under the pressure. But you didn't. You made sure, when it was time for you to come, that it was on your terms. When you decided, for your own life, it was the right thing to do."

She glanced up at him but didn't look convinced.

A breeze kicked to life, sweeping in a chill from the lingering snow. Underneath the quilt, Cara shivered.

He watched her battle to accept his words. But there was confusion and terror there, simmering in her deep blue gaze, holding her back.

"We should get you inside, out of the cold." He took her coffee cup from her hands and claimed his own sip before placing it on the small glass table beside her.

She didn't argue. Taking his offered hand, she let him pull her up. The quilt fell, bunching at her waist. She grabbed the edge, taking it with her as she swung her bare feet around. Though she tried hiding it, he caught the slight tremble in her legs as she stood.

For a moment, he was brought back to the young girl she used to be. He saw her in her pigtails, running over the ranch with him and his brothers, always so sure she could never show them a hint of fear. She would fight it with the best of wills, even when they could see the evidence of its existence. To her, fear was a weakness she wasn't willing to show. So she'd jump right into whatever challenge she faced, fighting it back, because she couldn't be weak. Wouldn't stand for it.

It was a trait she obviously had never grown out of. The beautiful woman standing before him still carried so much of the young girl he remembered.

Cade gathered the quilt in his hand before tossing an easy, comforting arm around her slender shoulders. He led her through the back door and into the bright, cheery kitchen, out of the morning chill.

"Hattie has your room ready." He dropped the quilt on the back of an overstuffed chair in the main room as they passed through on their way to the stairs, still holding her close, needing the reassurance she was finally safe and sound where she belonged.

****

*Her room.*

Struck by the thought of it, Cara paused for a moment on the way up. How long had it been since she'd slept inside the room that had been designated hers so many years ago? Before the night of Jacob's death. Before her life had changed so drastically.

Still it remained, after all these years, just that…her room. Her own space within the Grady home. Connecting her to those who had always been so much of her life, her childhood. The very person she had grown to be.

The upstairs hallway was quiet, empty except for her and Cade, their footsteps lost in the thick beige carpet. They stopped at the partially open door with Cade so close his warmth danced around her. Reminded her of all she'd fought hard and long to forget.

She peered through the opening, finding both comfort and dread.

The room was how she remembered it. Soft teal in the thick comforter covering the queen size bed and in the delicate curtains hanging over the double windows looking out over the front drive of the house.

The dark oak vanity table on the opposite wall held

so many memories of the mornings she'd sit there, preparing herself for the new day. The small, lounging chair in the corner brought back the hours she'd rest with a book and enjoy a few moments of silence.

This room had been as much hers as the one she'd claimed at her dad's place. Yet, even in the memories, the peace it offered, she found herself hesitant to enter. To be alone with her thoughts. Her growing fears.

She needed…she wanted—

Cade shifted, leaning a broad shoulder against the wall at her side, and she knew.

She wanted him. Needed everything he was. All that he offered.

"You should get some sleep." He reached out to tuck a stray curl behind her ear. There was such softness in his hazel eyes, gentleness in his touch.

Reaching up, she wrapped unsteady fingers around his wrist. "I don't—"

Oh, this was wrong. So wrong. She knew it but couldn't stop it. "I don't feel like sleeping." She looked hard into his eyes, refusing to waver on her decision.

She knew he saw the desire burning in her eyes but still he hesitated.

"What do you feel like?" Tugging free from her hold, he traced a delicate line along the curve of her cheek.

Wide-eyed, she stared at him, her emotion-filled gaze saying what she struggled to put to words.

He stayed silent. Waiting. Refusing to push her to say what he needed to hear.

She struggled with it. Wanting was one thing. Opening herself up to him in such a way was something else, all together. There was a moment of temptation to run from what moved through her. Deny it so she didn't have to face it.

But the need was too powerful.

"I don't want to be alone. I don't want to lie in that room and think about all the horror and darkness." Her voice shook. Sounded shaky even to her own ears.

She flattened her hands against the firm lines carving his chest. His tantalizing heat spread up her arms, pushing harder to satisfy the needs exploding inside. "I want to forget. I want to be reminded what it's like to enjoy. To be swept away in the good rather than all the ugliness that has hit since I've returned to Snow Ridge."

"I just want to be alive, Cade." Tears stuck in the corners of her eyes. Her voice caught on a sob. "And only you can give me that."

She saw the need battling with hesitation in his hazel eyes. She wanted to show him, wanted him to feel what raged through her. But there was so much she couldn't say. Could only hope he knew and understood.

He grabbed her hands roaming over his chest and held them prisoner at her side. Stepping close, pushing until not a breath of space stood between them, he held her captive with his gaze. "Are you sure this is what you want? Because once we take this step, I'm not going back."

The tip of her tongue snuck out, licking her lips as she nodded. "I'm sure. I want this, Cade. I want you."

With a low growl exploding from deep inside, he curled strong arms around her waist and backed her into the room.

Kicking the door closed, he left them nothing but this moment when their long, painful dreams would come true.

****

Closed inside the room, Cade caught the flash of doubt teasing in Cara's gaze.

"No." He backed her up against the wall, pinning her motionless. "No second thoughts."

He anchored his arms around her sides and nipped at her bottom lip. "This is right. This has always been right." He took her mouth, threatening to bruise with the force of his kiss. He didn't wait for her to accept or deny. He pushed forward, claiming what he wanted.

Trapped between him and the hard wall at her back, she surrendered her last bit of doubt. He felt it as it seeped from her, encouraging him.

He deepened the kiss, demanding more. She answered, giving all she could as she melted into him. He pressed against her soft curves, teasing an ache desperately needing to be satisfied.

This was what he needed. Had been without for far too long. He nearly lost his breath as she folded her hands over his, pushing close, giving all that she was. His for the taking.

With a painful groan, he ripped his mouth from hers. "God, Cara." He found the sensitive line at the side of her throat and pressed his lips against her heated skin, trailing a path from her shoulder to below her ear.

She tasted sweet, tempting. He tightened. The thought of having her, claiming her as he once had, became almost too much to bear. "You drive me crazy. You always have."

A trace of frustration mixed with barely controlled desire. With her, he was never on stable ground. Never able to find the control he depended on. She took that from him. Left him exposed, vulnerable.

He wanted, needed, to do the same to her. Let her know what it felt like to be so bare. So open there was no stopping what was to come. He wanted her to need with the same desperation he had known for so long. To understand what it felt like to want so badly you physically ached with it.

Spearing long fingers through the soft fall of her ebony hair, he held her still while his mouth again found hers. The taste of her, so sweet and tempting, raced through his veins. Kicked up his pulse.

A growl erupted from deep inside as he took from her all he desired. All he craved. Tugging his hands free from her long, silky hair, he flattened his palms against her spine, pressing her tight against him as he backed away from the wall.

He needed more. Feel more. Touch more. Discover more.

Counting on his memory of the room, refusing to break the kiss between them, he edged them toward the bed. Hands roaming, he lifted the hem of her shirt, finding smooth, bare skin beneath his touch. She felt soft, so delicate, as he skimmed a path up her slender sides and found the gentle curve of her breast under the lacy cover of her bra.

Cara fought for a breath, fire licking through her veins. She wanted, she needed.

*Cade*. It was always Cade. No matter the fight or the struggle, it always came back to him.

He drove her crazy. Irritated her like no one ever could.

He was so…him. A man so handsome, so annoying and tempting, it was damn near impossible to make sense of her feelings. Except for now as heat curled through her gut and spread through her limbs. The backs of her knees made contact with the edge of the mattress as the pad of his thumb brushed seductively over her hardened nipple.

She gasped as she arched into him. Hard, carved muscles pressed against her softer curves, tempting her with what waited. She wanted to feel it all. Wanted to feel every inch of gorgeous tanned skin.

She wanted to be reminded what it was like. His hands raking over her naked body, molding every curve. His body becoming one with hers, fitting as if he was made just for her.

"Please, Cade," she whispered against his probing lips, flattening her hands against his spine and pulling him even closer. Needing…seeking more. Always more.

Her fingers falling lower, she sought and found his waistband, tugging the ends of his shirt free.

Yes. That was what she needed. Heated skin, smooth, sleek muscle underneath her touch.

With a moan, Cade pulled his mouth from hers. His head falling back, he closed his eyes for a moment and she watched him, held there in the catch of all that burned between them.

Molding her fingers against his broad chest, she took in all that he was. The feel of him, the heat burning through. She was his, needing everything he had to offer.

She sighed, so soft it was almost a whisper, as he lifted her arms above her head. Pulling her shirt off in one swift move, he tossed it carelessly to the floor.

Capturing her wrists in one hand, he used his other

to work her jeans free, then slid them down her legs and kicked them out of the way.

And there she stood, in nothing more than tiny scraps of matching blue lace, staring wide-eyed at him as he took her in, his heavy gaze burning against bare skin.

Desire took her under, leaving her desperate to experience the feel of him again, buried inside her. Taking her to heights she knew she would only catch in his arms.

Dropping his mouth to the throbbing vein at the side of her neck, Cade used his weight, pressing her back onto the mattress.

Trapped by the force of his body on top of her, she could do nothing but lie there and feel everything. Every sensation. Every tantalizing touch as he flicked his fingers over the clasp of her bra, working it free.

He curved a hand around her breast, licking his tongue over the hardened nipple. She gasped, lodged her heels into the mattress, and pushed up into him.

"Oh yes." He lifted his head to smile down on her. "I remember."

Keeping his heated gaze steady with hers, he swept a light circle around the sensitive circle surrounding her nipple and rubbed his thumb over the hard nub. "I remember feeling you." He dropped his mouth, his tongue trailing a path where his thumb had been. "Tasting you."

His fingers crept down, over the curve of her stomach, beneath the blue lace between her legs. He found the place where she ached for him. Heat throbbed as he explored, pushing her desire deeper.

"Cade." His name escaped on a surprised whisper.

Instinctively raising her hips, she sought more, exploding with his touch. She reached for him, needing to feel. Wanting to give as he was.

"No."

She moaned in protest as he pulled away.

He grabbed her hands in his, lifted them above her head and held them there. "Let me—"

He dropped his mouth to hers, a quick, fevered kiss drawing every last breath from her lungs. "Let me have you as I've wanted for so long."

His hazel gaze caught hers and held, leaving her only able to nod in response. Never looking away, he dropped a hand, tugging on the blue silk and sliding it down her legs.

He tossed her thong carelessly aside and again found her most sensitive spot. His fingers firm, probing, he explored. Built the excitement until it threatened to be more than she could handle.

She writhed underneath him, curling her fingers into the comforter at her sides. It was already too much. He knew her. Knew every inch of her body. There was no hesitation, no pause, as he took her higher, igniting her blood to lava. Leaving her reckless and desperate under his touch.

"I can't—"

Her mind spinning, every nerve on fire, she struggled to form a single word. A coherent thought. "I need—"

He continued his sensual torment. His fingers gliding over her, teasing, bringing her to the edge. Dropping her swiftly only to build her up again.

She arched her hips, pressing hard against his palm. Fire caught and spread through her limbs, leaving her desperate and needy for more.

"Please." She reached up and wrapped her hand around the back of his head, bringing him down to her. Her mouth caught his in a kiss desperate with the need ignited inside. A passionate plea to give her the relief she sought.

He lifted his head and smiled. So seductive. So tempting. Pushing up and away, leaving her chilled, desperately wanting him back, he stripped away his clothes and tossed them to the floor.

For a moment, he stood at the side of the mattress, bared to her hungry gaze. Tanned skin stretched gloriously over well-toned muscle. So much power. So much strength. The sight of him alone was enough to flare even greater the flames burning inside.

He bent a knee on the mattress, gently cupping his palms around the inside of her thighs, opening her. His piercing eyes caught hers, stayed steady as he pushed between her legs, his need burning hot in the hazel depths of his gaze.

His fingers traveled slow and gentle over bare skin, curling around her waist. Lifting her hips from the mattress, he bared her to him in the most intimate of ways.

Hot and swollen, he brushed against her, teasing, building the desperation. "Look at me, Cara," he demanded as she closed her eyes with the sensation of him pushing in slowly then pulling back.

She forced her eyes open and watched the strain tightening the lines of his face as he held desperately to his control. Sliding inside, inch by slow inch, he then withdrew until only the tip of him remained.

"No more." She knew she begged but didn't care.

The torture had to end. She needed him buried deep inside, giving her all he promised.

Reaching for her hands, twining his fingers with hers, he lifted them above her head and sank deep inside.

The sensation almost did her in. Fighting for a breath, she wrapped her legs around him, pushing him further. Holding him still. Keeping him deep inside.

"Damn it, Cara." His growl vibrated around them as every muscle tensed. "I can't—"

He collapsed against her. Skin to skin, connected in the most intimate, deepest of ways, they were one for a stolen moment. The past and the present rising up, swirling in a hot wave around them, bringing them here, to this point. Where everything they ever knew came together in one desperate joining.

They were just Cade, just Cara, knowing one another on a level most never had the chance to experience.

With his heart beating frantically against hers, she pressed her hips against him. His eyes widened. His mouth took hers as he lost the last he had of his control.

Taking her as only he could, he pushed hard and deep, over and over. He cupped his large palms on the sides of her cheeks, holding her captive. She was unable to do anything but stare at his dark, hungry gaze as he buried himself deep inside, withdrawing only to push in even deeper.

Curling her fingers into his back, holding on for all she had, she met his every thrust. Rising to close him in, she held him close before he pulled back and pushed in.

Again and again.

Heated desire took over, setting every nerve ending on fire. She rose with him, higher and higher. Her heart beat hard against her ribs. Every breath became a struggle.

Uncontrolled pleasure exploded. Screaming Cade's name, she wrapped around him, grasping tight as time lost all meaning and she shattered into a thousand pieces underneath the seductive pull of his body rising and falling above hers.

As she tightened around him, vibrating from the force of her eruption, he tensed, shoved deep, calling her name as he exploded inside her.

They rode the hazy aftermath, slowly coming back to Earth. Unable to hold himself up another second, Cade collapsed on top of her. She could feel his heart pounding frantically against her. Found another moment of satisfaction knowing she had the power to do that to him.

She didn't know how long they lay there, still connected as one before she shifted gently beneath him. Coming out from the weight of his body, she curled into his side.

He wrapped a firm arm around her slender shoulders, holding her tight. She sank into him, needing the moment, the feel of being wrapped tight in his hold. He pressed a kiss to the top of her head and she melted into him, needing that small show of softness.

She let it carry her as she slowly drifted off, knowing the dreams that would come would never match the ones she'd just lived through.

Chapter Fourteen

He'd inhaled so much coffee, Luke was sure he would float away.

Sitting behind his desk at the station, he stared with a weary gaze at the pile of paper scattering his desk. It was the top sheet, though, causing him worry—a faxed missing person report that had come in less than half an hour ago.

A frantic mom in Nevada had contacted the police when her daughter, Sherry Cooper, failed to return home from her road trip. A full description was included in the report. But catching his attention was the mention of a slender gold cross she wore around her neck.

One like the necklace left for Cara.

Damn. Who was this bastard?

They sure as hell didn't have much to go on. When it came to leaving a traceable clue, he'd been successful at leaving them close to nothing. No fingerprints. No DNA. Not a trace to lead them back to who he was.

He was local. Of that, they were pretty sure. But there wasn't much else.

Common sense said he'd lived in Snow Ridge for some time. Including Cara in his sickness hinted at the fact he'd, more than likely, been around before she left.

Which meant over half the town fell into that category.

But, he reminded himself, working his frustration back down to a controllable level, it was less when it came to who knew the ranch well enough to leave a body where he did.

Not that it still helped much.

The Double 'G' was known and visited by many. It wasn't surprising someone had figured out the more private areas along the fence line.

Which left them all at a loss of where to begin. His own squad. The state troopers. Nobody had definite answers to go on.

"Got a minute?" Charlie Moore, one of the newest members of the squad, stuck his bright blond head through the door. Barely out of the academy, he was just a kid as far as Luke was concerned.

"Yeah." Luke motioned him in. "Whatcha got?"

"The picture of our missing person came in." He dropped it on the desk. "Thought you'd want it right away."

"Thanks." Luke picked up the picture of Sherry Cooper. And there it was, gently resting between her collarbones, the delicate gold cross they had taken from Cara's apartment.

It was one in the same. He was sure of it.

A heavy punch hit his gut. Another girl missing. Another link to Cara.

She was the connection, somehow. But why?

Shuffling through the files, he pulled out Gina's, opened it next to the information he had on Sherry. He took their pictures, laying them side by side.

There was something there. The look of them— dark hair, blue eyes, fair skin. Their traits were, he realized, similar to Cara's.

It was far from an exact match. But it was close enough to give him pause. Grabbing a picture in each hand, holding them out at arm's length, he brought an image of Cara to mind, then looked at the two women.

It was a stretch. But at this point, it was all he had.

Picking up the telephone at the edge of the desk, he called the ranch. It was time to talk to Cara. Time to see if she could make the connection.

**\*\*\*\***

Caught in that moment between sleep and awareness, Cara pushed deeper under the covers and curled into the hard warmth at her side, comfortable and content.

The crisp, teasing scent of sunshine and wilderness surrounded her. A gentle peace hovered, encouraging her to linger at the edge of dreams.

She couldn't think of a single reason why she needed to get out of bed. Not when the temptation to stay was so strong.

The heat at her side shifted beneath her and realization slowly returned. Reluctantly opening her eyes, she found her body curled against Cade. Her head rested on his broad chest. Legs tangled with his.

Sunlight peeked through the center slit of the curtains, reminding her morning had come before they'd ever found their way to bed. Brought back the dark memories bringing her to the ranch in the first place.

Refusing to deal with them, she chased it all away, concentrating instead on the feel of Cade's firm, hard body snug against hers.

She arched her neck and caught him staring at her.

"Morning." Satisfaction shimmered in the hazel

depths of his eyes as it pulled a sly smile over his full lips. He looked content, almost cocky, lying there looking down on her.

He tightened the arm curled around her, pulling her closer. Lowering his mouth, he found hers, dragging her into a heated kiss, full of the passion they'd shared not long ago.

There were things, she knew, she had to think over. But not now. Not with Cade's lips working their magic over hers, drawing back the heat never fully disappearing with sleep.

After all that had happened, she'd take this and savor it. Worries and second guesses could wait till later.

Anchoring her heels at the bottom of the mattress, she pushed up and turned to deepen the kiss. He felt good, so right, underneath her. She couldn't imagine a better way to wake up.

Thoughts of round two kicked up her pulse. Cade shoved his fingers through her hair. Pulling her back from the kiss, he stared without a word.

She smiled, slow and seductive. Keeping her gaze locked with his, she curled over him, trapping him underneath her as she locked her legs around his sides.

Lowering her mouth, she took him in a kiss of her own control. Groaning, he closed his arms around her, holding her tight against his warmth.

She could take him now. A short slide down his broad chest and she'd settle over him, taking him and all he offered. Feeling him throb inside as they again became one, finding the heat that spiraled uncontrollably between them.

Deepening the kiss, she vibrated against him. Bare

skin to bare skin. Fire igniting, fueling the need.

She was ready. Needing to feel.

A few sharp knocks shook the door.

"Damn." Cade pulled his mouth from hers, looking at her a moment more before rolling out from underneath her.

As he fumbled on the floor in search of his clothes, it took her a moment to realize she was sprawled out naked on the bed. A clear shot for whoever waited on the other side of the door.

And then it hit—realization weighed down by memories.

Her and Cade, together in bed. The knock at the door bringing the news of Jacob's death. A sharp fist closed around her heart as she pushed off the edge of the mattress and grabbed her clothes while Cade yanked jeans over his long, muscular legs.

Leaving his shirt untouched at the side of the bed, he waited while she threw her clothes on before he opened the door.

She nearly collapsed back to the bed when his dad's familiar face filled the space.

*Just like last time.*

Holding herself steady, she forced a smile when his eyes looked past Cade and landed on her. "Luke called. He'll be here in about an hour. Says he wants to talk to Cara."

Cade glanced over his shoulder. "We'll be ready," he promised, closing the door before turning back to Cara.

There was worry in the gaze he rested on her. "You okay?"

Though it was a lie, she nodded. "I'm going to take

a shower." She sucked in a deep breath and turned for the bathroom, desperately needing an escape.

****

She wasn't going there. It was a road she'd already traveled too many times.

Tossing off the clothes she'd quickly thrown on minutes before, she stood in front of the mirror, the aftermath of Cade's lovemaking staring back at her.

Lips swollen from his demanding kisses. Cheeks rubbed red from the morning stubble he hadn't had the chance to shave. There was no question she'd been thoroughly satisfied. Anyone who saw her could see that.

Including Patrick, standing at the door and looking at her as he had that day long ago.

*Again*...she wasn't going there. Certain memories were better left in the past. Reliving them would never bring Jacob back or change what had happened that night so long ago.

Or what had happened only a few short hours ago.

Had she been a fool for going back? Back to Cade's arms. To the unbridled passion she wasn't sure was for the best.

Hell. She didn't know. And at this moment, she really didn't want to know.

Scowling at her expression looking back at her, she turned for the shower, hitting the knobs with more force than necessary. Water sprayed as she set the temperature higher than she usually would, needing the extra shot of heat to wash away all she tried to forget.

She'd stepped in and tilted her head back, heated water running gloriously over her shoulders when she heard the creak of hinges.

She didn't have to look to see. She already knew who it was.

He didn't ask permission, didn't hesitate, as he stepped into the shower. His large form sucked up what little space there was.

Her eyes widened as he stepped underneath the water and pressed their bodies together. A whisper of a touch. Enough to tease. To hint at what they both knew simmered below the surface.

"Cade, I—"

He pressed a finger to her lips. "No words, Cara." He replaced his finger with his mouth. Slow and gentle, he took her in.

And she was lost. Unable to fight against what he promised.

Shuddering underneath his kiss, she raised her hands from her sides, sliding them over his shoulders and catching them behind his neck.

"So beautiful," he murmured. His mouth strayed from hers, gliding over the curve of her chin, the slope of her neck.

He teased there, finding the sensitive spot below her ear and brushing a gentle tongue over it. Again and again, until her head fell back with a gasp of pleasure.

Hot water sliced over them. Steam gathered, closing them in their own little world as he moved lower over the curve of her collarbone, trailing the shape of her breasts.

Dropping her hands into the tumbled fall of his whiskey-brown hair, she fought to stay on two feet as his tongue teased a hardened nipple, drawing it into the warmth of his mouth.

She melted into him. Every part of her was his for

the taking. His hands, rough from working the ranch, roamed, lighting a fire over wet, bare skin.

Over the curve of her waist. Around her hips. The inside of her thighs. He teased. He tasted. He touched until she was sure she could take no more.

"Please, Cade." Her knees weak, she tightened the twist of her fingers in his hair, holding on with all she had.

He looked at her. Hazel eyes dark with desire, he smiled before lowering his mouth to her other breast. Taking it as he had with the first, teasing with his mouth and tongue.

And his hands roamed. Every inch of her body. He took, he touched, without mercy. Pushing her higher and higher. Building the desperation until she was sure she would burst from it.

"You're mine." He pressed against her, sliding slowly up her body until they stood face to face. Water streamed over them, burning flesh already on fire. "You've always been mine."

Using his weight, he eased her against the porcelain wall at her back, pinning her there. She gasped at the sensations running through her threatening to take control and send her over the edge.

Off balance, her head spinning, every nerve ending tingling, she reached between them and wrapped her hand around his hard length. He throbbed against her palm, driving her desperate need even higher.

Groaning, Cade cupped his hand behind her head, bringing her to him as she stroked and teased just as he had. She didn't stop. Couldn't stop.

She needed to make him feel what she did—the desperation seeping through her bones tangling with the need roaring out of control.

"No more." Strong, firm fingers grabbed her wrist, yanking her away. "I need you. Now."

Curling his hands beneath her shoulders, he lifted until her feet no longer touched the floor, the wall at her back her only anchor.

Nipping at her bottom lip, forcing her to open to him, accept his kiss, he lowered her, inch by agonizing inch until she closed around him.

Every last breath pushed from her lungs. Her heart beat rapidly against her ribs. She couldn't think. Couldn't do. Only feel.

He swelled inside her, filling her until she was sure she would burst. Curling her nails into the hard lines of his back, she held on for all she had as he began to circle his hips beneath her.

Water covered their sleek bodies. Steam billowed, closing them in as one, existing only in that moment. Aching, pushing, throbbing for more. For that magic only they could create.

She held on for as long as she could, staying with Cade, matching his every thrust. He melted against her, pushing her higher until she was no longer sure where he ended and she began.

"Oh...God...Cade." Losing control, she held on desperately as she shattered. Wave after wave of dark pleasure took over, dragging her under until she knew only the feel of him shaking beneath her. He grabbed her tight, her name escaping on a desperate whisper before he tumbled over the edge.

Chapter Fifteen

Though the sun still shone outdoors, here, inside his private sanctuary, there was only dark. So thick he saw nothing. Moved by memory rather than sight.

He'd thought of her—the one waiting for him. Ready for him.

But he couldn't just disappear for the day. People expected things from him, would question if he was gone.

So he'd waited patiently, knowing it would be worth it in the end.

He flipped the switch, bright light filling the modest bunker, and found wide eyes full of fear staring at him.

Ahh…she was awake. That was good. She could watch while he prepared.

Too drugged to speak or scream, she lay motionless on the skinny bed pushed into the farthest corner. Shackles caught her wrists and ankles.

She was his, for whatever he chose. Ready for the sacrifice. Ready to do her part as he offered another. Preparing—always preparing—for the moment when Cara waited for him. For his control, taking her to places she'd never imagine.

He took great satisfaction in knowing she watched as he pulled a vat of holy water from the sealed cupboard, kept safe from contamination.

Acquiring it from Saint Mary's hadn't been easy. Not under the eagle-eyed watch of Father Frances.

His latest treasure had proven even harder.

From the long stainless steel counter where he worked, he picked up the heavy silver-laden crucifix. Wondered if its absence from Father Frances's personal collection had been noticed yet.

He'd taken it from his old, drafty office during his long, tiresome sermon last Sunday then sat through the remaining service, proud to have taken such a valuable piece from one who claimed to know and see all through the Lord.

Running his thumb gently over the intricate carvings, he understood the prize he held. Knew his use for it. Saw it clearly.

But first the holy water. He needed her pure, cleansed of all dirtying her soul and fouling her very being.

The thrill of her eyes following his every move, terror clear in their blue depths, pushed him to hurry. Only long ago learned patience held him back, understanding the steps in any religious rite were important.

He'd already sanitized the bowl he'd used for Gina. It sat, cleansed and ready, at the sink. Pulling the thin cloth off, he folded it into a perfect square and laid it in its place at the counter's edge.

Next came the boiling. The single burner was saved and used only for the holy water so as not to taint it with other evils.

Confident, sure of his every move, he whistled, an old hymn he'd learned from *Her* many years ago. She would be proud of him as she'd made it all possible.

Gave him the blessing to know what was meant—for him, for *Her*—for Cara.

It was good. All his preparations—followed carefully and methodically. Everything was ready. Ready for the one who would satisfy him for now before leading to even greater as Cara came closer and closer to being his.

****

If she was honest, the last thing Cara wanted to do was leave the bedroom.

There was something therapeutic about being caught up in Cade's arms. Loved by him until she was nothing more than a pile of mush unable to move a muscle or speak a word.

Behind the door, caught in the haze of mind-blowing sex, she could forget the reality looming. Pretend none of it was true.

But the minute she stepped out into the hall, Cade close at her side, everything returned, forcing her to face what she'd been able to avoid for a few short, glorious hours.

Voices met them at the top of the stairs.

"Sounds like a party down there." He pressed a hand to her back as she paused, hand on the rail and feet hovering at the edge.

A party she wasn't sure she wanted to join, especially when the unmistakable sound of her father's voice drifted up. Happy as she was he was out and about more, this was a time she wanted him back at home, watching his news program on the television.

Adult though she was, it didn't sit well, thinking what she and Cade had been up to while her father waited in the kitchen.

And he'd know, just as the others would. There was no getting around the truth. No matter how hard she might be tempted to try and deny anything happened.

Reluctantly, she allowed Cade to guide her down the stairs and into the crowded kitchen. They were all there. Patrick and her dad gathered at the far end of the table. Jake and Luke sat across from them.

Penny, busy at the counter with Hattie, smiled at her when she entered, a knowing twinkle in her eyes. The two worked quickly over Hattie's famous Strawberry Cream Cake, arranging it on a large platter.

"Hi, Dad." Unable to meet his gaze, she dropped a kiss on his rough cheek before taking the seat beside him.

Refusing to leave her side, Cade took the chair next to her and squeezed close as Hattie pushed through, placing the cake-heavy platter in the center of the table next to a pot of fresh-brewed coffee.

"You okay?" Her dad dropped a large, protective hand over hers resting on the edge of the table.

She forced what she hoped was a reassuring smile. "I'm okay. Better now than I was."

"What the hell is going on?" He turned his attention to Luke, fear dancing dangerously close to anger in his voice. "Who the hell is doing this to my girl?"

Looking as if he hadn't slept in a month, Luke shook his head, frustrated. "I wish the hell I knew." He opened the plain brown folder sitting on the table in front of him.

"I know you said you didn't know Gina." He pulled her picture from the folder, sliding it across the table.

"But what about her?" He grabbed the corner of another picture, placing it beside Gina's. "Her name is Sherry Cooper. She was reported missing this morning."

She slid both pictures closer to study them. Her heart froze, a chill chasing up her spine when her eyes passed over the delicate cross hanging from the neck of the second woman.

"The necklace." She swallowed hard over the knot forming in her throat. "That's the necklace that was left in my apartment last night."

No. Her head ached from the truth creeping in.

She looked again at the missing woman staring up at her. To think of what might have happened to her. Of how the necklace ended up hanging off her painting.

Her mind didn't want to go there, refused to follow the path of the dark thoughts drumming to life.

"What the hell?" Cade grabbed the picture, holding it up for a better look. "Do you think the one who left the necklace for Cara is the same one who took this woman?"

Gentleness filled Luke's hazel eyes as they rested on Cara before passing on to his brother. "Yes. We believe there's a connection."

"What the hell does that mean?" Cade demanded, fear getting the best of him. He was angry. She felt the heat of it burning against her as she sat there beside him. There was no question he was set on making sure somebody paid for what was happening.

"It means, right now, we're investigating the theory the person who murdered Gina is also the one who left the cross in Cara's apartment. And, more than likely, abducted Sherry Cooper."

"I don't understand any of this." She pressed firm fingers to her temples, fighting off the headache quickly forming. "Who would do this? What do I have to do with it?"

Luke turned his attention back to her, his gaze reflecting the same anger she'd felt from Cade. The same determination to protect her from whatever danger she faced. "There's a connection. It's weak, I admit. But it's all I've found so far."

"What is it?" Her hands shook as she grabbed an empty coffee cup and filled it to the rim. It was something to do, to distract her from fully accepting the truth staring her hard in the face.

Luke took the picture from Cade and laid it back with Gina's. "The three of you have similar looks. They aren't extremely close, but they're enough to notice."

She hadn't seen it. Hadn't noticed before. Setting her coffee cup beside her, she slid the pictures closer, looking carefully at the two women who, as strangers, had webbed themselves into her life.

Both were younger, at the beginning of their twenties rather than the end. And nothing in their overall appearance struck Cara as similar to her own.

But she saw what she guessed Luke had. The hair. The eyes. They were close to her own. Enough so that a sense of unease slid over her.

"I can't do this right now." She shoved the pictures away, out of sight, and pushed up from her chair. "I'm sorry. I just can't think about any of this at the moment."

Feeling weak, like a coward, she headed for the back door. She stepped out on the back porch, sucking in large, greedy gulps of fresh air.

The idea of the cross and the young women with the same hair, same eyes as her—what it meant terrified her. Left her wanting to do nothing more than bury her head under the covers and forget it all.

Standing at the low railing, staring out over the ranch, she couldn't imagine how any of this was happening. Not here. Not where small mountain town life was supposed to offer the comfort of freedom from such horrors.

The echo of the door closing vibrated behind her. "So." Cade dropped a gentle arm around her shoulders, tugging until she nestled close to his side. "I was thinking we should get you out tonight. Away from all this."

She started to shake her head, but he stopped her. "No stubbornness. Not tonight. You deserve a break. Let me give that to you."

She thought of the earlier temptation to shove her head under the covers and found it more tempting. But a glance at the stubborn set of his jaw, the determination shimmering in his hazel gaze, made it clear arguing would be useless.

"Okay." She let out a long, slow breath. "What were you thinking?"

"You'll see." He dropped a kiss on top of her ebony curls. "Trust me."

\*\*\*\*

Just as Cade had hoped, the pub was full of life.

Jake, a true lover of their local bands, had done good tonight. The lively, fiddle-rich music from the Irish country band poured through the doors, surrounding them the minute he and Cara entered.

Beer flowed. Laughter filled the air. And a smile finally graced Cara's lips as she saw those waiting for her gathered around a group of tables in the back.

"Oh. This is perfect." She squeezed his hand before stepping off ahead of him to greet Jackie and her husband.

He liked this. Liked to see the spark of happy return, knowing he had something to do with it.

If he could, he'd make sure she never lost it. If there was a way, he would keep her shielded from all the craziness surrounding her. Protected so nothing dark or dangerous touched her.

It was part of what he'd always known. The responsibility of taking care of her. To look out for the little, pig-tailed tag-along he couldn't shake even when he'd wanted to.

But there was more striking harder, hitting deeper since knowing danger came so close.

He'd felt it earlier in the privacy of her room, holding her tight. Getting her back into his bed had been his main goal. But something had changed. An emotion he wasn't ready to accept, but knew was there, just the same.

"She looks better." Jake slung an easy arm around Cade and stole a glance at Cara on the other end of the table.

"Yeah. She does." Cade grabbed the pitcher of beer from the edge of the table, pouring himself a generous glass. "It's a good escape. At least for a little while. Thanks for that."

"Hell, all I did was spread the word and move a few tables around. No thanks needed for that."

Cade moved his gaze from where Cara sat with

Jackie to take in the others who had come. His dad and Luke talked over their beers while Jimmy and Seth enjoyed a good laugh with the hands they had brought along from the Double 'G' and Moonshine.

Colin raised his glass in salute as Cade's glance passed over him before turning back to the pretty blonde from the coffee shop sitting at his side.

It's what he'd wanted. An easygoing crowd. Out for a good time. No worries. No fears. Just laughter and booze and some good times with friends.

It's what Cara needed, deserved.

He looked back at her sitting at the other end of the table and caught her eye. For a moment, it was just them, trapped in the memory of what they'd shared only a few short hours ago.

Drawn to her, unable to stop the need to touch, feel all that she was, he filled a second glass with beer and brought it to her. "Thought you might be thirsty."

She smiled at him. "Thanks." Her fingers brushed his as she took the glass, bringing back images from earlier. Of water slicing over her as she clung to him and the world shook underneath him.

Well, hell. He needed to get a hold of himself. If he didn't, he'd be dragging her right back out of the night he'd planned. Racing her back to bed as quickly as he could.

The answering spark of memory in her own blue eyes tempted him even further.

"We need wings." Jackie's insistent voice broke through the heated haze holding him hostage. "Lots of them."

She poked Cara, giving her the look, one understood in friendships as long and close as theirs.

"Yes. Wings." Cara looked up at Cade. "That sounds good. Would you get us some?"

He was being played. He knew it but chose not to argue.

\*\*\*\*

"Okay. Spill it." Jackie jumped the minute Cade was out of the way.

"Spill what?" Cara knew but preferred to stall, not sure she was up to sharing details yet.

"Something's happened. Between you and Cade. I saw it. Right there. Clear as day in the way you two kept looking at each other."

It was useless to deny. Jackie would know she was lying. And she wouldn't hesitate to call her out on it. In fact, she'd probably enjoy it.

"Sex is a good distraction when you have some crazy lunatic breaking into your apartment."

"Uh-huh." In the way she always did, Jackie waited. Knew the full truth would come if she had patience.

"I didn't want to be alone. I started it. Enjoyed it…a lot."

"And now?" Jackie folded her hands on the table and looked carefully at her. Waited for what she wasn't saying.

"And now." Cara took a long, slow drink from her beer, stalling for as long as she could. "I don't know. It was sex. It was good. Really good." She beamed, the smile of a woman well loved.

"But I know better than to let it become anything more." Even to her own ears, it sounded false. But it was what it was. What it had to be. To allow more would be to lose all she'd worked so hard to become after leaving Snow Ridge behind.

Jackie didn't look convinced. Taking a slow sip from her iced tea, she set determined, all too knowing eyes on Cara over the rim of her glass. "So it was just sex. Nothing more."

"Yes," Cara answered for her own benefit as well as her friend's. "Just sex. *Really good sex*. But, still, nothing more."

Jackie stared at her, doubting her words. Still, she didn't argue or push for more. "We will, sometime soon, talk more," she promised instead.

"After all this." She swept her hand in a wide circle. "When what you have on your mind is not crazies stalking you but just the bare facts of sex…with Cade."

Nothing would change by then, Cara was certain of it. But she didn't argue.

From the corner of her eye, she caught sight of Cade, hands heavy with the load of wings he carried.

It didn't matter much about the later talk Jackie promised. Didn't matter about where sex would or wouldn't take her and Cade. What mattered, in the here and now, was this chance to forget that Cade had given her. A chance to sit back and enjoy life with a good drink and great friends.

More had gathered around the table, ramping up the party atmosphere and the light edge of fun surrounding her since the moment they had stepped foot into the pub.

And this is what she would enjoy. All other thoughts, confusion, questions, fears, could wait till later.

Much later.

\*\*\*\*

It was perfect.

He sat with them. Shared a drink, a toast, a good song.

And they never knew. Never guessed at the fact he was among them. The one they searched and hunted, labeling him as dangerous and unbalanced.

They didn't know. Didn't have a clue.

Chugging his beer, he watched Cara. The tilt of her chin as she listened to the conversation of others. The bright spark in her blue eyes when she laughed.

Oh yes. She was all he needed...wanted.

There was so much beauty. So much desire. Just like *Her*.

He'd done right. Made the true decisions giving him the right to come closer and closer to taking what was truly his. What he had waited for so long for fate to finally make true.

And just like Gina, this last beauty he'd had was for Cara. For her to understand, before the time came, she was important enough and special enough to be worthy of the practice he pushed on himself. So that he would be perfect for her. Be all she deserved and more.

And it was time for her to discover the truth of his latest conquest. As she had discovered the truth of Gina. He had his plan in mind. Knew what it would take. What he must do.

Soon, she would know and experience it all.

Just as it was meant to be.

Chapter Sixteen

"We could push the opening to a later date." Jackie pulled an oddly shaped vase from the box at her feet, wondering how it was some things could actually be considered art. "Nobody would blame you."

"No." Cara crumpled a sheet of bubble wrap and tossed it to the side. "We open at the end of the month, as planned."

Frustration itched at her, pushing her patience to the edge. She'd spent two days locked up at the ranch. Protected from some sick crazy who, she was sure, was taking great joy in the chaos he created.

That was all the time she was willing to put her life on hold. She had responsibilities. A shop she believed in, deserving her attention. There was no way she was going to let some invisible jerk take that away from her.

Precious Gems was what she had sweated, worked, and thrived for. Nobody deserved the power to take that away from her. She knew when it was time to move to the ranch for her safety. But that didn't justify giving up on her shop or the future it offered.

Besides, only a fool would try something now.

She glanced at the lanky redhead making himself comfortable behind the counter with the morning paper and a cup of coffee. Ordered by the chief himself, Officer Mitch had been assigned as her personal shadow whenever Cade or one of his brothers couldn't be with her.

She was never alone. *Never*.

After ten years free from the overprotection of her childhood, it was hard to accept. But it was necessary, she knew. And so she didn't argue, even when the urge came on strong.

"Okay." Sensing the frustration running through her friend, Jackie dropped a gentle hand on Cara's shoulder. "We open as planned. But, fair warning, if I'm in labor, you won't be getting my butt here to help."

"Really?" Cara smiled at her friend, feeling better at the thought of a new baby. "Let's hope, then, he's not a latecomer like his mother."

"We can hope." Laughing, Jackie went back to her unpacking, Cara doing the same.

And it felt right again. Being here. Doing what she had set out to do. A crazy might lurk outside. But here, inside her shop, laughing with her best friend, all was good.

\*\*\*\*

Cade trusted Luke. Knew he'd placed one of his best in charge of looking out for Cara.

Still, worry ate at him as he tended to the chores the ranch demanded. Those he could no longer pass on or ignore altogether.

At the main barn, tucked inside his office, the strong smell of leather and fresh hay surrounded him as he flipped through the ledger for their latest sales, estimating what they had coming in. Worked around the costs they would face come end of summer when he acquired Balton—a magnificent stallion he knew would be a prize for the ranch.

The snow had melted away. The sun's bright rays peeked through the open barn doors, filtering into his office as he fought to concentrate on the work in front of him.

It was hell, trying to focus while images of Cara pranced through his head. He saw her, the fear and terror on her face when he'd entered her apartment after the necklace had been left.

The desire and heat burning in her deep blue eyes as she pulsed underneath him while he exploded inside her.

So much to try and set out of his mind. Too much.

With an aggravated growl, he shoved aside the ledger and pushed up from his seat.

He'd walk it off then get back to work.

The neigh of the horses in their stalls called to him. Only a few were forced to remain indoors on such a beautiful spring day. Injuries restricted them, making them restless behind their closed gates while the others had been let free to run.

He would go to them, soothe them, working thoughts of Cara from his mind with simple acts so that he could get back to the work waiting for him.

Casper, one of his favorites, popped her nose over the stall as his footsteps echoed inside the barn. A dark spotted mare, her spunk and stubbornness finally got the best of her. Deciding she didn't feel much like having a rider on her back, she'd reared up during a ride along the fence line. Nearly tossing off the ranch hand in the saddle, she came down into a forgotten bundle of barbed wire hidden in dried bush.

The hand had escaped unharmed, but Casper required fifteen stitches to close the gash on her front leg. Stitches now keeping her locked inside the barn, where she hated it most.

"Poor girl," he soothed, running a gentle hand down her nose.

She swept a hoof against the ground, kicking up dust.

"I know. You'd rather be anywhere but here." He patted her smooth neck. "And if you stop trying to throw off my hands, this should be your last lock-in."

Her head bobbed, agreeing with him or defying, he had no clue. With one final pat on her neck, he turned to go then stopped when a strange flash of light caught his attention.

It came from the backside of the stall where shadows made it hard to see the cross on first glance. It wasn't until silver caught the sunlight, reflecting it back to the dim interior of the barn, that he got a good enough look.

*What the hell?*

Flipping the latch on the gate, he kept a comforting hand on Casper's sleek coat, letting her know where he was as he moved behind her. He didn't want to spook her and get a kick in the gut for it.

His heart stopped. An icy chill ran up his spine as he stared at what was shoved in the corner.

Aware of the risk if he scared Casper in such a confined space, images of Joe's accident hitting hard, he bit back the angry curse words hovering on his lips.

With a hand itching to form a fist and punch something, he wrapped his fingers around the crucifix dangling from a loosely pounded-in nail with a heart-wrenching photo dangling beneath it.

Holding his temper, a task that was far from easy,

he backed out of the stall, the carvings along the crucifix biting into his palm.

Latching the gate, he grabbed his phone and held it to his ear while he stared at the picture. It was her, the missing woman from the picture. The one wearing the necklace left for Cara.

She was naked and bound at the wrists and ankles. Her blue eyes were wide with fear.

Impatient, he waited through the rings on the other end, relieved when Luke's voice broke through.

"Call the officer you have with Cara, make sure she's okay," he demanded, refusing to waste a second on ridiculous greetings. "The sick bastard struck again."

"Damn it." The anger in Luke's tone vibrated through the phone, matching the emotion boiling hot through Cade's blood. "Are you at the ranch?"

"Yeah. The main barn. He left another surprise in one of the stalls."

"Don't let anyone touch a thing," Luke barked, frustration weighing heavy in every word. "I'll call, have Cara brought to the ranch, and be on my way."

Relief swelled, knowing Cara would be back under his watch. "I'll wait for you here."

Dropping the phone in his pocket, he stormed into the office. He didn't like this. Didn't like it one bit. Thoughts of his hands wrapped around the throat of whoever was responsible for this horror ran through his mind as he straightened up the little work he'd been able to do.

He would be even further behind now but didn't give a damn. All that mattered was Cara and keeping her safe from the threats refusing to end.

\*\*\*\*

She was pissy. Cara didn't try hiding it as she shoved open the passenger door of the police cruiser.

After all that had happened lately, she and Jackie were making progress, unpacking and stocking shelves. They had hit a nice rhythm, one rudely interrupted when Officer Mitch announced he had orders to return her to the ranch.

She'd argued. But in the end, it hadn't done any good as she and Jackie were escorted to the cruiser and safely tucked away inside.

It was Cade's doing. She was sure of it. And just more proof why things between them could never go any further than where they were.

Without waiting for Jackie or Officer Mitch, she stormed past the main house. The fast pace of her steps matched the impatience and irritation simmering through her veins as she made her way to the barn.

Over and over, the tirade she planned on unleashing repeated in her head. He had to accept she had a life to live outside the fear hanging over them. One that involved being out of his sight, his protection, no matter how much he hated it.

Oh yes, he was going to get an earful. And then, she was going straight back to Precious Gems and continue her work.

She had it all there, puffed up inside and ready to explode, as she broke through the line of aspens between the house and barn.

The barn, where flashing red and blue sirens shoved the truth back at her. A handful of uniformed officers were coming and going from the shadowed interior. Low, intense voices drifted her way.

A heavy fist hit hard. Dark, frightening images

returned, taking her back to what she'd spent the day trying to forget.

She saw Cade a second before he looked up from his conversation with Luke, hazel eyes locking with hers. And in his gaze, she felt everything she wanted to be over hit in full force all over again.

He reached her in seconds, grabbing her hands. Pulling her close, he held her as if afraid to ever let her go. "You okay?" He pulled back enough for his eyes to peer deep into her own.

"I'm fine." She offered what she could of a smile. All the angry words she'd collected on her way to the barn slipped away. "What happened?"

He didn't want to answer. She saw it clearly before he diverted his gaze to look back at the excitement behind him.

"Tell me what's happened," she demanded, taking a step back from his hold.

Cade looked at her, wishing he could shield her from whatever was happening, she knew. "Something was left in one of the stalls."

She didn't respond. Only stared, waiting for the rest.

And she'd wait, for as long as it took.

"I was walking the barn, stopped to check on Casper when something caught my eye inside her stall. When I went in, I found a crucifix hanging above a picture of the woman reported missing."

Cara remembered the picture she'd been left when Gina was missing. She could only guess the one Cade found had been just as horrifying. "It was from him, wasn't it?" She glanced past, watched Luke in deep conversation with one of the officers. His face was dark and troubled.

It was a nightmare, refusing to end. Whoever the monster was, he'd proven he knew no limit to his evil. "He's killed her. Like he did Gina."

"We don't know."

"You know." Her voice rose in a mix of fear and frustration. "You might not have the proof, but you know. We all know. He took her like he did Gina. Killed her."

She knew he wanted to deny it. Wanted to reassure her everything was okay and she had nothing to fear.

But he couldn't. She saw the understanding as it settled over him. He wouldn't…couldn't lie to her. No matter how much he was tempted.

"Yes. We all know." His anger snapped at her. She wanted to push back, challenge him, but Luke's arrival at their side prevented her from doing anything but flash him a quick look of disgust.

"We have a lead." He spoke to Cade though his gaze centered on Cara. He laid a gentle hand on her arm, consoling even as the dreaded words left his mouth.

"Father Frances from Saint Mary's told one of my officers he was missing a crucifix from his collection."

*Saint Mary's.* Cara's heart constricted at the name.

She'd heard her dad's stories enough to recognize the church. Her parents had been faithful, constant members until her mother's death. Until it had become too hard to walk through the doors and remember all he'd lost.

It had to be a coincidence. *It had to be.* Because the alternative was too frightening to consider.

"I'm headed there now to find out what I can." He

tightened his hold on her arm before dropping his hand back to his side.

"I want to go with you." She turned away from Cade, centering her attention on Luke.

"I'm not sure that's a good idea." A tough cop though he was, he faltered when it came to her demands. It was, she knew, a plus in her favor.

She needed to be part of taking down whoever brought this horror. Needed to feel as if she was doing something to fight against the fear threatening to take over and control her.

"I'm sure it is a good idea." Her gaze wide, pleading, she felt only the smallest bit of shame for using their past to get what she wanted.

Reaching up, she flattened a palm against his broad chest. "I need to be there. Hear what he has to say." She refused to falter under his determined gaze. "It's more than just another church to me. You know that."

He didn't like it. Not one bit. She saw it in the firm set of his mouth and the hard shift of his shoulders. Still, she recognized he was giving in. Knew him well enough to see it in the softening of his gaze as well as the frustrated hand he shoved through his hair.

"Fine...damn." He backed away, shaking his head. "I don't like it. But I'll allow it."

Satisfied, she turned, ready to go.

He stopped her. "I'm letting this happen because of who you are and what you mean to me. But don't think, for even a second, that I'm going to let such feelings change anything if I believe, for any reason, that it's time for you to go."

"Okay." She understood his struggle. Respected it.

"I mean it, Cara. If I say you're out of there, that's

exactly what you do, without question."

He showed the battle raging inside. Guilt rose, tempting her to change her mind. "I promise." She reached for him, joining her fingers with his. "If you say go, I'll do it."

Satisfied, he turned back to the officers waiting for him.

She turned back to Cade and caught Jackie hovering behind him.

And there, at that moment, her terrifying present and painful past clashed, threatening to bring her to her knees.

But she wouldn't do it—refused to give in to the rush of emotions surging forth.

For whatever ugly reason, she'd been brought into this hell. And she would face it. Fight it.

Because that was the woman she'd become.

Chapter Seventeen

Though she knew she'd once sat in the pews, Cara had no memory of Saint Mary's other than the street view when she'd pass by.

Sitting proudly, tucked a block away from Main Street, Snow Ridge's oldest church held the beauty of another time. Of another generation, when careful attention was paid to every detail.

Gray stone with intricate carvings gracing the dark wooden doors, the building radiated a peaceful, serene grace that invited in lost souls, offering solitude and redemption within the sturdy walls.

A marble-carved statue of the Virgin Mary greeted those who approached with soft, knowing eyes that watched over all who came and worshiped.

Luke and Cade at her sides, she stood on the old yet sturdy stairs. A sense of dread poked at her as she stared at the big doors waiting for them to enter.

She'd wanted to come. Demanded it.

Yet, standing here now, she wasn't as sure as she'd been.

"You okay?" Cade took her hand.

She had to do this, doubts or not. For her own sanity and self-worth, she couldn't change her mind. "I'm fine." She stepped forward and flattened a palm against the wooden door, giving it a determined shove.

Shadows surrounded her. An eerie silence hovered.

Thick red carpet, stretching from one side to the other of the modest narthex, muffled her steps.

Though the walls were painted a pristine white, it did little to help brighten the space. Dark wood paneling and deep colored stained-glass windows drained the light and left an uneasy chill raking up her spine.

From the shoebox-size front office, a tight-curled, gray-haired woman peered out. A mixture of greeting and curiosity danced in her dull brown eyes. "Can I help you?"

Luke brushed past, holding out his badge. "Is Father Frances available?"

Her gaze widened at the sight of his badge. She looked from him to where Cara and Cade stood a few feet behind, her brows drawn together in concern.

"I believe he's back in his office. Let me check." She backed through the small door, the muffled fall of her steps drifting back into the heavy silence surrounding them.

Cara's hand still locked with Cade's, she knew better than to try and pull away. He'd been testy since they left the ranch. She knew he battled his need to protect her and treat her like the child she once was compared to the woman she'd become. Knew what he wanted was so much different than being here, at the church with her, waiting for answers.

Thankfully, there wasn't much waiting to do before the older lady stepped back into the narthex. "Father Frances asked that I take you to his office." Her steps brisk and quick, she circled around them, leading the way toward a side hall edging the outer wall of the church.

The confines of the hallway, thick carpet casting an eerie echo to their steps, left Cara feeling dizzy as she walked at Cade's side, a step behind Luke, deeper and deeper into the church.

Three short, skinny steps at the back of the church, behind the sanctuary, brought an end to the red carpet and dark wood paneling. Standing in the small space surrounded by clergy offices, she was thankful for stark white walls and plain gray linoleum along the floor.

No longer surrounded by the uncomfortable dark shadows, she drew in a long breath, chasing away the uneasiness that had come over her the minute they had stepped inside.

"This way."

Led to one of the few open doors, they hovered outside until given permission to enter.

Father Frances wasn't what she expected.

In her mind, she'd seen gray hair and a short, stumped figure. Wrinkles creasing a face that had been around for decades.

What she found instead was a man not much older than her. Thick black hair was cut short around a firm, oval face, drawing a woman's attention from the first look.

His smile, though troubled, held a certain charm to it. The sparkle in his emerald eyes gave a hint to much more hidden behind those long black robes.

"I must say, Chief, I'm a bit unsettled you're here." He worked his way behind his desk, waving his hand at the chairs on the opposite side, urging them to take a seat.

"Why is that?" Though Cade and Cara claimed two of the four plush leather chairs, Luke waited until

Father Frances sat before claiming his own.

"I had intended to call the station before Elise let me know you'd arrived." His steady gaze passed over the three, landing hard on Cara. She resisted the urge to squirm as he stared, feeling as if he peered straight into her soul, searching for the many sins residing there.

Relief swelled when he turned away to grab the envelope on the corner of his desk. "This was left in the front office an hour ago." He reached across the desk and handed it to Luke. "One of the crucifixes from my collection has recently gone missing, so it disturbed me."

"Is this your missing crucifix?" Luke held up the sealed evidence bag, handing it to Father Frances for a better look.

"It is." His dark brows drew together, lines creasing his forehead. "Where did you find it?"

"At the Double 'G' Ranch, along with this." He held up a second evidence bag, the disturbing picture of Sherry Cooper secured inside. Tossing the bag on the desk, he waited for Father Frances to pick it up, watching his reaction.

Eyes wide, face pale, Father Frances pinched his fingers around the edge of the bag. "I've seen her before. There." He jerked his head toward the envelope Luke held. "I thought…I believed she was merely sleeping or intentionally a part of a rehearsed pose, hoping to make a statement."

Cara tensed as Luke slipped his finger under the lip of the envelope. Reaching across the armrests, Cade caught her hand, holding it firmly in his.

He kept a steady eye on his older brother as he pulled out the contents.

*Another picture.*

Luke cursed before handing it to Cade. "You said this was delivered an hour ago?"

Father Frances nodded as her frightened gasp filled the office. His concerned gaze bore into her, but she couldn't look at him. Couldn't tear her eyes away from the picture Cade quickly moved from her sight.

It was too late. She'd seen enough. And just like the first picture of Gina, it was an image she knew she'd never fully get rid of.

He'd repeated his ways. The picture of Sherry looked as if it drifted over the first. She was naked, hands folded serenely over her ample breasts with the stolen crucifix resting between them, silver dancing against nude skin.

She did look as if she was sleeping at first glance. But Cara knew better. Had no doubt life had long ago left by the time the photo was taken.

But even that knowledge wasn't what sent the icy chill up her spine. It was the image behind it clasping a tight fist around her heart, draining the air from her lungs.

The cemetery. She knew it well. Wished she didn't.

Unlike Snow Ridge Memorial Hills, the main cemetery for the town, Golden Oaks was smaller, more personal, serving only a select few in the community.

Few…like Jacob's family.

A decade might have passed since she'd stepped foot on the sacred grounds but she remembered it like it was yesterday. Remembered that final day when Jacob had been laid to rest.

She couldn't—

Every breath was a struggle. Needing space, the

walls suddenly feeling as if they were closing in, she pushed up from her chair. Avoiding the concerned stares of the men around her, she made a quick dash for the door.

Leaving behind the low murmur of their voices, she retraced the way they had come. Down the stairs, through the dark hall, until she reached the double doors and shoved hard.

Stepping into the sunlight, she sucked in large, greedy breaths of fresh air, used them to calm the nerves jumping recklessly through every inch of her body.

She stood alone for only a moment before Cade burst through the doors. He didn't ask questions. Didn't try using words to soothe her.

He just grabbed her. Pulling her hard against his comforting warmth, he folded strong, protective arms around her. She fought not to lose it.

She didn't know. Had no way of knowing. It could be a coincidence. What were the odds he would know? Would use that?

She already knew the answers she didn't want to admit.

Cade's comforting arms encouraging tears she refused to shed, she flattened her hands on his broad chest, pushing back from his hold. "I'm okay."

There was no missing the doubt in his eyes, but he didn't argue. He gave her space, still holding her arm, as if needing to feel her for his own sanity.

"We don't know," he started, swallowing the rest back as he saw the reality shimmering in her blue eyes.

She knew. And she wouldn't accept anything suggesting otherwise.

"Luke was making the call as I left the office, bringing in his best." Reaching out, he tucked a stray strand of ebony hair behind her ear before dropping a soft kiss on her forehead.

"We'll go with him. As soon as he's here. The cemetery is close. We'll know soon."

Yes, they would know.

They would know what was already a frightening truth to the both of them.

\*\*\*\*

The cemetery sat a few blocks away from Saint Mary's.

Luke didn't like the idea of Cara being where civilians didn't belong. He wanted her back safe at the ranch. Cara saw that truth clearly in his eyes as he approached.

"I feel like a broken record." His hand curled tight around her arm, he pulled her to the side as soon as they reached the small, quiet cemetery tucked on the edge of town. "I'm telling you again, I don't like this. And I have final say. No matter how much you might argue."

"Okay." She pushed onto her toes, leaving a kiss on his cheek.

He caught her. "I mean it. I love you too much to repeat what happened the last time when we searched for Gina. I don't want you stumbling on to another scene like you did then."

She curled a soft hand against his cheek. "I promise not to venture anywhere alone. And I'll let your officers," she swept her other hand toward the street where, with their lights flashing, squad cars collected against the curb, "lead the way. Wherever it might be."

He wasn't happy. Just like back at the ranch, she saw it clearly. Still, he leaned down and dropped a quick kiss on her lips.

"Stay with her," he tossed at Cade before turning on his heels to collect the officers climbing out of their cars.

Her mind a jumble of so many different emotions, Cara stared at the wrought iron gates allowing entrance to the graves tucked inside.

Would they find something? Anything?

How could they not? The last picture sent, the terrifying one of Gina, had been the one and only link they'd had to find her body.

She didn't believe for a minute this would be any different.

Though the arm Cade dropped around her shoulder was gentle, the look in his eyes was anything but. Anger simmered there, barely held back from exploding to the surface.

She wasn't sure if it was directed at her or at the one who brought them here. Figured it was best not to find out.

"As much as you might hate it, you're staying with me." His harsh voice rubbed hard against nerves already working on overdrive.

Her temper rising, threatening to escape, she fought it back as Luke and his officers hurried past. "I already made my promise to be a good girl," she bit out, falling into step behind the group moving quickly ahead of them. "That should be enough."

It wasn't. Not by a long shot.

Cade didn't want her here. Didn't want her anywhere close to what was happening.

And what the hell was wrong, anyhow, with dragging her back to the ranch, no matter how much she might scream in protest?

He'd heard it before. Had dealt with it. Just because he'd hit some damn understanding of what she fought for when it came to defining who she was didn't mean he had to let her walk into something like this.

He was ready, more than prepared to tell her that. But a single look in her eyes had him biting back every word he wanted to say.

She needed this. He saw it in her troubled gaze. She needed to feel part of trying to end this craziness whether it was logical or not. To Cara, it was what she clung to.

He wasn't going to be the one to take that away.

The slow setting sun danced shadows over the headstones as they moved deeper into the cemetery. Though the breeze swirling between the mountains brought with it the sweet-scented flowers scattered around, he knew Cara only noticed the path in front of them and where it led.

Though it had been ten years since she'd been here, he knew she forgot nothing. Could still clearly see that fateful day. He imagined they had walked this same path behind Jacob's casket. Knew the pain of that day was hitting her all over again, reminding her of everything that had happened and dragged her down so low.

Afraid she was close to stumbling from the weight of it, he tightened his arm around her, keeping her steady.

He hadn't been with her then, on that dark day. It was just another way he'd failed her through that time.

And he wondered now if he was failing her again, not fighting harder to take her back to the ranch and away from all of this.

He heard Hattie's voice, knew what she told him, but it wasn't so easy to accept her wisdom while he felt Cara shiver under his hold. Finding this balance of supporting her while protecting her was proving so much harder than he believed it would be. And which solution was truly right when he felt her struggle beside him.

Especially as officers fanned out around them to search, finding nothing. Every step grew heavier as they headed farther in and the fear of what they would find. Where they would find it.

"They know." She looked at him. "They're heading for Jacob's grave."

As much as he wanted to, he couldn't deny it. "We can wait here." He tightened his hold around her. "There's no reason for us to follow. If we were anybody else, Luke wouldn't have even let us get this far."

"I need to go. I need to know."

Determined, Cara forced one step in front of the other, following the folds of blue uniforms ahead of them.

She knew when it happened. Heard it in the harsh orders barked out in the seconds before she and Cade reached them.

*Jacob.* Just as she expected.

There, propped up against the pale brown headstone, overflowing pots of Petunias at her sides, Sherry sat in the image of a woman in prayer. Knees pushed up to her full breasts, her hands were crossed delicately over their curved tops.

She was bared, as Gina had been, black hair a stark contrast against the white of her skin. Blue eyes stared lifelessly from a face frozen forever in time.

"Damn." Too late, Cade spun her away.

Suddenly weak, tempted to collapse on the hard ground, she leaned into him, forcing a breath through her constricted lungs.

She'd asked to be here. Be a part of this. She couldn't fall apart now.

Grabbing another breath, she forced her legs to remain steady. "I'm—"

She gulped air. "I'm okay. I just need a minute."

"You're far from okay." He jerked her farther away, swearing under his breath.

"You aren't fooling me." She trembled under his hold. "Or yourself."

Controlled chaos exploded. Voices rose. Feet clamored over the path, quick and steady. Another crime scene. Another murder.

And again, Cara centered it.

She fell even deeper into his hold. He pulled her close to his chest, holding her there as Luke broke free from the mass of frantic blue jumping around Jacob's grave.

The concern in his eyes matched what she saw in Cade's. They worried like they always had and always would.

"Shouldn't have let this happen." Self-disproval fell heavy in Luke's voice. "Never should have agreed to let you come along. See something like this."

He pressed a gentle hand against her back. "I want you to go. Back to the ranch. Let Cade, Hattie, and Dad take care of you."

Pulling her head from the comforting warmth of Cade's chest, she looked at him. "I'm okay," she lied to him as she had to Cade.

"It's time to go." He glanced over his shoulder to watch his officers securing the area around Sherry's body. "You made me a promise. I expect you to keep it."

She didn't have it in her to argue, didn't have the desire to. There was nothing she could do. Nothing that would change such a cruelty against another innocent woman.

"Okay." Stepping out of Cade's firm hold, she looked at the two of them, seeing the worry clear in their matching hazel eyes.

She needed to go. For Luke. For Cade. And most of all…for herself.

**** 

Though safe, Cara wasn't altogether sure the ranch was the best place for her.

Her head spinning, she sat in one of the lounge chairs on the back porch, staring up at the stars winking at her from the black sky above.

It hadn't just been Patrick and Hattie waiting for them when they'd returned from the cemetery. Her dad and Penny joined the fray. Worry and concern bubbled over, threatening to drown her under the force of it.

There was so much fear. So many questions. She was surprised she didn't burst from it.

And what could she say as their voices rose, higher and higher, as reality set in? Yes, there was some crazy killer out there taking the lives of innocent women. No, she didn't have a clue who he was or why he seemed set on involving her.

She understood love pushed them. Drove them to the hysteria she and Cade walked into.

But she'd been grateful when the fear edged away, and the questions slowed. And had almost cried tears of thankfulness when she'd finally found the chance to sneak away and take a break from it all.

Which she was going to take advantage of as long as she could. Closing her eyes, a soft breeze brushing over her, she pulled in long, deep breaths of fresh air, fighting back images of Sherry's naked body posed over Jacob's grave.

She heard the creak of the door. Seconds later, Cade stood at her side, pressing a glass of wine in her hand. He didn't say a word, just grabbed his own chair and settled beside her, taking a large draw from the beer he'd brought for himself.

She sipped the wine, thankful for it. Silence settled as she stared out over the quiet ranch, wishing she felt the same peace that surrounded her.

"He knows me," she finally spoke. "More than I thought. Using Jacob's grave proves that. He knew the message it would send."

He dropped his hand over hers and squeezed. The look he gave her left little doubt that he had come to the same horrifying conclusion. Whoever he was, the killer had enough personal connection to know her life ten years ago to remember it even when she returned.

"We could go away," he suggested. "Just you and I. We wouldn't have to tell anyone where we're going. And you'd be safe until Luke figures this whole mess out."

For a moment, she was tempted. To go and get

away from all this sounded wonderful

But, she'd run before. She wasn't going to do it again. She was putting her roots back in Snow Ridge. She wasn't going to let anyone chase her away again.

She shook her head, knowing Cade already expected her answer. "I'm not going to let him, whoever he is, chase me away. I just hate not knowing who *he* is."

"We'll find him. I promise." Finishing the last of his beer, he pushed up from his chair and set the empty bottle on the table in front of him.

Grabbing Cara's half-full glass of wine, he did the same before pulling her to his side. "For now, let's walk."

"Walk?" Caught off guard, she didn't protest when he took her hand in his and led her off the porch, away from the main house.

"Yeah. When's the last time you and I just walked around the ranch because we had nothing better to do?" Cade led her away from the barns, the corrals, to the open pastures lingering in the distance.

Under the light of stars, they walked to the river.

"Cade, I—"

She hung back and pulled on his arm, stopping him.

He saw confusion mixed with fear in her clouded blue eyes. Understood the battle she struggled with. Feeling helpless while so determined to do and take care of herself.

Knowing her like he did, coming to understand her in a way he never had before, he didn't doubt for a second the words she tumbled over weren't ones he wanted to hear.

Before she had a chance to continue, he wrapped a firm grasp around her arms, yanking her against him. "Not tonight, Cara." He caught her mouth with his, greed and desperation pushing at him.

He pulled back and caught her gaze with his. "Tonight, let's just be. You and I. Walking along the river's edge. Enjoying the evening like two people without a care in the world."

He waited, heart hammering against his chest until she nodded, soft but sure. "Okay."

Relieved, he took her mouth again. Curling his arms around her, he pressed her smooth curves tight against him. She melted into him, opening to him. Giving back all she received.

This. Right here. It was right. What he had needed, without ever knowing, for the long years she'd been gone.

He'd been a fool, and she'd had her moments of foolishness. But none of that changed what had been set in motion that long ago night of her high school graduation.

This was them. This was, if he had any say in it, what they would always be.

\*\*\*\*

He didn't like this.

Watching from a safe distance but still able to feel the heat in the embrace between Cara and Cade, he shook his head in disgust.

He'd seen it before. The closeness shared between them. Who hadn't? Anyone who'd been around long enough knew the relationship between Cara and the Grady brothers, especially Cade.

But this.

The kiss. Hands roaming. Bodies tight.

There was more to it. He saw it clearly from where he stood in the thick growth of evergreens. Something had changed between them. And as he watched, there was no question what that *something* was.

The idea she had tainted herself with someone like Cade Grady disgusted him. How could she? He'd never been foolish enough to believe she was pure. But to realize she hadn't learned her lesson, had walked right back into her reckless mistake from years past—it was disappointing.

So disappointing.

He'd considered taking another before making Cara his. But now he saw clearly that wasn't an option.

Their time was coming quicker than expected. What he watched proved that.

But, unlike with the other two, this would not be a surprise to her. He'd make sure before he ever brought them to their fates, she understood the redemption coming for her.

Yes. It was time. He had to act now and save Cara from the dark path she traveled.

Chapter Eighteen

They walked the river hand in hand, like two love-struck teenagers without a care in the world.

By the time they returned to the house, some of the peace Cara had hoped for surrounded her, leaving her hesitant to let it slip away.

She heard the voices from the kitchen as they climbed the stairs of the back porch and knew walking back into that would chase off her calm.

She tugged on Cade's arm, stopping him before he entered. "Let's not go in that way," she pleaded with her voice as well as her eyes. "I'm not up for it at the moment."

He didn't argue, didn't say a word.

Retracing their steps, he led them off the porch and around to the front of the house. Standing at the door, he rested a hand on her shoulder. "Stay here. I'll check and make sure nobody is lurking around."

He stuck his head in and then turned back, grabbing her hand. "We're clear."

He rushed them through the front room and up the stairs. She couldn't help the laugh bubbling up, threatening to escape, as they ducked into her room and closed the door before they were seen.

"That felt a bit sneaky." She pushed her fingers through her hair, leaving it to cascade down her shoulders. "Like kids sneaking around behind their parents' backs."

Which wasn't too far from the truth, she realized as she made sure the door was locked, since their fathers' voices followed them up the stairs. "Guess we should make it worth it." She flattened her palms against his broad chest, and then brushed them up, curving over his wide shoulders.

The fear she'd battled eased with their walk. She wanted to take advantage of it, to enjoy a stolen moment of delight without having to put her thoughts on the one killing innocent women.

And until now, she realized, she'd allowed Cade to have most of the control when it came to sex. Perhaps it was time for it to be her turn.

The thought drew a seductive smile. Finding his mouth, taking it as he had done to her just a bit ago, she pushed them back toward the bed, nipping at his bottom lip as the back of his knees hit the mattress. Sliding her hands under his cotton shirt, she lifted it up and over his head.

Wide, hazel eyes stared down at her as she tossed the shirt aside and yanked her own off, adding it to his. "This is good," she all but purred, brushing soft lips across the hard lines carving his chest. "So good."

She slid her hands up his sides, enjoying the tremble beneath her palms. It was nice to know she affected him in the same way he did her. That her simple touch brought forth such reactions.

She pushed on him until he bent at the knees and laid back on the soft, inviting mattress. He was amazing to look at. Sun-kissed skin outlining deep-lined muscles formed from hard work around the ranch.

There was nothing soft about him. He was firm.

Solid. Everything about him offered a delicious sight to the eyes. A temptation that had always been hard to avoid.

He was Cade. Hers in so many ways. She'd known him, seen him, in ways many others never had. The thought kicked her pulse higher, left her needing to touch. To feel him underneath her. Rough against smooth. Hard against soft.

She came down over him, pushing his hands away when he reached for her. "No. This is my turn."

Before he could reply, she lowered her mouth to his, taking him in with everything she had. Drawing all the emotions, all the sensations into one pulsing kiss.

"Cara." Her name escaped on a sharp breath as she pulled away and nibbled a path from his chin, down the strong curve of his neck, the long stretch of his shoulders.

Sliding her fingers down his arms, she twisted them through his, pulling his hands away to stop him from reaching for her and the need raging through her.

He groaned. A low, needy sound that pushed her desire to higher levels.

*Oh, yes.* This was what she wanted. Cade weakened beneath her. A prisoner. Just as he was so good at making her. She thrived on the power it stroked through her. Trembled with the knowledge she could hold such control over a man as strong, as vital, as him.

Soft and greedy, she followed the thin line of whiskey-brown hair trailing over his chest, down his abdomen. Her mouth seeking, giving, taking.

He yanked his hands free as she trailed her tongue over him, dropping them hard over her shoulders. The hard push of his fingers bit into soft skin as she took him into her mouth.

She took. She teased. Drawing him in. Pulling back. Pushing, demanding, until Cade was sure he'd lose it all. With a violent growl, he grabbed her, yanking her over his body until she fell with her back flat on the mattress.

The sight of her was almost his undoing. He bit back the surge fighting for release as he pinned her under the weight of him.

"No." She shook her head, tumbling ebony hair over ivory skin, shoving weakly at his shoulders. "This is my turn."

"Darling." He dropped his head to bite at her neck. "Much more of your turn and there won't be anything left."

He molded his hands to her slender hips and lifted her, rubbing against her. Slow and smooth, so she felt what she'd done to him. Suffer from it as he was.

It was good. Seeing her head fall back. Hearing her needy sigh. He dipped low, sucking a nipple between his lips and lavishing it with his tongue.

She tasted so good. So perfect. She fit to him as he fit to her. There were no substitutions. No others that came together in the way they did.

"Oh. Please, Cade." Her plea swarmed around him, driving his desire even higher.

His hands, trembling now, still wrapped around her hips, held her steady. Staring into her eyes, wanting to see the moment when he sank deep inside, he pushed. Held back. Pushed deeper.

Inch by painful inch, he took her. Drawing her up and around him until he filled her completely.

She gasped and wrapped her arms around him,

holding him even closer. She was soft. Delicate yet strong. All of it. Everything that drove him crazy and set his heart racing. Everything that had his pulse thundering in a way he'd never known before.

Where he was. What he experienced. He wanted to take her there with him.

Against his own thunderous need, he started slow. Cupping her face, he held it with his hungry gaze when she went to turn away.

He wanted her to see him—see them—in the way they were meant to be.

He rose. He fell. Grabbing her, he took her with him through every sensation igniting between them.

He held her gaze. Her mind. Her body. Driving them higher and higher with every thrust.

This was his. It was hers.

Never turning away, he held tighter as her breath hitched and her body trembled. He wanted to see, know, all of this.

Holding back his own release, he pushed in hard, and then pulled out slowly. Teasing, tempting. Giving her everything he could to make her understand she was so much a part of him. A part that could never be replaced by another.

Her hands curling around him, nails biting into his back, she stared hard into his eyes, letting him in like she never had before as she exploded. His name was an erotic whisper on her lips. Her surrender more than he could ever hope for.

He lost it then. Holding her to him in the most intimate of ways, he surrendered while calling out to her. Pulling her in, he refused to let go as he shuddered from the force.

He collapsed on top of her.

She took his weight. Folding her arms around his heated, sweaty body, she held him close. His head nestled between her breasts. The steady beat of her heart lulling him back down to reality, he savored the moment.

Knew it was one he would never forget.

\*\*\*\*

By his own rules, Luke tried hard not to take work home with him.

He rarely succeeded. And after today, after all that had happened, such rules were nothing more than shattered expectations he couldn't possibly live up to.

It was well after midnight. He saw it on the digital clock at the corner of his desk.

Tucked inside his own house on the ranch, he flipped through the file gathered for the one who had now killed twice, twisting Cara deeper and deeper into his sick little game.

That frightening picture—the one delivered to Father Frances an hour before they arrived—it was proof of so much.

The timing of it wasn't coincidence, coming right after Cade's discovery of the crucifix.

Whoever left the clue knew what was happening at the ranch—took advantage of it—leaving the next step in his twisted game. And he knew Cara, more than they ever imagined.

He grabbed the coffee at his side, taking a slow sip of the now tepid liquid. He knew her past. Knew about Jacob and what his death had done to her.

This wasn't random killings by a lunatic. It was personal. And Cara was the key.

His gut sank. Emotions threatened to take control. Something no officer of the law could risk.

He saw her for just a moment, from a spring evening many years ago. She couldn't have been more than ten at the time. Young enough to have her thick black hair pulled back in lopsided pigtails—Joe's attempt at controlling her curls when she was a little girl.

He remembered his car. An old Mustang he'd worked his butt off to afford. As a teenage boy, it had been everything. And the young girl he'd convinced to take a ride with him had been almost as good as the car.

Susie. He remembered. A sweet-faced sophomore with crystal blue eyes that reached right down into a guy's gut. Teased and taunted him.

She'd wanted the kiss. He would never forget that. Right there underneath the big oak hanging over the front drive. For an over-hormonal teenage boy, it had been everything.

Until the laughter erupted from behind.

Sweet Susie pulled away, chasing off the crazy ideas running through his head. Cursing, he'd turned and caught Cara and Jackie trying unsuccessfully to hide behind the evergreens lining the back of the house.

Jackie had pulled on Cara's arm, urging her to run. But she'd stayed where she was. Knowing she was caught and plastering an innocent look on her young face.

He'd been angry. Especially when Susie made her excuses and headed home. But Cara didn't care as she emerged from her hiding place, approaching with a smile gracing her lips.

"What were you thinking?" He scowled, kicking at

the rocks at his feet, cringing when they rained against the rims of his Mustang.

Reaching his side, she looked at him with those big blue eyes. "I was thinking you looked pretty silly slobbering all over her like that."

"I wasn't slobbering."

"Yes, you were." In the cockiness only children knew, she backed up against the front fender of his Mustang, crossing one small foot over the other. "You were slobbering all over her. And she was slobbering all over your fancy new car."

"That was all right with me." His anger fading, he joined her, staring out at the setting sun.

She looked at him, surprise in her eyes. "It doesn't bother you that she liked your car more than you."

He laughed. "Nope. Cause I like my car more than I like her."

"Then why were you kissing?" She shook her head, unable to understand such thinking. "Seems to me, you two would have been better off making out with your car instead."

She had a point. He bumped a hip against her. "What made you so smart?"

"I was born that way." She stuck out her tongue, earning another hip bump. "Plus, you don't have to be all that smart to know it's way better to be slobbering over someone who likes you more than your car."

"So you were just looking out for me?" He tugged on a pigtail, earning another one of those child-innocent smiles.

"Of course." She pushed up on her toes to drop a quick kiss on his cheek. "We're friends. And that's what friends do."

*Yeah. That's what friends do.*

Pulling out of the memory, Luke grabbed the Saint Mary's membership directory Father Frances had given him. The list was long, but his gut told him, somewhere in there, was the one he looked for.

He'd go through every single one. Pull apart, pick into pieces, every little bit of their lives.

Because that's what friends do.

Chapter Nineteen

He'd been careful not to wake Cara.

After what the day before held, Cade knew she deserved whatever sleep she could get.

And for him…he needed coffee.

Stumbling into the kitchen, the sun barely peeking over the horizon, he nearly wept with joy when Hattie greeted him with his own personal mug, filled to the rim with fresh, glorious coffee.

"Come." She nudged him with a bony elbow. "Sit."

He figured he must look as bad as he felt. Sleep had come in short, brief spurts. Interrupted every time the realization returned that some sick crazy had set his sights on Cara.

Fear and anger were a bad combination.

"You've got yourself a look about you." Hattie shook a finger at him as he claimed a chair at the table. "One that doesn't speak well about your state of mind."

"This will help." He held up his coffee, providing what he hoped was a reassuring smile.

"Hmmph." Unconvinced, she stuck her head in the refrigerator, pulled out a large platter of eggs, and a gallon of milk.

After grabbing a bowl from a high cabinet, she cracked an egg over the edge. "Only thing that's going to help is making sure that girl up there," she shook a finger toward the ceiling, "is safe from all of this."

He couldn't argue.

Uneasy with sitting and doing nothing, he pushed up from his chair to join her at the counter. "Let me help." He grabbed an egg and cracked it as she had.

"I don't need no help." She looked at him, her gaze piercing, seeing more than he wanted.

"But I need to help. I need to be doing something."

He was hurting. Hattie saw it. Heard it. Nodding, she stepped to the side, giving him room. "You take care of these eggs. I'll start on the bread."

It broke her heart, seeing her young ones in pain. Suffering as they were with such craziness. Her job had always been to protect those trusted in her care. Those whose own blood had counted on her to look out for them.

But sometimes—just as now—that job wasn't always easy.

"You're doing good." She grabbed the loaf she'd baked the day before from its place on the counter and curled her fingers around her favorite knife. "Being there for Cara when she needs you."

"I'm not trying to do good. That's the last thing I'm thinking."

Knife pressed against the bread, she looked at him and saw all she needed to. "So you've finally figured it out."

"Figured what out?" He sent a disgusted look her way, true to the surly man who'd entered her kitchen seeking coffee.

"Figured out you love Cara. In a way, now, so much different than what you once felt." She pushed the knife into the soft bread, slicing off pieces perfectly sized for her famous French Toast.

"Yeah. That realization's already come." He went back to cracking eggs. "I'm dealing with it. Doesn't make it any easier with what's going on. Makes it harder actually."

Hattie hid her smile, knowing it wouldn't be something he would enjoy seeing. She didn't wish hardship on any of them. But seeing one of her boys struggle with problems of the heart lifted her spirits. Hinted at the true love they were headed for.

Because love didn't come easy. Old souls like her knew that. Relationships were meant to have problems. Ups and downs. If it were easy for them, she'd doubt the truth behind their words.

But when love drove them crazy, left them surly and testy as they tended to eggs in her kitchen, she knew it was the real thing.

Unable to help herself, she set the knife down beside the half-cut bread and moved over, dropping a soft kiss on his cheek. "Hard or not, I'm happy for you. For both of you."

"Yeah...well." Cade shook half an eggshell at her. "Don't be so happy just yet. I could very well screw this up before it's all said and done."

With more force than necessary, he dumped the shell in the trash. "This whole independence thing of hers isn't something I'm sure I won't completely mess up."

"Messing up is okay." Hattie poured a generous amount of milk into the bowl and shoved a whisk in his hands. "It's what you do after you mess up that counts."

Dumping some sugar and cinnamon into the mix, she went back to her own task. "When it comes to issues of the heart, not one of us is perfect."

"No. We aren't." Cade stirred with all the frustration, fear, and anger, boiled up inside. "But it's much harder to justify mistakes when you've already made more than your fair share in the past. Screwing up now is just more fuel to the fire."

Coming back to him, Hattie grabbed the whisk before he took her French Toast mix to a place she couldn't recover it from. "Seems to me, you both made your mistakes in the past. Doesn't matter none in the here and now."

She shook the dripping whisk at him. "What matters is what the two of you decide to make out of today."

**\*\*\*\***

"Your dad's worried. More than he's letting on." Penny shoved plates in Cara's hands, motioning for her to set the table. "It'll be good for him, having you here for dinner."

Cara set places for the three of them, adding two wine glasses for her and Penny and a cold beer from the fridge for her dad. "Thankfully I was sprung from protective watch, as long as I promised to stay safely tucked away inside."

"Which you will." Penny handed her the bottle of wine she'd had breathing on the counter. Cara poured them generous glasses, handed one over and then sipped from her own.

Setting the fresh garden salad she'd made in the center of the table, Penny took hers with her to the window and peered out at Joe flipping the steaks. "Damn stubborn man he is. Couldn't get him to move away from the television for months. Now I can't get him to take a rest in front of it."

"Gonna grill up some steaks for my little girl, he says." She shook her head as Cara joined her. "Decides he can do it without help. Forgets he's still got healing to do. Still needs that help whether he wants it or not."

Sipping her wine, Cara watched her dad. His wheelchair pushed up to the grill, he held his spatula in hand. He was stubborn. She would give Penny that. And she couldn't stop her own worry at his insistence to take care of the steaks on his own.

But there was good, too. Seeing him out there, as he'd been in so many of her childhood memories, manning the grill like the expert he was, knowing the secrets to turning out the best steaks in all of Snow Ridge.

"You're the reason for this." Penny nudged her. "His worry for you, for what's been going on, is driving him to be out of that wheelchair and steady on his own two feet."

The idea was bittersweet. She prayed so long and hard for something to push at her dad after his accident. Something to give him reason to want to get out of the wheelchair and be back in the heart of the life he'd once had.

But this…this wasn't what she wanted. Worry and fear pushing at her dad. It wasn't a wish daughters usually carried around for their fathers. "He isn't overdoing it, is he?"

"He has his moments." Penny rested a comforting arm around her shoulders. "Don't you worry. I'm keeping a good eye on him. I know how to knock down that stubbornness of his when it needs to be."

Thankful for her, Cara dropped a kiss against her cheek. "You're good for him."

Watching her dad cautiously pile perfectly grilled steaks onto the platter resting in his lap, she stepped away from the window and swung the back door open. "Looks good. Though I think you cooked for an army."

He waved her off. Using one hand, he guided his wheelchair, the other holding the platter steady until he reached the table. "Been awhile since I've grilled. Needed to make it worth it."

"You did that and then some." Penny grabbed the platter from him, giving him no time to protest as she set it next to the salad.

"You won't be griping once you taste it." He wheeled up to his plate and grabbed his cold beer for a long, slow drink. "And this here," he tapped the neck of the bottle, "makes it that much better."

They sat and filled their plates. Cara was relieved to discover her dad still had his magic touch with the steaks. Since she wasn't driving anywhere, she poured a second glass of wine and savored every bite of perfectly grilled ribeye.

It felt good, to be so close to normal with her dad. This was all she'd wanted. The spark back in his blue eyes. The returning thirst for life he'd carried.

She liked him stubborn and a bit grumbly, just as he had been through her childhood. She liked sitting at the table, enjoying his food, talking with him about the day. Always knowing, trusting in his love for her.

"Can't take credit for this." Penny pulled a Banana Cream Pie from the refrigerator after they'd cleaned away the dinner mess. "Hattie made it. Said it was your favorite, Cara. That it would be sure to make you smile when I served it up."

It did. Hattie made the best. And coming at the end

of a fabulous meal, the smile was easy in coming and didn't fade as it tended to do these days.

This she liked. A night with her dad. With Penny. It was almost normal enough to make her forget the ugliness.

"You still have some time to hang out with your old man?" Her dad pushed his wheelchair away from the table, folding his large hands over his full stomach.

"I do. I'm not on any time schedule tonight."

"How about coffee on the front porch?" He glanced over at Penny, already rising to start the pot. "We can do decaf if you're worried about sleeping tonight."

"The hard stuff is fine with me." Cara joined Penny at the counter and collected three cups, dangling them from her fingers while they waited for the pot to fill.

After pouring the hot liquid into a simple black carafe, Penny led the way outside. She pushed on the screen door and paused halfway out.

"What in the world are those doing here?" Pressing the carafe into Cara's hands, she moved out the door and gathered a bouquet of white orchids resting at the foot of the stairs into her hands.

Nearly blending with the delicate petals, a simple white envelope was shoved down in the center of the bouquet. She closed her fingers around a corner and pulled it free.

The lip wasn't sealed, offering easy access to the linen paper concealed inside. Cara watched as she slid the paper out and ran her eyes over whatever was written there.

Gasping, Penny dropped the paper, the envelope, and bouquet, jumping back as if fire licked at her.

"What the hell?" Setting the carafe and mugs to the porch at her feet, she reached for the dropped paper.

"Cara. No."

But it was too late.

She saw it there. In bold black lettering contrasting against soft white linen—

*In white there is purity. There is innocence. Our time is coming. Soon you will know the true glory of one who is pure and innocent. My eyes are always on you.*

She didn't want to believe. Searched frantically through her mind for an explanation that did not carry the dark reality slapping her in the face.

The orchids could be for anybody. The note could mean anything.

Even as she thought it, tried to justify it, she knew better.

The truth of it knocked her back, leaving her desperately sucking air through her lungs as she searched frantically through the darkening night.

Was he out there? Watching her?

The very idea left her sick.

Her legs weak, heart hammering, she sank into the nearest chair, burying her head between her knees and willing and wishing for it all to go away.

\*\*\*\*

Luke felt his frustration growing as he stood there with his brothers and fellow officers on the front porch of Joe's place.

Chaos invaded the quiet night, the ranch again a place to be investigated. This was Grady land. These things didn't happen here. Especially not to those who were family. If he couldn't keep his own safe, how could he keep all of Snow Ridge safe under the responsibility of his badge?

Not that now was the time for such thoughts. His concentration belonged only on Cara and the newest terror she faced.

"Who knew you were coming here tonight?" Hitched on the back rail of the porch, he did his best to be gentle with his questions.

"Only Cade, your dad, and Hattie." Cara glanced over as the screen door hinges squeaked, Penny pushing through with more coffee and mugs, signaling a long night.

Jake inched around her to help Penny with the load weighing down her arms. He held up the carafe in offering, began pouring as those in need of caffeine headed his way.

"How long were you here before you found the bouquet?"

"I don't know, exactly. It wasn't there when I arrived. And Dad grilled, we enjoyed dinner before we came out to the front porch. So, that could be..." She shrugged, looking to Cade for help.

At her side, as he had been from the moment he arrived, Cade looked at his brother. "She was gone a couple hours before we got the call."

"Okay." Luke scribbled in the little notebook held firm in his large hands. As chief, he didn't normally get so personally involved. Knew the dangers any officer of the law faced if they allowed their emotions to surface and take control.

But, for Cara, there was no getting around it.

He looked at her. Saw the fear she tried hard to hide. It left shadows at the corners of her blue eyes and strained the lines around her delicate mouth.

Thank goodness for Cade, he thought, as he watched one of his men carefully tuck the bouquet into an evidence bag. She needed to be protected, no matter how much it irritated her.

He trusted his brother. He'd been part of making him tough. If danger came at Cara, Cade would be sure to take care of it. The knowledge took a load off his already heavy shoulders knowing that.

"You should let Cara go back to the main house." Shifting close to his brother's side, Jake kept his voice low so not to be overheard. "After the last couple days, I worry she's had enough. I'm not sure how much more she can take."

"She's a lot stronger than she looks." Luke pulled his brother's cup of coffee free from his grasp to take his own satisfying drink. "Stronger than she was when she left us. But you're right, she's probably best to head back to the house, away from this."

Returning the cup, he turned his attention back to where Cara stood at her dad's side, wrapped firmly in Cade's arms. "I've got all I need for now. Anything I don't have, I can always get from you later."

He grabbed her hand, catching her troubled gaze with his. "Why don't you go back to the main house? Get some rest."

"I don't know if I should." Cara looked down at her dad.

"Don't you be using me as an excuse not to get away from this." He shook a finger at her, worry evident in his eyes even as his face hardened, leaving no room for argument. "I don't want you here now. Not with this going on."

She wavered between a smile and tears. "But this is going on because of me."

Her dad grabbed her hand, pulling hard. "Don't you be thinking that, not even for a minute. This is going on because some sick individual thinks he's going to get away with terrorizing my little girl."

Tugging, he brought her closer, curving a rough hand around her cheek. "He's come too close to my own. Go. Be safe away from here. If not for you, for me."

She couldn't speak over the knot in her throat. Nodding, she straightened. "Okay." She looked at Cade, saw the same concern and worry brewing in his gaze. "I'm ready to go."

His arm still tight around her shoulders, he led her away. She tried not to look as they passed by where the bouquet had been left. Fought back nausea as the words that were left swam through her mind.

She swayed. Cade caught her up, holding her steady as she cursed such a show of weakness.

She would not give in to this. Would not give in to the fear somebody was trying to bring into her life. Whoever he was, he would not win. She'd make sure of it.

Cade tugged her along as her steps slowed with her thoughts. For a moment, she was tempted to go back, make a stand, just in case he was watching.

As if reading her thoughts, Cade paused, turning so he faced her. "You need to let Luke and his men do their thing. We will only be in the way there. We'll go home, crawl in bed, and I'll see what I can do to take your mind off all this."

It was a promise she couldn't resist, especially

since he was right. If she went back, she would only be in the way. It was better to let Luke do what he had to and find the one who haunted her.

****

His place. His girl. He'd stay until the end.

Joe had said as much to Penny when she'd tried encouraging him inside. To Luke, when he'd reassured him they could finish up without him.

Not a one of them understood this was all he could do now. The only thing he had to offer his daughter from the suffocating confines of his wheelchair.

Feeling more useless than he ever had, he bit back the need to hit something—anything. Whatever he could find to ease the frustration. The fear. The knowledge somebody was after his little girl, and he was worthless to stop it.

So, he waited. Sat there in his wheelchair, pushed to the edge of the porch, watching while they swarmed over every last inch of his place and the land surrounding it.

They picked, and they gathered, finding nothing he could see of any interest. A broken twig here. A hint of a boot mark there.

It was a fully-functioning, busy working ranch. People came. They went. There was never a lull in the buzz it took to keep a place like this running.

What could they possibly find to hint at one who had darker intentions than the rest? Especially if that one camouflaged themselves in the everyday practice of the others.

To think of that. To think of one lurking just outside his knowledge, threatening Cara, peaked his anger to new levels. It had been near a decade since he'd quit cigarettes. But, at that moment, he craved one like he never had before.

He settled for a beer instead, snagging one of the officers in blue, convincing him to fetch one since Penny had retired inside and would know no better.

Sipping on it, watching them work, he stayed as he said he would until Luke set a scuffed boot at the top of the stairs, looking at him with a mixture of respect and worry. "We're done here, Joe."

"Looks that way." He nodded, lifting the bottle to his mouth for one final, long draw of the amber liquid.

"Do you want me to help you inside?"

He set the empty bottle down on the table next to him with more force than necessary. "Don't insult me, boy. I took care of myself just fine back when you were barely out of diapers. I can do the same now."

Nodding, understanding the reason behind his surly response, Luke waved himself off, leaving him alone in the quiet darkness.

He sat there, knowing he should go in but finding no desire to do so. His temper still raged. Worry burned.

He despised the limitations set on him. Hated that he sat stuck in a wheelchair while threats piled on his daughter.

He'd come out of his accident with the heart to do nothing. To sit like the worthless man he believed himself to be, slowly fading and withering away into nothing.

Now he cursed that pity-driven soul who hadn't worked harder, done more from the start to recover from the hand he had been dealt.

If he had, perhaps he'd be of more use now.

Frustration and stubbornness creating a dangerous mix, he curled thick, long fingers around the armrests of his wheelchair and held on with the strength to turn his knuckles a ghostly white.

It took all he had to slide first one foot, then the other, from their rests, settling them on the porch below. The pain of that alone had him sucking in his breath, waiting impatiently until the worst of it faded.

Though he willed his legs to straighten and bear his weight, it took more than he imagined. Gone was the man who stood and sat, ran, and rode without a second thought.

Though he could get his mind to think it, want to do it, it was hell forcing his limbs to respond. Somewhere inside him was the disconnect he battled. The proof of the injuries he suffered against his spine and head.

Still, he refused to give in. Seeing Cara's face, frightened and pale, when she'd seen those flowers and read that note. There was no choice to give in. No more excuse to give up and let it be.

Feeling every bit like a grown-up baby as he whimpered, he used the strength he'd gained in his arms, forcing his butt up and out of the wheelchair.

It was hell. Every small movement. Every inch he drew closer and closer to standing.

Hovering like a fool, half sitting, half standing, he had to stop and wait out the pain blazing like a wildfire through his limbs.

It hurt. *Damn, did it hurt.*

Red shifted at the edge of his gaze, his heart thundered against his ribs, and he sucked in the worst of it through harsh, desperate breaths.

With one final shove, he stood. Shaky and unsure, but he stood.

"Holy hell," he growled as what felt like a herd of wild horses trampled over his spine, hitting each vertebra with a violent kick.

As much as he hated to, he had to let go, sinking back into his wheelchair.

It had only been mere seconds he'd stood on his own two feet. But he'd done it. And he would continue to do it. Giving not a damn about whether or not those in charge of his care thought he was ready.

He would do it for Cara. Do it so she would have back the father she'd always deserved and once had. So that he would never again be helpless when it came to protecting his own.

Chapter Twenty

"I love them dearly, but Hattie and Penny don't have a clue what to do."

Sitting at the kitchen table, morning sun streaming through the windows, Cara held tight to her coffee cup.

"Doesn't mean I don't." Sitting across from her, close to drooling, Jackie grabbed another of Hattie's homemade cinnamon rolls from the platter centering the table. She nipped off a corner of the warm dough, sighing in delight as she popped it in her mouth.

"You've taught me well when it comes to setting up the store. I know exactly what should go where." Caring nothing about manners, she licked gooey cinnamon from her fingers. "Hell, it's the kind of crap I dream about these days."

"What about my dad?" Still not willing to give in and accept the plans for the day sprung on her when she'd entered the kitchen, she looked at Cade. "He's doing better. But that doesn't mean he can be left alone for the day."

"My dad's already got plans for them." His answering smile held more understanding than she was comfortable with. "He'll spend the day picking his brain, using him for the very reason he was hired. Old Joe is still the best when it comes to our Quarter Horses. About time we take advantage of that again."

Cara couldn't argue with the good it would do her

dad to feel needed again. To be part of ranch business, back in the heart of it, working side by side with Patrick Grady. Creating the best of the best when it came to the Double 'G' Ranch.

Still.

"The store's mine. My responsibility." She lifted her coffee to her lips, looking at both Jackie and Cade over the rim. "I can't expect Hattie and Penny to give up their own responsibilities to take care of my job."

Not that there was much of that responsibility left. In the week since they had found the orchids on the steps of her father's porch, the excitement had all but drifted away.

No new notes. No more missing women. Nothing but the everyday hum of life in Snow Ridge.

Taking advantage of it, with Cade or Officer Mitch always at her side, Cara had put all her fear and uneasiness into unpacking and stocking the shelves.

It had given her an escape. Not to think. Not to fear. Not to put anything into the horror staring her down. To only know Precious Gems and the success she wanted it to be.

She'd worked hard, long hours. Exhausted and worn by the time she stepped foot back on the ranch. Her mind only on sleep and the work waiting the next day.

Still, it didn't sit well—this plan shoved at her before her day had barely started.

She should have known. Should have figured something was going on when she saw Jackie sitting with Cade at the table, their voices a low murmur as she stumbled in, needing her first cup of coffee to start the day.

If she'd been more alert, more awake, she would've known by the mirroring looks they had shot her way they were up to something.

But with little sleep and no caffeine, she hadn't caught on until it was too late.

"Told you she'd be arguing." With the rush of one on a mission, Hattie breezed into the kitchen and sent a scolding look Cara's way. "Darn stubborn streak is what you have."

Resisting the urge to sink back into her chair like a scolded child, she drew up what confidence she could. "I'm not trying to be stubborn. I just don't see it as right. Cade and I running off for a day away while others take care of my job."

"How about others wanting to take care of you." Hattie opened the refrigerator and pulled a hunk of roast beef from the lower shelf. "And you making it difficult by refusing."

*Okay*…she hadn't been prepared for that. Cara looked over at Hattie, at Cade beside her and Jackie across from her.

The look in their eyes told her all she needed.

Hattie was right. She was wrong.

Which didn't exactly sit well. Especially not with three sets of knowing eyes rested heavily on her.

"Okay. You all win." She offered a half smile, half sneer, finding little comfort in the satisfied looks she received in return.

Nodding in approval, Hattie pulled a large knife from the block at the edge of the counter. "Now that's better." She sliced into the roast beef. "I'll make you and Cade up some lunch for the day and then go and fetch Penny."

Understanding better than the others what it took for her to give in, Jackie pushed up from her chair. Coming around the table, she wrapped a friendly arm around her shoulders. "And tonight, it's you and me. At the pub. A girl's night to celebrate."

"And what exactly are we celebrating?" Cara looked up at her best friend, hoping she understood her reluctance had nothing to do with her confidence in her to take care of things.

"Does it matter?" She jabbed her with a bony elbow. "If we must have an excuse, we'll make it a last celebration of freedom before this little one comes around." She rested a hand against her pregnant stomach. "And Precious Gems opens for business."

For the excuse of a girl's night, it worked well enough for Cara. Though she knew it wouldn't be a typical girl's night. It couldn't be when she was permanently assigned a male of some sort at her side. Whether it was a Grady brother or one of Luke's officers, it was a constant she'd come to accept. Though she hated every minute of it.

"As long as I get to buy the drinks," Cara pushed up from her chair and grabbed her empty coffee cup, "it's a deal."

And that was that. Rinsing her cup and setting it on the top rack of the dishwasher, she accepted all her arguing had been for nothing. She had a day with Cade, a night with Jackie, just as they had planned.

She would take it. Enjoy it. Because she knew, better than she ever had before, it was best to take what she could when there was no way of knowing what horrors tomorrow might bring.

\*\*\*\*

She needed this.

The thought struck hard. Sitting on top of Mischief, riding at Cade's side over the spring-kissed land, she was swept back to those moments when all she ever desired was a saddle, her horse, and the land to ride.

The little girl in pigtails, on her first allowed ride without her dad. Cade on one side, Jake on the other. Feeling so grown up. So free.

A preteen, unsure of herself, hating the gangly, flat-chested girl staring back at her in the mirror. Finding confidence every time she saddled up her horse and headed out for the land she knew so well.

And the brokenhearted teenager, fresh off a fight with Jacob. Tears drying on her cheeks as she rode fast, chasing away the pain with each pound of hooves against the hard ground. Finding the calm she needed in the wind whipping around her. The cool air brushing against her skin.

*This*. This is what she'd missed. What she'd needed from the first step she'd taken back in Snow Ridge.

Cade pulled back on the reins of his beloved stallion, Midas and motioned for Cara to do the same. "Look." He pointed into the overgrown bush at the river's edge. "Do you see?"

She did. Tucked back into the thickening leaves, a white-tailed deer gazed out at them. Behind her, carefully under her protection, two newborn fawns fumbled on four legs, their red-brown coats helping to hide them from prey.

It was a sight she'd seen often growing up. One that still amazed her with the beauty of it.

"I'd forgotten," she fell back into step beside him

as Cade moved Midas on, "how much there could be in a simple ride. So much freedom. So much worry shoved aside."

For a moment, she felt like the young girl she once was. Her childhood so simple and innocent. Knowing only the life of the ranch. The Grady brothers she grew up with.

She'd made herself forget the day she'd walked away.

It was easier that way. Better to say goodbye with a block of all the memories she had. All the joy she'd known growing up here.

It helped her believe and hold on to the myth that Denver was her home. Not this old ranch tucked away in the heart of the mountains.

Cade smiled at her. His hazel eyes holding an emotion she was afraid to give thought to. The wind caught his whiskey-brown hair. Sun danced across the hard-carved lines of his sun-darkened face.

She'd been with him in the most intimate of ways. Now knew the man he'd become, matured into. Yet, her heart still caught. Her breath hitched as she stared at him.

It was like seeing him for the first time. A ridiculous thought altogether. But he drew her in. Her pulse quickened. Her body warming with the reminder of what he felt like buried inside, taking her to places she never imagined existed.

This was Cade. All that she had ever known. All she had come to know.

And she was seriously losing it with what ran through her mind just by the look of him.

Desperate to chase it away, she gave Mischief a

soft kick and took off ahead of him. "I need to ride," she yelled back. "Really ride."

She heard the echo of Cade pushing Midas at a faster pace. Felt him behind her.

He didn't try to stop her. Didn't try to pass.

He let her go. Gave her the freedom she desired as Mischief broke out into an easy gallop, sweeping them both along the river's edge. Rider and horse an amazing sight to see.

She didn't slow. Didn't hesitate. A childhood full of riding giving her the ability to ride as fast and as hard as she desired.

It felt good, riding without a care. The wind pushed back on her. The sound of the river flowing rushed along beside her.

She didn't stop till she reached the clearing cut away below the tumble of boulders forming a small, yet breathtaking waterfall. As she slowed Mischief and walked her in circles to cool her down, she glanced over her shoulder and laughed.

The simplest and innocent of sounds. It was real. It was from the heart. And it was the truest Cade had heard from her since she'd returned to Snow Ridge.

"That was amazing." She shoved a hand through the careless tumble of her ebony curls. "Damn, I missed that."

He couldn't help but laugh as she stopped beside him. Her cheeks were flushed, her chest rising and falling hard from the excitement.

She bent over Mischief, wrapping her arms around the horse's long neck. "Thank you," she patted her sleek coat, "for a ride I won't soon forget."

He wasn't sure if she was talking to him or the

horse.

Deciding it was best not to know, he swung a leg over Midas and hit the ground softly. "After that, I'm ready for one of those sandwiches Hattie packed."

Cara didn't move, just turned her head to look at him as he worked the flap open on the saddlebag. "Give me a minute, and I'll join you."

He understood she wasn't ready to get down, needing a few more minutes of savoring before putting an end to it.

A few feet away, he spread an old flannel blanket along the bunchgrass growing freely along the riverbank. He returned for the goodies Hattie sent along. Roast beef sandwiches and fresh fruit, cubed cheese and a bottle of champagne.

Her eyes widened at the last as she watched him pull the bottle out and yank two plastic cups after it. "Champagne? For lunch?"

"Hattie must be hoping I get you tipsy so I can have my way with you." He winked, slow and smooth, enjoying the chance to tease.

"Or she's hoping it will dull my constant irritation with you." She slid from the saddle, moved his way, and took the champagne from his hands. "Or keep you from coming back to the house groaning about how frustrated you are with me."

Settling on the blanket, surrounded by food, he patted the spot next to him. "Somebody might think she knows us a bit too well."

Laughing, she eased down beside him and grabbed a bright red plump strawberry from the plastic tub in front of her.

The soothing sound of water flowing over the

rocks worked up and over the bank, surrounding them. A slight breeze caught in the trees, bringing the scent of pine and wildflowers in a sweet mix.

A deep blue sky, intense here in the Rocky Mountains, hovered above. Small puffs of white scattered it, creating the shapes and forms he and Cara used to spend so many hours of their childhood watching. Finding animals, faces, whatever they could in the soft, drifting clouds.

"Here." He handed her half a sandwich, taking the other half for himself. Easing back, propping his arms behind him, he stared off into the distance. "I couldn't imagine living anywhere but here. I don't know how you did it all those years in Denver."

Memories came of the life Cara had left behind. "It might not make sense to you, but I loved it there. There was so much. To see. To do. I went overboard when I first got there, trying to take it all in and do it all."

She saw herself. The young girl she'd been. Running from Jacob's death. From the judgment. The heartache.

And running from Cade.

It had been everything she'd never known, never even imagined to expect. Surrounded by brick and steel buildings, new and old. Skyscrapers and condos, shops and hotels, all clamoring for space. It was like a world of its own.

It felt sheltered, closed in. Yet, so free and amazing. Here was this always busy, vibrating life. So many people. So much energy. From one block to the next, it was always there, giving her a taste of something different than what she'd known.

There, she was one of many. Her face lost in the

crowd, unknown and unseen in so many ways. It was like choking for so long and finally having the chance to grab a huge gasp of air. Taking that desperately needed breath that had drifted out of reach.

"Do you miss it?" He pushed up and grabbed the champagne. "Living there?"

Pointing the bottle away from them, he pushed his thumbs against the cork until it popped, bubbles pushing up, drizzling over his hand.

She took the glass he held out while thinking about his question. "I did at first. I love my dad, and I knew I had to be here to take care of him. But I hated that it meant leaving Denver and giving up the life I'd built."

Memories of that final day drifted back. The tears staining her cheeks as she stood there, surrounded by boxes, knowing it was time to go. The painful twist to her heart when she placed the keys in the hands of the young couple moving in, doing her best to accept it was their home now.

But somewhere in the past few weeks, there had been a change. Even in the center of all that was happening, she'd come to realize the stab of sadness she'd felt was weakening, more and more.

"I'd forgotten, during the years I was gone, that Snow Ridge would always be my home. No matter how far away I moved."

She turned away from Cade, pulling in the vivid blue beauty of the columbines growing a few feet away from where they sat.

It was these moments, sitting here at the river's edge, taking in some of the most amazing wildflowers she'd ever seen, she was reminded of where her heart truly settled.

The vibrating life and constant buzz of living in a place as busy and thriving as Denver had given her so much. She'd found a new part of herself, being there, discovering so much that was new.

And it would always be part of her, just as Snow Ridge was. She'd found her independence there. Realized she was a woman who could take care of herself. Who could count on her own wits and smarts to survive.

She'd enjoyed what came with living downtown. The nightlife. The culture. Even the risks. It had a certain excitement to it. A spark that ran through her, offering a new kind of life so different from the one she'd existed in.

She would need to go back. There was no questioning that. For a visit here. A rekindling of memories there. But she'd come to accept the fact that she'd returned home…right where she belonged.

"I used to think of you, all those years you were gone." Cade twisted long fingers around the skinny neck of the champagne bottle and refilled their glasses. "I'd wonder what you were doing. If you were okay. And I'd tried to imagine you living like that. So different than what you knew."

Reaching for her, he pulled her close. "At first, I was sure you'd return before the first year. Standing on your dad's front porch with your bags, more than ready to be home."

"And then I thought the second year. Or maybe the third." She heard the grief he fought hard to keep away. Didn't like knowing she was the one who caused it. The thought her leaving would cause him pain was one that didn't come during that time of her life.

"Then I stopped thinking. Told myself I was done caring. You weren't coming back. And there was no reason to waste my time thinking so."

Not sure she wanted to go where he was headed, she worked free from his hold, grabbing a cube of cheese as her excuse. "Coming back would have been admitting failure. That was the last thing I was willing to do."

"Don't you get it?" She turned so she faced him, her gaze full of all those old emotions set to life that fateful night. "I'd always been so sheltered, so protected, that I had no idea how to handle life when I actually had to face something so difficult. Something different than what I had ever known being surrounded by you and your brothers. My dad. Your dad. Even Hattie."

"And you were suddenly gone. Damn—"

This was not where she wanted to go. Wiping a stray tear from the corner of her eye, Cara pushed to her feet and hurried to the river's edge before she lost even more control.

How did they even get here? Talking about the past they were better to leave behind.

They had already discussed what happened. Back when she'd first returned to town. There was no reason to take that road again. No reason at all.

Yet, she felt it there. Back in that place of what she hadn't said, hadn't been brave enough to admit. There was something still to be done when it came to them. A truth to be bared.

"That night we first had together." She curled arms around her sides, fighting off a chill that made no sense standing under the bright sun. "It was more than I ever

261

expected, or would have ever dreamed I could feel or experience."

She heard Cade move behind her and sidestepped out of his way, not ready for his touch. "I was a stupid eighteen-year-old, putting into my head all these foolish ideas of how wonderfully everything would change after we'd had sex. I played with marriage and babies and happily ever after."

She glanced over her shoulder, saw the wide-eyed surprise in his expression and couldn't help but laugh. "It was the thoughts of a young, naïve teenager," she offered in her defense. "What did you expect?"

"Not that." He shook his head and let out a long, thoughtful breath.

"Yeah well, you were a young, naïve boy yourself who did more thinking between his legs than anywhere else."

"I think I'm still guilty of that." He dared a step closer, standing only inches away as they both stared out over the running water. "But that doesn't mean the head on my shoulders doesn't do a fine job of thinking for itself as well."

"I believe that...now." She smiled at him, feeling better. The sudden rise of tension easing, she held out her hand.

He took it. And together they stood there as one, looking out over the land they had grown up knowing so well. Never having a clue what was to come for their futures.

She didn't look at him, and he didn't look at her. Their hands the only connection between them, silence fell for several minutes before she found her voice again.

"When your dad came to the door that morning to tell us about Jacob, it wasn't just guilt that hit me. It was shame. Here I was, lying in bed with you, thinking these thoughts of happily ever after, while my boyfriend was dead."

Her heart grew heavy, as it always did with memories of Jacob. She had loved him in the only way her young heart had known how. "And then you were gone, too."

"No." She tightened her hold when he went to pull away. "I don't say that as blame. Not anymore. We both hold our own when it comes to that night."

Still feeling the guilt of it heavy on his shoulders, Cade wasn't sure he agreed. In his head, his memories, blame was what he earned after what he'd done.

He sensed, though, Cara wasn't looking for words from him, accepting or denying what she shared. All she needed, right then, was for him to listen.

He would give her that.

"When it first happened, I blamed you." She looked at him, emotions running free through her deep blue eyes. He saw the pain and loss she'd suffered. But he also saw more—an acceptance he wasn't sure had its place in that part of their past.

"And when I moved to Denver, I wasn't only running from everything that happened with Jacob's death. I was running from you, too.

"And I've been mad at you for a very long time. Even when I first moved back, I still held that anger. It was much easier than any truth I'd learned."

"Cara." He tugged on her, drew her slender frame to his chest, and held her there. "Where are you going with this?"

She laughed, but there was no joy in it. Only uncertainty and old pain. "I'm not exactly sure." She looked up at him, her gaze open and vulnerable. "I was trying to explain why I couldn't turn around and come back after I'd moved away. But I'm having a hell of a time trying to get there.

"But I will." She sucked in a breath, pushing her full breasts into his chest, kicking into gear thoughts that had no business in this conversation.

He thought she would, but she didn't pull away. She turned her head, staring back over the river as if it gave her the strength she needed.

"I was so mad at you when I left. I had a point to prove. That I could make it without you. That I didn't need you, especially not after you turned away from me.

"So, I couldn't come back. Not even when I was tempted during the beginning." She looked back at him, flattening her palms against his shirt. "And then, after time, it hit me. I still had a point to prove. But it was to myself, not you."

He watched the struggle she battled, knowing there were some things she would never share with him about that time of her life. The truth of it knocked him harder than he expected.

"And I did it. Though there were times it was hard as hell." Her fingers closed into fists, grabbing folds of shirt. Her expression was open and raw as she stared up at him, hiding nothing, giving him a rare glimpse into all she was and all she'd become, as if she knew the thoughts he'd just had. "So many times, I wanted to quit and come back home. But I wouldn't let myself. It was just me, depending only on myself. It was frightening and freeing all at the same time."

He didn't answer. Folding long arms tighter around her sides, he held her close to his warmth. Her cheek pressed to his chest, the steady throb of his heart beat with hers.

His chin resting on top of her head, he let the quiet and peace surrounding them respond in the way he couldn't yet put into words.

She looked up at him and smiled, soft and sweet. In her gaze, he saw a mix of the child who'd first stolen his heart and the woman he'd fallen madly in love with.

He wanted her. The burning he'd carried since the moment she'd stepped foot back onto the ranch never faded.

But he understood now, at this moment, it wasn't the time for that.

"Come on." He led her back to the blanket, refilled their champagne, and settled beside her.

This was what she needed. Quiet and peace.

He held her close while staring out over the river, imagining a life where she never left his arms again.

Chapter Twenty-One

"I'm amazed." Cara lifted her beer as she shook her head in surprise.

Unable to quench her craving for the pub's famous wings, Jackie dropped a cleaned-off bone in the basket, licking stray sauce from her fingers. "I'm telling you, we should have had Penny and Hattie helping us from the start. Those two together are like a mini whirlwind when they get going."

Cara had seen it herself when Cade dropped her by the shop before finding their way to the pub. Seeing the results of their work, she'd nearly cried. With all they had accomplished, opening on Memorial Day weekend wasn't such a crazy thought.

"Told you we'd be having a reason to celebrate." Jackie lifted her glass of iced tea, tapping it against Cara's beer mug.

"And it's almost like a real girl's night out." Cara glanced over her shoulder, taking in the small table settled in the center of the pub.

Cade sipped from his own beer. Luke and Officer Mitch pulled cheese-loaded chips from the nachos centering the table. They pretended she and Jackie weren't there. Just as she did her best to convince herself there weren't eyes on her at every moment.

Not that it worked. She craved freedom. Wanted a moment, a second of time, where she wasn't aware of eyes following her, whether they were protecting or threatening her.

"None of that." Jackie put a finger on the bottom of her mug, urging it to her mouth. "You're getting the look of the pouty. And that simply can't be allowed tonight."

Doing as she was urged, Cara took a slow drink from the beer. Setting the mug on the table, she grabbed a wing from the overflowing basket. "Okay. Let's talk baby."

"Oh please, no." Jackie shook her head even as she curled a protective arm around her swollen stomach. "I love this little one. But I don't think I can handle another minute of baby talk. Between my mother and mother-in-law, there is no other topic."

Cara offered a sympathetic smile. She couldn't even begin to guess what it was like, married with a baby on the way. Such things felt foreign to her. "So, what should we talk about then?"

"Sex." Jackie's grin reached from ear to ear. "Specifically, sex between you and Cade."

Yes. Leave it to Jackie to dig right in.

Though she knew he couldn't hear a word they shared, Cara cast a hesitant glance back at the table where Cade tried forgetting she was there.

*She knew better.*

"I already told you sex with Cade is amazing." She grabbed her beer and lifted it toward the bartender, signaling for another.

Jackie grabbed her own glass, looking at Cara over the rim. "Uh-huh. Now go into detail."

She nearly spit out the beer in her mouth. "I'm not going into detail about my sex life, best friend or not.

There are some things not even you should know."

"I'm not talking about sharing your favorite positions. Even I have my limits." Snagging another wing, the gleam in Jackie's eyes held a little too much enjoyment. "I want to know all the gushy stuff. You know, those pesky feelings you like to pretend you're immune from. Especially when it comes to Cade."

"Did you really say gushy?" Cara couldn't help but laugh.

"It's the pregnancy hormones talking. Now get to it." She waved her half-eaten wing. "Tell all."

She'd never struggled in sharing her feelings with Jackie. There had never been a wall or a limit between them.

Yet, when it came to talking about Cade, she struggled. How could she not when she didn't even know herself the truth behind what tossed around inside her head and heart.

"I think," she finished the last of her beer and pushed the empty mug to the edge of the table, "that I'm going to enjoy it while it lasts."

Though she'd had more than enough wings, she grabbed another, needing something to keep her hands busy. "Being with Cade, not just for the sex, is good for me. For him too, I think. We can irritate each other and love each other all in one sweep.

"But I'm also level-headed enough to know the two of us together for too long of a time wouldn't be a good thing."

"Yes." Jackie's nod was long and exaggerated. "Because it can never be good when two people connect in the way you and Cade do. Hell, love experts warn against such things all the time—don't you dare plan a future with someone you fit just right with."

Reaching over, Jackie grabbed her hand, cupping it between hers. "Are you sure you're not letting your fears rule, pushing you to walk away from something that could be good for you? You and Cade have always had that special...something. The kind of connection most people spend their lives searching for."

She had fears. Plenty of them. But she wasn't willing to admit they controlled her. More like they kept her cautious and aware of the risks.

"I'm not sure the connection between Cade and I is such a good one." She looked over her shoulder and caught his eye. He smiled. A simple, quick motion meant just for her.

The flutter in her heart only helped to prove her point. "What he wants, I don't think I can give. He wants the girl who left Snow Ridge. Not the woman who returned."

"He's told you this?"

"No." Cara shook her head and wished for a refill on her beer. Glancing over, she caught the bartender's gaze, again signaling to her glass, hoping he understood.

"But that doesn't mean the risk isn't there. And I can't become her again, Jackie. I can't become that person who fled to Cade, to all the brothers, like some helpless waif. I fought too hard to change. And being with Cade, for too long only increases the chances I'll become her again."

"So, it's not really Cade and his wants that frighten you. It's what you believe of yourself." There was a bite in Jackie's words.

Cara's head snapped up, eyes narrowing, at the

tone and the words. She opened her mouth, preparing to defend herself, but snapped it shut when Adam from behind the bar set a full mug of beer in front of her.

"This one's taken care of by the man at the end of the bar." He pushed it in front of her.

"What man?" Cara turned, seeing no new faces from the last time she'd looked over her shoulder.

"Well, hell." Adam shifted back on his heels. "Don't know where he went. He was there a few minutes ago. Paid for your beer and said to tell you it was on him. That he's looking forward to you two being together very soon."

Cara's heart sank. Fear clouded her vision.

Willing her heart to take a normal beat, knowing this was not the time to lose it, she turned, the look in her eyes saying all that was needed to urge Cade from his chair.

His worn boots echoed against the wood floor, so loud in her head as the walls felt like they were creeping in. The air suddenly became hard to breathe.

No. She wasn't going to lose it. She wasn't going to give whoever was doing this the pleasure.

"What's going on?" He pulled her hand to his and looked at her, at Jackie, at Adam, searching for answers to the fear he'd seen.

"Don't know." Adam shrugged, stepping out of the way as Luke pushed up to the table. "She tapped her glass." He nodded at Cara, too new to the pub, to Snow Ridge, to know her by name. "Let me know she needed another round."

His shoulders slumped as he caught sight of Jake working through the crowd, heading their way. "I might have taken longer than I should. But as soon as I got the chance, I started working on bringing her another beer."

Seeing the uncertainty in his gaze, Cara felt sorry for him. "It wasn't the beer. And it wasn't you." She offered what she hoped was a reassuring smile.

She wasn't sure it did much good as he just about shook in his boots when Jake reached the table, looking at her and Jackie, his brothers.

"What happened?" He turned to Adam, his gaze intense, sending the poor guy backing up.

"I was just saying how I got a beer for her." He looked again at Cara. At the beer she pushed out of the way. "I was starting to pour when some guy comes up to the bar. Says this one's on him and smacks down a ten-dollar bill. Tells me to keep the change."

"What guy?" As she had, Cade turned back to look over those enjoying their drinks and food.

"He must have left while I was coming to the table. I didn't think nothing of it. He wanted to make sure I let her know how much he was looking forward to being with her. Made me think he knew her personally."

Adam stood like a deer in headlights as three sets of hazel eyes stabbed through him. He shook his head, looking confused as they said nothing, only stared, as if he held some magical answers.

"Did you recognize him?" Luke stepped past his brothers, taking the lead.

"No. But I don't recognize most at this point. I've only been in town a month, and this is only my second week working here. The faces are still pretty new to me."

Cara's hope drained. If only he'd known him, recognized him. Maybe then this horror would be over.

"Can you describe him?" Luke continued, glancing

at Cara and Jackie, their girl's night ruined. "Anything about him you remember?"

"Nope. He was another average, everyday customer I see over and over again. Couldn't even get a good look at his face. He had an old straw hat pulled low hiding most of what there was to see."

And wasn't that just how it kept coming out.

Cara bit back the frustrated groan threatening to escape. There was never a clue. Never a hint as to who it was killing innocent women while setting their sights on her.

Fear found another hold, curling ruthlessly through her limbs, suddenly making her feel so tired. Exhausted.

As much as she fought to be strong, weakness threatened to take over. It scared her just as much as the man who'd sent the beer.

****

This whole crazy mess was taking its toll.

Cade saw the proof in the dark shadows underneath Cara's eyes. The exhaustion ringing in her every word.

"It was him." She didn't look his way, keeping her gaze on the darkness passing by as he turned into the ranch and headed for the main house. "I want to deny it, but I can't."

He wanted to lie and tell her they couldn't count on anything. That it might be nothing more than an innocent admirer buying her a drink.

But they would both know it wasn't the truth. And as much as he wanted to say different to protect her, he knew—they both knew—they were long past that point. No words, true or otherwise, would change what she faced.

He slowed in front of the house. "It was him." He threw the truck into park and turned to face Cara, the porch lights casting shadows over her slender frame.

"But he couldn't get closer than the end of the bar. He won't get closer than that," he promised, reaching for her.

She jumped when his hand settled on her thigh, looking at him as if just realizing he was there. She sucked in a harsh breath, her chest rising and falling heavily with the force of it.

"How do we know he hasn't already been closer? We don't know who he is." She shook her head and looked toward the house where the front lights burned a soft glow over the porch. Petunias, caught in them, showed signs of life in their planters.

He sensed her need for the comfort and peace waiting for her." Let's go in." He pushed the door open, stepping out into the brisk night.

She crawled out before he made it around the front of the truck, meeting him on the path. Taking her hand, he held it firmly in his as they made their way up the stairs and through the front door.

Familiar scents—polished wood, fresh baked bread, the hint of a fire burning in the hearth—surrounded them, easing the nerves left over from the night.

Cade closed the door and locked it. At the foot of the stairs, he stopped, pulling her to him. Gentle, almost cautious, he dropped his lips to hers. Pulling her slowly into a kiss, he tried to chase away the ugliness, leaving only his love for her in its place.

Sighing, she melted into him. Winding her hands around his neck, she pushed on her toes, deepening the hold.

Pulling away from the kiss but still holding her close, he worked them slowly up the stairs and down the hall. They passed his room where he'd not slept under the covers of his own bed since the first night Cara came to the ranch.

And he was okay with that. More than okay. Because the tradeoff was holding this incredible, tender beauty in his arms every night. As he would do again tonight.

But first, he was going to cherish every inch of her.

At the door to her room, he paused long enough to find her inviting mouth again, capturing her in a kiss that was as tender as it was passionate, hoping she felt what he still hadn't put to words.

He backed her up, kicked the door closed behind them, and moved them toward the bed while his mouth tasted, explored.

"I want you to feel." He trailed a delicate line over the curve of her cheek and nipped at her ear.

Her clouded gaze reflected the need that pulled inside him. "I am feeling. Oh—"

Cara's head fell back on a sigh as he traced his tongue down the pulse beating against her neck. She curled unsteady hands around his shoulders. He eased her gently to the bed and tugged her shirt free, exposing soft, firm breasts spilling from a red silk bra. "I need you to feel everything tonight." He gathered one in his hands and ran a lazy finger over the hard nipple. "Every inch of your body. Every sensation I can create with my touch."

Caught in a new flash of heat, she could only stare while her heart hammered against her ribs. Every nerve became a pinpoint of pleasure.

He was slow, easy, gentle. Finding her mouth again, he pulled her in. Teasing, playing until she was nothing more than a melted pool of desire beneath him.

He drifted then, his lips trailing a seductive line over her shoulders, molding her breasts with soft, delicate kisses. His fingers were like lightning rods, pulling forth seductive tremors along her bare skin, igniting a path over her stomach, dipping beneath the line of her jeans.

A master at his touch, he stripped away the rest of her clothes. Exploring with hands and mouth, he never gave her a chance to recover before sending her on another rise of fierce heat and uncontrolled need.

He took. He lavished. Exploring every inch of her body there was to find. Brushing off her hands every time she tried to touch him, tease him as he did her, he took and then took some more until she was sure she'd burst from the sweet agony of it.

She hadn't even noticed he'd done away with his own clothes until he hovered above her and slowly slid inside until he filled her completely.

Her breath stopped. And for a moment, all she could do was hold on as a force of sensation took over, burning through without mercy.

He was slow, achingly so, as he took her. Loving her with the force of his gaze, the soft strokes he pushed inside, as he had with his hands and mouth only minutes earlier.

Unable to turn away, she stared, trapped, into his eyes, watching him with every move that drove him deeper and deeper inside. Brought them as close as they had ever been.

It was almost hypnotic—lost in him like she was.

And then it was there. That burn Cade expertly brought to life, finding new strength and another firm hold as it wound its way through her body. Her heart found a quicker beat. Her blood heated as it rushed through her veins.

He held her. Watched her. Driving her higher and higher. Caught in his hold, his eyes, she slid closer and closer to the edge.

And then there was just Cade, holding her so tight she didn't know where she began and he ended. Desire darkened his gaze as he watched her tumble over the edge. She cried out his name as desperate release took over, shaking her from head to toe.

Seconds later, he fell with her, letting her see it all through his eyes. Feel it through his embrace as he clung to her while the tremors waved over him.

Unable to suck in a steady breath, he collapsed on top of her, burying his head in the crook of her neck.

Wrapping her arms around his back, she held tight, wishing she never had to let go.

****

He couldn't have asked for better.

Tonight had been as perfect as he'd hoped for. Everything had fallen into place, giving him the opportunity to carry out his plans.

Grady's bartender had been the new boy, just as he'd hoped. And he'd been careful to keep his appearance hidden without making it obvious. It wasn't hard. With so many crowding the pub, nobody gave him a second glance. He blended with the rest. Another local coming in to join the night.

It had been priceless, slipping out and coming back

in as one they recognized and expected to be there. He'd made it in time to see the shock haunting Cara's face when she'd been delivered her drink. He relished the wave of concern spreading through the pub as they searched for the one who sent it.

*Oh yes.* Perfect.

Hidden in the thick darkness, he stared up at the main house and imagined Cara naked in bed, waiting for him, wanting him as he came to her and brought her body to life.

Her image tangled with another. The one she mirrored in so many ways. She'd waited too. Wanted him though she could never admit it.

But he knew, from the moment he'd seen *Her*, she'd been created, brought to him.

Just as Cara now was his. Another offering laid at his feet.

He hardened with the memories he carried. The images of what he had yet to create.

Impatience now became his battle. He was ready. There was nothing left to do but finally bring to Cara what was meant from the moment he'd set eyes on her.

Satisfied with his accomplishments, he wished her a night of sweet sleep before sliding deeper into the trees, his mind and heart settled on the truth.

It was time.

## Chapter Twenty-Two

He was done with it. Done with this crazy mess.

Luke reached for the coffee on the edge of his desk, wincing as ice-cold black sludge slid down his throat. Moving away from his desk for the first time in hours, he refilled his cup.

Reclaiming his chair, he shifted through more papers, knowing the answer was in there somewhere. He only had to find it.

"You been in here all night?" Jake stepped into his office, shaking his head.

"Since I left the pub." Luke barely spared him a glance, pulling a paper from the pile dangling dangerously at the edge of his desk. "Going home isn't going to get this son of a bitch behind bars."

Cutting over to the coffee pot Luke always kept freshly brewed, Jake poured a cup of the tar the department liked to pass off as coffee. "I hate knowing he's one of us." He settled a hip against the edge of the desk, staring down at the storm of papers spread everywhere. "Someone we could very well trust and have never been suspicious of."

"It's someone we trust. You can bet on that." Luke raked tired eyes over the membership for Saint Mary's. Though he had no proof, he knew the answer was there, in the long list of names. So many he recognized, knew for years. A part of Snow Ridge just as he and his family were.

He used thick black lines to mark off those he didn't suspect. Women and children. Those too old or sick. The names left were still too long. So many without answers.

"He has to have his own place." He thought aloud, moving his gaze between the membership list and the photos of the women killed. "What he does takes privacy. He needs time alone, without the threat of being caught, to carry out his torture."

Jake took another sip of coffee. "Most around here have their own places. That's going to be a hard list to narrow down."

"It's here." He concentrated again on the member list before typing names into his computer, searching property records. "I've got him. I only have to figure out where to go to nail him."

****

By mutual agreement, they spent a lazy morning in bed.

Cara chased away the reasons why she should get up and head over to Precious Gems as Cade ran down for coffee and some of Hattie's blueberry muffins.

He had his own responsibilities as well. Running Double 'G' Ranch was a constant demand. And yet, since this had started, he'd done nothing but look out for her, staying by her side as much as he possibly could.

Which meant he'd had to put his responsibilities in the hands of others. Something she knew wasn't easy.

"Thank you." Twisted in the sheets, she leaned over to drop a quick, soft kiss on his lips. He tasted like coffee and blueberries, and the intoxicating flavor that was unique to him.

Surprised, he looked at her, the bite of muffin in his hand forgotten. "For what?"

"For being here...always. For doing what's hard for you and handing over the running of the ranch to others."

"For you, it's easy." After popping the rest of his muffin into his mouth, he bent over, returning the favor of her grateful kiss. "The ranch is important to me, I won't deny that. But you mean more. I'd give up much more than my responsibilities to keep you safe and make you happy."

The soft yet determined tone of his voice, the way he looked at her, caused a friction of unease to crawl up her spine. Needing a distraction, she twisted over the edge of the bed and grabbed her coffee cup where she'd left it on the nightstand.

Patient, he waited until she turned back. Shifting over the crumpled bedspread and twisted sheets, he worked himself around until he faced her. "Seems making you happy is about all I'm able to think about these days."

"Yeah...well." Cara inched back, needing space to breathe, not so sure she liked the sudden shift in their conversation. "I'm not sure that's a healthy way to think."

He only smiled as she inched back, seeming to like her growing discomfort. "Seems pretty damn healthy to me. In fact, I'm rather liking this new change. Thinking about making it permanent."

"Permanent how?" Fear began a slow creep through her. His words, the look in his eyes, promised he was about to venture into a place she didn't want to go.

"I was thinking along the lines of the marriage and babies you were talking about yesterday. Seems pretty permanent to me, that way."

"I was talking about the foolish thoughts of a teenage girl." Uncertainty jumping forward to join the fear she already battled, she scooted off the edge of the bed, grabbing her discarded shirt and bra from the floor. "It had nothing to do with our relationship today."

She hooked her bra, tugged her shirt over her dark curls, and then turned, searching for her jeans. Reaching out, Cade stopped her, pulling her back to the bed.

"To me it did." He yanked on her arm, tumbling her down beside him. "Like it or not, you've got me hooked. Hell, you always have. I just took some time realizing the truth."

Reaching out, he ran a gentle finger along the tension lines around her mouth, easing them away. "You can take your time coming to accept this. It took me some time. So, I expect the same with you."

"But," he held tight when she made a move to get away, "I won't be giving up. Not on you or us. That's something you're going to have to deal with."

"Damn it, Cade." She wrenched away and quickly fled the bed. Finding her jeans, she yanked them over her legs. "I don't need this. Not now."

"I'd believe you, feel sorry for you even, if it weren't for the fact it wouldn't matter what was going on, you'd still use the same excuse to run and hide from the truth between us."

And that did it, stroking the temper burning inside. Her gaze flashing angry sparks his way, Cara cursed under her breath as she slammed her way into the bathroom.

Behind the closed door, she yanked her hair into a ponytail and swiped her toothbrush through her mouth.

How dare he? Who in the hell did he think he was?

Silently calling him names, feeling the urgent desire to land her fist in his gut, she jerked open the door and stared, hard and angry, at where he continued to sit at the edge of the bed.

Without a word, she made her way to the bedroom door.

"Where do you think you're going?"

She considered not answering, just simply walking out and leaving him to his questions.

But she knew him well enough to know if she didn't respond he'd follow her out the door and carry this on wherever he caught her. Be damned who might be around to hear or witness such a stupid, foolish fight.

"I need to get away from you before I do or say something I regret." Anger weighed heavy in her voice, flashed dark in her eyes. "I'm going to spend some time with my dad."

"Not alone you aren't." Cade jumped up and grabbed his clothes.

Yanking his shirt over his head, he moved for the door. "You're not foolish enough to believe you're safe going out there alone." Stumbling on his feet, he pulled his jeans up.

"I don't want you near me. And you can't get Officer Mitch here in time." Shrugging, she stepped out into the hall and hurried toward the stairs.

Refusing to let her get too far, Cade rushed out of the room right behind her.

"You can watch from the back porch." She paused on the top stair without turning back. "Make sure I get there all nice and safe and sound."

She finished the stairs and burst into the kitchen, earning a startled look from Hattie, busy at the sink. "What in the world are you up to?" Soapy bubbles up to her elbows, she reached for a towel.

"Just going to visit my dad." Cara didn't slow down on her way out the door.

"She's being stubborn, that's what she's up to." There was no use trying to hide his frustration as his words bit back at Hattie.

Her muffled response followed them out. Though he hated to do it, he knew better than to insist on staying with her. He'd sent her for a spin. One she hadn't been prepared for.

He didn't regret it. Just wished he would have remembered the stubborn streak of hers didn't always react in the way he expected.

Though she'd demanded the porch, he followed her halfway down the path, refusing to let her get too far away. He knew she was aware of his presence not far behind, but she never stopped or looked back.

Watching her storm into her father's house, he waited on the path and watched a bit longer.

He would give her what she wanted. *For now.*

Retracing his steps, he found his way back to the main house. He would take some paperwork out on the back porch and do some catching up while he kept an eye on things. He'd put a call into Luke, see where he was in the investigation, and then do a casual stop by at old Joe's place.

His daughter might be fuming mad at him and try

to cast him out. But Joe, he would have none of that. And Cade would be right back where he could keep an eye on her, no matter how mad it made her.

****

What in the hell was Cade thinking?

Sitting at the kitchen table with her dad, Cara did her best to appear as casual and at ease as she could. But inside...inside she was fuming, silently cursing Cade and the ridiculous path he'd decided to try and take their relationship.

Why couldn't he leave well enough alone? They were good where they were. No commitment. It was easy. Simple. How she liked it.

If there was one thing she knew, it was that she and Cade spending a lifetime together wasn't the answer. She'd moved past such ridiculous fantasies. She wouldn't be going back regardless of his promise to wait until she was ready.

"I wish you'd go back to Denver for a bit. Take Cade with you, if you need him." Misreading her uneasy silence, her dad reached over the table and grabbed her hand. "Till this passes. Till we know you're safe."

Shaking off the mood she'd arrived with, she tried a smile, hoping to reassure him. "You taught me better than that. Running won't solve anything."

He was going to argue. She saw it in the hard stare he shot her way. But the quick, loud rap against the back door stopped him before he had a chance.

Even as relief filled her, she tensed as the sudden knock kicked back a reminder of fear.

The breath she hadn't been aware she'd held escaped as Jimmy's familiar face peered through the screen door.

"Sorry to interrupt." He offered an apologetic smile as Penny swung open the door. "Patrick said I should talk to you about plans to expand next year's breeding. Thought I might catch you alone. If it's a bad time, I can always come back later."

Cara pushed up from her chair and headed for the coffee pot. Pouring Jimmy a cup, she ushered him to the table. "It's not a bad time at all. I'm just hanging around, being a nuisance. Not enough reason to put off work."

Her heart lifted at the very idea of it. Her dad again involved in the daily operations of the ranch, guiding the hands with his visions for the future, as she'd seen him do many times during her childhood.

"Let's go out back." Understanding the men needed their work time, Penny laced an arm through Cara's. "You can tell me your thoughts on starting a garden in that empty patch sitting so ugly at the edge of the yard."

"Already told you, we don't need a garden here." Her father's voice trailed after them. They ignored him, stepping out into the bright May sun.

The late morning sky held a deep brilliant blue. Birds chirped their lazy songs from the branches above. The scent of columbines and thimbleberries brushed in with the gentle breeze.

It was a beautiful start to the day. On mutual agreement, Cara and Penny chose to enjoy it, discussing plans for a simple garden. Moving on to the idea of lining the backside of the lawn with sagebrush and junipers, offering privacy without blocking the beautiful views of the mountaintops in the distance.

The yard had lacked a woman's touch for far too long. Cara was thankful for Penny's input and ideas to soften the look, creating a peaceful oasis to escape the hard realities of the day. And though her dad might complain, she knew, in the end he'd be thankful for it.

She was also thankful for Penny, who'd brought her own feminine touch to his life. Brightening it in ways, Cara knew, he hadn't quite figured out yet.

The familiar ring of her phone caught her by surprise as she realized the stretch of time they had spent outside, creating and planning a beautiful mix of color and shape sure to bring new life to the neglected yard.

"It's time," Jackie's nervous voice jumped through the phone before Cara could finish her hello.

"I've had contractions all morning." She sucked in a harsh breath and let out a small, frightened laugh. "They're getting stronger and closer together. The doctor says it's time for the hospital."

Headed for the house, Cara fought down her own nervousness. "Okay. I'll meet you there. Do you need anything?" She didn't know what the proper etiquette was for a guest attending a birth. Her experience with running to a friend in need always involved grabbing a bottle of wine and a pint of ice cream on the way.

Jackie's laughter on the other end of the phone sounded much better. "Are you kidding? We've had everything we need packed for weeks, ready to go. All I need is you. Hurry."

Her steps quick and impatient, Cara burst into the kitchen, Penny close on her heels. "I'll be there soon. I promise."

Turning away from his conversation with Jimmy,

her dad looked at her. "Everything okay?"

"Jackie's in labor." She drew in a long, deep breath. She didn't get to be the nervous one. "I need to get to the hospital."

Carrying a calmness she was far from feeling, her dad refilled his coffee and sipped slowly from the dark brew. "I'm sure Cade would be glad to take you."

The idea didn't sit well. "No. He's done enough."

"Well, you can't go alone. It isn't safe." Her father's voice hit the familiar strict tone she'd known well as a child. "Give Luke a call and have him send over one of his officers."

"That will take too long. I promised Jackie I'd get there as soon as I can."

"I'll take you." Jimmy looked from Cara to her dad. "My truck's over at the main barn. It wouldn't be nothing to pile you in and give you a ride."

Cara considered it only for a second before nodding. It was a short trip from the house to the hospital. She would be safe enough. And once she reached the hospital, there would be too many people around for anyone to be foolish enough to try something.

"That would be great." Moving behind Jimmy, she hugged her dad goodbye. "If Cade comes looking for me, will you let him know where I'm at."

"Maybe you should let him know before you go."

"No." Her earlier flash of anger returning, she knew it was best to keep her distance. Talking to him, for any amount of time, would only lead to more disagreement. Jackie didn't need her showing up in a mood while she was in the middle of labor. "He doesn't need to know my every movement. I'm not going out alone, so everything is fine."

Though he didn't look convinced, her dad didn't argue.

Thankful for his quiet reluctance, she turned to Jimmy. "I'm ready when you are."

Crossing the kitchen floor, he held open the back door for her. "Let's go then. I'll have you there as quick as I can."

Chapter Twenty-Three

Luke didn't like what he was seeing.

Hours of papers cluttering his desk, combing through the church member registry, led him down a path he never expected. One leaving an uneasy feeling in his gut.

Ignoring the constant ringing of a telephone outside his office, he studied the property records on his monitor while glancing at the fax machine from the corner of his eye, impatiently waiting for the information he'd requested.

"Chief." Her small size barely filling the door, Luanne, his loyal secretary since the day he'd taken the oath, waited for him to turn away from the monitor. "You've got a call on line two. A Detective Savila. Says he's from Santa Mara, New Mexico. He's insisting it's important he talk with you."

More than a little surprised, Luke reached for the phone pushed to the edge of his desk. He'd been expecting a fax, not a phone call, from the Santa Mara Police Department. His original request had only been for background information, nothing that should have warranted the time for a personal call.

"This is Chief Grady."

And then he heard it, the truth he didn't want to admit.

There was a killer on the Double 'G' Ranch.

\*\*\*\*

He'd given her longer than he first planned.

Lining up the edges of the papers he'd worked over, Cade slipped them back into the file and stood to stretch his cramped legs.

He'd known he was behind on ranch work. But the extent of it was beyond even what he'd imagined.

So he'd worked, and given Cara the time she'd wanted.

But now, her time was up.

The thought of seeing her again brought an extra bump to his steps. A fool was what he was. *A damn fool*. Letting all caution go when it came to Cara and her feisty spirit and amazing heart. Even her steadfast determination to keep her independence.

Hell. There was nobody like her. Nobody meant for him in the way she was.

Sooner or later, she would figure that out.

Lost as he was in his thoughts, it took a moment to register the noise growing louder and louder in the distance. Stopping, he turned toward the front drive, saw the cluster of flashing lights barreling down the road, and realized what it was he'd heard.

Sirens. And they were headed straight for the ranch.

An uneasy feeling settling deep inside, he looked down the path at Joe's place and then back to the line of police cruisers.

Luke led, tires kicking up pebbles and dust as he stopped a few feet away from Cade. The fierce look on his face was enough to send his pulse into overdrive. "What's wrong?"

"Where's Cara?" he demanded rather than

providing an answer.

"She's visiting her dad. Been there all morning."

"We need to get to her. Keep her safe." While officers filed out of their cruisers, Luke turned for Joe's house, signaling them toward the main barn.

"Damn it." Cade stepped in his brother's path, wanting the answers he wasn't getting. "Tell me what's going on."

Moving around him, Luke continued toward the house. "Jimmy's our killer. I'm sure of it. He's been on the ranch, under our noses, the whole time."

"What?" Shock pushed hard. Suddenly desperate to get to Cara, he matched his brother's frantic pace. "How is that possible? We've known Jimmy for years. We would have seen some sign."

"We didn't know him well enough. He caught my attention when I saw his name on the church registry and then learned he owned a place just off Double 'G' land." He didn't look at Cade, his eyes firmly locked on the front door of Joe's house.

"Owning property outside the bunks we provide our hands doesn't exactly make someone a cold-hearted killer."

"It doesn't." Luke took only a moment to look at him, his own fear reflecting in his gaze. "I ran a background check on everyone who fit my criteria. Jimmy's was the only one that came back incomplete."

Cade's nervous pace pushed him a step ahead of his brother. "Incomplete, how?"

"The information I found only went back a few months before we hired him. There was nothing showing he existed before then." Luke widened his steps, catching up. "So I did some checking, put in a request to the last known town I could find in his background. The one he originally told us was his hometown when we hired him."

Cade didn't like this. Not at all. Dread filled him as he reached for the doorknob. "And?"

"And Jimmy had a history of murder before he ever found his way to Snow Ridge."

The truth fell like a brick. Needing more than ever to see Cara, he pushed open the front door without bothering to knock. His only concern was being close to and keeping safe the woman he loved.

It was quiet inside. Almost too quiet. No hint of Cara's gentle voice or her addicting laugh.

Luke's questioning gaze landed on him, sending his uneasiness up another notch. "In the kitchen, I'm guessing," he offered as an answer to his brother's silent question.

Relief swelled at the sight of Joe and Penny around the kitchen table, only to sink quickly when it was clear they were the only two there.

"Where's Cara?"

The demand in Cade's voice earned a surprised look from Joe. He looked from Cade to Luke, uncertainty resting in his eyes. "She left a bit ago. She's headed for the hospital. Jackie went into labor, called and begged her to come as soon as she could."

"How in the hell did she leave the house without me seeing her." Cade looked from the front door to the back door and found his answer.

Kicking himself for believing, even for a second, it was okay to leave her on her own, he pulled in a deep breath, trying, unsuccessfully, to calm his nerves. "How did she get there? She knows better than to go out alone."

"She didn't go alone." Penny pushed up from her chair, waving them to the table. "Jimmy was here when she got the call from Jackie. He took her."

*He took her.*

Cade's world went dark, fear and anger clashing. Clenching his hands into fists, he fought the urge to punch the wall beside him. Just to let it out before it exploded inside.

Spinning on his heels, he started for the door, Luke's hand around his arm stopping him before he took more than a step. "No." His brother moved around until they stood eye to eye. "I know what you want to do. I don't blame you. But you going out, crazy and worked up, won't do any good."

"He's got her," Cade repeated the dreaded words, each one striking a new chord of fear. "You can go to hell if you think I'm going to stand here and do nothing while everyone runs around working up some crazy strategy to save Cara."

"What do you mean, save Cara?" Joe's voice broke between them. "What's going on?"

Though it was clear he was reluctant to, Luke let go of Cade, turning back to the table where Joe's fierce blue eyes showed the first signs of worry.

There was hesitance to let Joe know the truth. Cade saw it in his brother's expression while he impatiently stayed where he was.

"I've got a good reason to believe Jimmy's the one who murdered those women and has been terrorizing Cara."

Joe turned pale, his eyes the only color left in his face as they lit with anger. "He was here. In my house."

Shoving his wheelchair away from the table, he came closer to where Luke and Cade stood, watching him. "I let her go. Didn't think nothing of it."

"You couldn't know," Luke tried reassuring him. "None of us had a clue, Joe. Hell, I remember being there the day he was hired. Never thought twice about it."

"I don't give a damn about any of that." Frustrated, he waved his hand in the air, the lines around his eyes and mouth growing deeper. "I just want my daughter back here...safe."

"We'll get her." Luke looked between Cade and Joe, leaving no doubt his words were meant for both of them. "I promise."

"I've already got my men searching the barns and the bunks. And I have another team on the way to his place. He won't get far. We'll find her."

Cade was sure they would. But his biggest fear was when they did, it would be too late.

## Chapter Twenty-Four

It had all fallen into his lap so easily.

He'd watched from the breeding barn as Cara made her way down the path to her dad's place, loving the sight she created. Long ebony hair trailing behind her, catching the beauty of the morning sun and tossing it back at him.

And she'd been alone. No Cade at her side as he always seemed to be.

He hadn't planned on anything more than taking a chance to be near her and build his excitement for when their time came.

Then Jackie called, and he knew he was given the chance he'd prayed for. After ten years of waiting, he'd finally been granted all he deserved.

And it had been easy enough, keeping her at ease, never letting on what his plans were. She'd given him a soft smile when he'd helped her into his truck and relaxed into the passenger seat as he left the ranch without anyone having a clue.

He'd headed for the hospital, just to be safe. He even turned into the parking lot before reaching over as if intending to offer a comforting pat on her leg. So intent on getting inside, she hadn't noticed the needle until it was too late.

The dose he'd given her hadn't been a full one. Unlike the others, he wanted Cara alert enough to understand every moment of what was happening. She couldn't move, slumped against the passenger door with her head turned in his direction. But she could listen and learn.

"This moment has been meant since I first saw you." He smiled and imagined her smiling back, her blue eyes lighting up with the same affection he'd seen when she looked at Cade. "I knew our time would come as long as I had patience."

The town rolled by as he found a back road and made his way to the home that would be theirs for a brief amount of time.

No. That wasn't right. Though Cara's time would be limited, her spirit would always remain. Making it theirs. The home they shared together.

The idea excited him, pushing him to quicken his speed. But he couldn't take the chance. Not when everything was working so well. "I've prepared for you. Those other women, they meant nothing. They were merely practice so our time together would be perfect."

And it would be. He'd made sure of it. Everything was ready, set up and waiting. He only had to get her home.

Coming around the final corner, his mind centered on his plans, it took a moment to register what he saw.

Police cars surrounded his house, uniformed men and women streaming in and out the front door, giving not a care to the growth they trampled or the path of dirt they brought with them into the house.

A sense of violation surged at the sight of them invading his personal place.

From where he slowed at the edge of the road, he couldn't see if they had found the bunker carved into the side of the mountain. If they hadn't, it would only be a matter of time. And then every bit of it would be ruined, tainted by their unwanted presence in a place so sacred. So protected from the touch of others.

Set off balance, he pulled a hard breath through his lungs, desperately praying for a calmness he didn't feel. Everything had been perfect—so perfect.

And now this.

Cursing, he curled his hands around the steering wheel, knuckles paling from the force. This wasn't how their joining was supposed to be. It wasn't right.

They had invaded where they didn't belong. Dealt a terrible hand to the fate that had been his from the moment he'd laid eyes on Cara.

No. Shaking his head, he brought his thoughts back from the dangerous road they traveled. They may have forced him to detour, but he wouldn't allow them to stop him.

Glancing over at Cara, her wide blue eyes staring back at him, he knew he'd come too far, waited too long, to give up now.

This was nothing but a setback. One he would take care of. Just as he'd been taking care of things since the moment he'd left New Mexico, and the secrets it held, behind.

****

There had never been a fear in his life matching what tore through Cade as he stood in the midst of chaos outside the main barn.

So many moved around him, faces he knew yet couldn't focus on. It was like existing in a muddled reality where nothing felt right or seemed real.

"We know Jimmy can't return to his house," Luke

pushed his voice over those who gathered, ready to help. It was no longer only a sea of uniforms. They came in droves. Volunteers. From the nearby ranches and the town, anywhere the word had spread help was needed to find one of their own.

"My guess is, he'll go to Double 'G' land. It's what he knows best." Over the heads of the others, he caught Cade's impatient gaze and the plea for him was clear to hold out for a bit longer. "The ranch won't be our only search, but it will be our main focus. We'll go out in teams and cover as much ground as possible."

Stepping aside, allowing officers to gather those assigned to their groups, he cut through the mass of bodies. "You two are with me." He waved a hand at his brothers. "We'll go on horseback, head out toward the south fence line. It's closest to Jimmy's place, and where I'm placing my bets he's most likely to go."

"I'm going with you." Patrick stepped up with his boys, knew he needed to be with them. He prayed hard for the best of all outcomes. But, if the worst came to be, his sons would not be alone. He would make sure of it.

He motioned for the hands to bring his horse, stepping back as Joe pushed his wheelchair between him and his boys.

His hard gaze passed over them, a terror only another father could understand heavy in the fierce lines pulling around his mouth and eyes. "Count me in. I'm going to find my girl."

Patrick tried to find words for his old friend, understanding the fear and need pushing at him, and hating the restraints working against him. "I'm not sure—"

"Nobody has to be sure about anything except getting me on a horse." Fierce determination setting his jaw, he curled long fingers around the arms of his wheelchair and pushed to his feet.

The pain was there. Patrick saw what Joe couldn't hide. Yet he stayed on his feet, fighting his way through it. "I know this land with the same passion as the rest of you. Be damned if I'm going to sit here useless while my daughter's life is in danger."

"Don't make me useless." The pleading look in his eyes reached through the connection of their friendship, asking what Joe was too proud to put to words. "I have a horse to take the lead, and I can do something for Cara."

The strain of staying on his feet drew beads of sweat along his wrinkled brow. Still he remained, waiting until Patrick nodded before waving for another horse to be brought over.

"Thank you." His voice nothing more than a mere whisper meant only for Patrick's ears, he held on longer, fighting the pain until the hands brought one of his favorites, Ace, saddled and ready.

It took three to get him up on the back. He didn't move, didn't speak. Just sat there with the feel and memory of being back where he belonged.

Pride and worry clashing, Patrick grabbed the reins and held them out for Joe. "Let's go find your daughter."

****

Whatever he'd shot into her was wearing off. Still, her arms and legs felt like heavy weights. Her thoughts were slow, like molasses moving through her muddled brain.

Cara knew, no matter how much she wanted to, making a run for it was out of the question. Her own body trapped her at Jimmy's side, leaving her captive to whatever ran through that crazy head of his.

His truck bounced along the far edge of Grady land, following an old dirt road, long ago left to nature. Deep ruts and grooves caught the tires, throwing her around inside the cab.

"They can't stop me. Can't stop this," Jimmy mumbled, staring hard out the windshield. Since pulling over on the side of the road, watching the police swarm around a simple log cabin set back deep in the mountainside, he hadn't made much sense.

Not that any of this made any sense.

She never would have guessed Jimmy as a killer. The thought of what he had done to those women was enough to make her stomach roll as her backside bumped painfully in her seat.

It was difficult, putting into truth the Jimmy she'd known and trusted was someone else altogether. Someone darker. More frightening than anyone she'd ever come across before.

"This was meant." He spared her a quick glance. "For us. Nobody can take it away. I've waited too long."

She wanted to ask him why. Why her? Why kill those innocent women? Why any of this? But whatever drug ran through her system held on, leaving her unable to create words from the questions running through her head.

She could only listen to his strange babble and pray the drug would soon wear off and give her a chance to escape.

"Won't be long before it's dark." He pushed harder on the gas pedal, making the bumps almost unbearable.

Too weak to brace herself, she had no defense in stopping her body from being thrown around, smacking her side into the door and falling back into the seat.

"That fool Luke will have organized the gangs to be looking for you by now. He did the same, didn't he, when our sweet Gina went missing." He shot a dark smile her way, teasing at the fear she struggled to keep down. "Never realizing, for a minute, I was part of the group searching for my own glorious work."

His laughter, cold and heartless, filled the inside of the cab. "I wish you could have seen it." There was a sickening darkness in the gaze trailing over her. "What I had set up for you. For the two who came before you. I planned so carefully and made sure everything was perfect. As it was meant to be."

"It's where we should be." His hands tightened on the steering wheel. "All my careful plans took us there. Brought our final moments to all I had prepared for what was destined."

Though following him was still a chore, she understood enough to turn her blood cold. There was something dark brewing inside. A sick belief leaving him to think they shared some kind of twisted connection.

And those women—was he really suggesting he killed them as practice for her? The very idea was too much to accept. Left her feeling ice-cold to the bone and nauseous from the very thought.

She couldn't think of it. Didn't want to think of any of this. Forcing better thoughts, she saw Cade, felt his gentle, loving touch, and heard the tenderness in his voice as he held her close.

He'd be looking for her. He wouldn't give up until he found her. The knowledge was enough to keep her hopeful she would escape whatever crazy intentions Jimmy had.

Without letting up on his speed, he jerked the truck off the treacherous road, throwing Cara around in her seat. "We'll have to walk from here." He pulled into a dense wrap of evergreens, hiding the large vehicle behind a wall of thick branches.

She gazed out the window and tried to make sense of where they were. They had followed the old, abandoned road for some time. Had they stayed on it, they would have reached the spring where once the horses had been brought to drink before Cade's grandfather had piped into it.

But that was still some ways away. Where they were now left her feeling disoriented. She rarely had reason to be on this forgotten road. Only a rare day on horseback, riding as far as the land would allow, brought her to this remote stretch of the ranch.

She knew it, though. It was part of her. Keeping that reminder in the back of her mind, she watched as Jimmy crawled out from his side of the truck and circled around the front bumper.

The hinges on her door creaked as he pulled it open and stood for a long moment, looking her over. "You can walk, I'm hoping. Had I known this change in plans, I would have been even more careful with the dose I gave you."

She wasn't sure how well she would fare with the use of her legs. But for the sake of slowing him down, she would take full opportunity of the situation.

Not that it was much of a stretch, she realized as he wrapped a firm hand around her arm and half dragged her out of her seat. Her legs buckled the second her feet hit the ground, forcing Jimmy to come behind her. Hooking his hands underneath her shoulders, he pulled her up.

Giving her a moment to gain her balance, he curled an arm around her and eased to the side. Her weight fell into him as she struggled to stay upright.

"If you can't walk, I'll drag you," he declared. Taking a step forward, doing as he promised, he pulled her along beside him. "We don't have time to wait around for you to get your footing back."

Though more feeling returned the longer she remained upright, she refused to show any signs, forcing him to bear her full weight.

Her feet hanging limp, she used the time to take a good look around, doing her best to determine where they were. Where they might be going.

"It shouldn't be like this." He hitched her higher, closer, doing his best to move through the thick overgrowth surrounding them, paying no attention to the long lines her dragging feet left in the dry earth behind them. "We should have better. Deserved better than what we've been given."

He stopped to look around and then turned to the left, breaking through a patch of thistle bush.

Though she searched for something familiar, a landmark she might recognize, nothing reached out to her or comforted her with the knowledge of where they were.

Still, she wouldn't give up. If slowing him down didn't work, she would think of something else. There would be an answer. A way.

She had to believe it because the alternative was too frightening to even consider.

## Chapter Twenty-Five

His heart hadn't slowed since he'd realized Cara wasn't sitting safely in her father's house.

Sunset was coming quick. From the saddle, Cade watched the reddish glow hover over the mountains. They'd found nothing yet giving them a clue where Jimmy had taken Cara. Losing the sun's light would only make it even more unlikely.

He couldn't think of that. Couldn't think of anything but finding Cara. And he would find her. There would be no quitting until he did.

The thought of Jimmy touching her, harming her in any way, made his blood boil. The son of a bitch would pay for terrorizing her.

"We should reach the old access road before sundown." His horse keeping pace with Cade's, Jake looked out at the darkening sky, his gaze reflecting the same concern and fear mixing dangerously with anger. "If Jimmy was desperate enough to get off the roads and out of sight, it would have been the closest escape for him to grab."

Cade only nodded, his mind too caught up in worries to answer. With his brothers at his sides, Joe and his dad a pace behind, he headed for the rise of mountains in the distance, praying she was there. Willing to give his own life in return for finding her in time.

The setting sun pulled the day's heat from the air, leaving a brisk cold settling over them. Trees and boulders pushing from the hard ground slowly turned to shadows, mocking them with the obstacles they would become once darkness fell over the ranch.

Each minute felt like an eternity as they rode on. Luke's phone buzzed nonstop, officers checking in, reporting the same status, over and over again.

There was no sign of Jimmy or Cara.

**\*\*\*\***

Night had fallen, chasing away even the smallest trace of light, as Jimmy dragged Cara up another rocky ridge.

They had been going for hours. Higher and higher. Boulders beat against Cara's legs. Long, spiny branches reached out, lashing at bare skin.

The drugs had long ago worn off, leaving her to feel every hit against bone. Every slice through tender flesh. It took all she had to prevent the tears wanting to come with the pain. She wouldn't give him the satisfaction. Refused to let him know how much she hurt.

Not that he seemed to be doing much better. By the time he dragged them to the top of the ridge, heavy panting vibrated through his body, washing a disgusting stench over her.

"We'll take cover here for the night." He stopped in front of a large dark hole cut into the side of the mountain. "It isn't what it should be, but it will do."

He had to bend to get through, taking her with him. Every muscle screamed in protest, begging for relief.

The night chill was thicker inside the dark cave. Though her eyes were more than adjusted to the lack of light, only shifting shadows met her gaze as he moved them in the confined space.

It wasn't like the caves she and Cade had explored when they were young. This one would have held their interest for a few seconds before they moved on. Space was limited. The back wall came up too soon for any true exploring to be done.

But for Jimmy's needs, it obviously worked.

He dropped her to the side and looked around before settling at the entrance, his eyes heavy on hers. Watching. Searching for something that made her want to squirm.

Instead, she pushed back and rested against the cool, ragged wall, putting as much distance as she could between them. Though beaten from the trudge over hard ground, she was feeling better, more in control.

She could walk—run if she had to. All she needed was the chance. A moment to use to her advantage.

Working up her confidence, she did her best not to let her thoughts reflect on her face. He smiled at her as if he knew what raced through her mind. Yanking his shirt loose, he exposed the slender pouch attached to his waistband.

"I'm going to assume you'll be good and won't try to get away. But in case you have thoughts of doing so," he pulled a long, angry knife from the pouch and held it out for her to see, "I'm prepared."

Frustration rolled over her in a violent wave. She hadn't seen a gun. Had assumed he was unarmed. Knowing better pushed the fear drumming through her veins even harder. But it didn't change her decision to do all she could to get away from whatever twisted plans he had in mind.

Pulling his legs up, he wrapped both hands around the hilt and rested the knife, blade up, on bent knees, a threatening barrier between her and escape. "This has been meant for us for too long. I won't let anything mess it up now. Not when our fates have finally come together as I knew they would."

"When you first came to work at the ranch?" She shook her head, trying to make sense of everything he'd said and mumbled since he'd taken her. "I don't understand why. I don't understand any of this."

"There isn't anything to understand. Just accept." The whites of his eyes glowed eerily as he stared at her through the dark. "Long ago, before we ever knew of each other, our paths were meant to connect. It was fated to be true from the very day I became a resident of Saint Pedro's."

She struggled, wishing she could make sense of all he'd shared. "Saint Pedro's?"

"It was my home for five years. Five long, lonely years. When I was still a boy, stupid to the truth I've learned since then."

He stroked a lazy finger up the side of the blade, his dark smile leaving no doubt to the craziness he lived by. "My dear mother lived a hard life, made worse by being saddled with a child she didn't want or need."

"She told me that often." There was nothing but cold, hard resignation in his voice. "Almost every day she made sure I knew I wasn't what she wanted. Far from it. I was the burden a night of drunk sex brought her. A constant punishment for the sins she'd committed."

She thought to tell him she was sorry but realized the foolishness of it. He'd come too far, committed too much, to care about one's sympathy for whatever hell he faced as an innocent child.

"I wasn't an easy child to be burdened with, either. I liked trouble. It gave me a rush. So I found it, created it, any chance I got."

He laughed, the sound of it dry and empty as it echoed through the cave. "I made it to twelve before being sent away. And that was a miracle in itself. I figure my mother was too wrapped up in her men and booze to put enough effort in it before that."

"Is that what Saint Pedro's was?" His head jerked as if surprised to hear her voice in the middle of his storytelling. "The place where your mother sent you?"

She couldn't tell his reaction to her questions, the shadows too thick to read what ran over his face. But the thought of keeping him talking was more appealing than sitting there in silence, praying for a chance to get away.

And maybe, just maybe, he would reveal something, giving her some kind of clue to what ran through his sick mind. What pushed him to kill two innocent women, and then take her as his next conquest?

"Saint Pedro's Home for Wayward Boys," he growled out the name. "My mother didn't send me there herself. Instead, she begged the judge to order it as my punishment. I'd been in front of him a few too many times, so he agreed, happily hitting that gavel down and sending me off with a triumphant smile from my mother."

Turning away from her, he stared at the far wall. "Never saw her again after that. Not that it mattered. Didn't figure I would. She'd gotten rid of her burden and could walk away without ever looking back."

"I'm sorry." Though it was hard to feel anything but hatred for him, there was a part of her that felt sympathy for the boy he was, long before he became the monster sitting with her now.

He looked back at her, saying nothing, his finger falling back down the side of the blade. "Nothing to be sorry about. Had that not happened, I never would have been led here. To you. To us."

Her stomach turned, but she fought it back. She couldn't let him know her fear or disgust at who he was. If he believed she cared, as sick as it was, he might falter and make a mistake. It would be all the chance she needed.

"I met her there." His voice dipped to almost a whisper. "The one who began my journey...Sister Abigail."

\*\*\*\*

Under the constraints of the dark shadows dancing, Jimmy looked at Cara and saw *Her*—the one who he'd first known. The one he'd first taken. Their images blended together, shifting him between past and present.

"Don't think I ever saw her smile. It wasn't her way. She thrived on control. On obedience without question from the wards she tended. There was no grace in her beliefs. Only law to be followed without question or complaint."

He still felt it, that first surprising sting against his cheek. He'd barely been an hour inside Saint Pedro's when the backside of her hand struck skin. "I'd thought she was too young to be a nun. Foolishly believed, since she wasn't graying and wrinkled like the others, she'd be easier on the strict discipline and constant repentance they demanded."

The memories swept back stronger than before. He was there again, inside those dark, icy halls. The constant smell of fear and despair heavy within the thick brick walls. "She took pleasure in bringing us into her office, letting us get a good look at the desk drawer filled with wooden rulers...her beating implement of choice when her hand wasn't enough."

"And she had her own special place out in the courtyard. A simple square of pebbles by the gardens. Her place for penance, she'd call it. Where we'd be saved from a spiritual death of our soul."

He thought of the scars covering his knees, pain returning at the thought of kneeling in the pebbles for hours. Never allowed to move. Not even an inch as they dug into tender flesh, growing more and more painful as time passed.

"She sounds horrible."

The soft drift of Cara's voice yanked him back to the present. Blinking hard, he brought her face back into focus, chasing away the competing image of Sister Abigail.

"No not horrible." He shook his head, old feelings of desire flickering back to life. "She was a lost soul waiting to be taken. Tamed. It took years for me to realize why she'd been brought to my life. Why I was destined to know her fury while loving her power."

There was an evil hitch in his voice, sending shivers up Cara's spine. The more he talked, the more she dreaded what he had to say.

"There was a connection between us. Just as there is with you and I. It took me time to find it with her, though. To understand the true quest I was meant for."

He stared down at his hands holding the knife, then lifted them to study the blade. "I took her one night. Freed her from the sins she detested. And it was right. It was meant as I knew it would be."

"True to her calling, she was a virgin."

The satisfaction she heard was enough to make her sick. She pushed farther back against the cold, hard wall.

"She fought me, as was expected. She couldn't go against her religious teachings so firmly bred into her." A sick twist of excitement carried with his words. "And I was young. A bit foolish. I didn't understand her fight, her fear, were part of what was to be."

He concentrated on the knife again, as if seeing the memories in the smooth blade. "I was a nervous, frightened boy. I overreacted, using more force than necessary with my hands around her neck. I only meant to silence her and ease her fight. Instead, her life ended in my hold."

"You killed her?" Chilled to the bone, she fought back the terror.

"Not intentionally. But the feel of it, a life draining away under my control, was a high I'd never known. I knew then I'd not only been meant to free her but myself as well. I had been given the miracle of sending another into death."

He rested his hands back on his knees, settling in deeper at the mouth of the cave. "I wish I could have stayed and watched the results of what I had brought. But it was too dangerous. Too risky. It wouldn't take them long to know it was me. And just like what happened here, I knew they'd never understand it was good that brought her death, never evil."

Cara tried to put it all into place. What had happened to him. What he'd done. Where he'd ended up. But her mind refused to function, always circling back to the realization he'd killed many and planned on doing the same to her.

If there had ever been an ounce of question before, there was none now. He intended to do with her what he began with Sister Abigail and continued with the two innocent women here.

"I stayed low after leaving Saint Pedro's." He looked at her, so much burning in his gaze, she felt the heat clear through to her bones. "Then I realized I needed more. Needed to continue what had been meant for me and for another. So I came up for air. Started to find a solution to becoming the new man I had discovered after freeing Sister Abigail."

He smiled, so quick and casual, it reminded her of the Jimmy she thought she knew. "I found someone to give me a new identity and began searching for an escape from New Mexico. Double 'G' gave me that."

He looked at her, desire and fury flashing a dangerous spark in his eyes, penetrating through the darkness, holding her captive. "And meeting you gave me a purpose and brand new hope."

Chapter Twenty-Six

It was dangerous to continue.

Guided only by the stars penetrating the black sky and the flashlights they held, Cade rode side by side with his brothers.

The risks didn't matter. Only Cara. The thought of what she faced was enough to keep him going. Every minute tested his patience, making the desperation worse. In the hours since leaving the main barn, they had found nothing. Not the slightest clue to where Jimmy might be keeping her.

It was enough to drive him crazy.

"It's impossible to know if anyone's been here." Luke pulled his horse to a stop in the middle of the access road. "It's too old and overgrown for there to be any signs."

He circled his flashlight around, searching for some kind of sign. "The spring's not too far from here. Not sure where he'd go from there, but it's worth checking out."

It didn't sit well with Cade, the thought of Jimmy staying so long on the road, in clear view. He had to know he was being sought. He wouldn't want to increase the chances of being found by staying so long on a beaten road restricting his speed.

Holding his flashlight in one hand, he used the other to steady himself. Sliding from the saddle, he planted his feet firmly on the ground. "He didn't make it to the spring. He pulled off before that."

He stood in the middle of the old, gutted road, running his mind over what he remembered about the path it traveled. Luke and Jake watched for a moment before climbing down from their horses to join him.

"What are you thinking?" Patrick called from the back of his horse as he inched closer with Joe at his side.

"I'm thinking he would have wanted off this road before someone saw him. He would have known the dangers of remaining exposed for too long." Cade turned in a slow, thoughtful circle, taking in where they were. What he knew of their harsh surroundings.

This wasn't the fertile land utilized by the ranch. It was a remote edge of the property, claimed by the Grady's but rarely used. The terrain was rougher. The ground drier. It was useless for anything other than the solitary road leading to the spring.

"The fence line follows the road from the gate to about fifty yards back before the property turns off for the mountainside." He glanced behind his shoulder, then back to where Luke and Jake stood, watching him closely. "If he were going to get off the road, he'd have waited until he had more land."

"So we walk the edges." Jake turned his flashlight back, running it along where dry dirt met vegetation. "Look for signs where he might have turned off."

Cade turned his own flashlight in the opposite direction. "That's what I'm thinking. If he came this way, he came off the road somewhere around here. I'm sure of it."

"I'll backtrack to where the fence line turns off and

start looking there. You and Jake spread out along this stretch." Luke stepped away from his brothers and turned to his dad and Joe. "You two ride up ahead, look for signs of them closer to the spring."

No words were needed as they separated to begin their search. Cade struggled to keep his mind searching and away from his fear for Cara. The images still came, of those other women and what Jimmy had done to them.

It nearly brought him to his knees, the thought of her having to face such a horror. The idea of losing her was too much to bear. He'd lived ten long years without ever realizing how much he'd put his heart on hold.

Until that day he'd seen her in the barn. Until he'd been hit with the painful truth of how much she'd taken the day she'd left Snow Ridge.

He couldn't bare losing it again.

"Here." Jake's voice drifted through the darkness.

Cade reached him first, heart beating against his ribs. "Did you find something?"

"Fresh tracks through the bush." Jake edged his flashlight, cutting a beam through the beaten-down path cutting off from the road. The pattern was thin and barely noticeable.

"Nobody should have been on this road for ages." Jake pushed to his feet as Luke joined them and looked out to the distance where his dad and Joe made their way back. "But this is definitely fresh."

"It's Jimmy." Cade didn't question how he knew, just accepted the truth. Pushing ahead, he searched deeper, fighting through the overgrowth, sweeping his flashlight from left to right.

The beam caught a strange reflection. A hint of

something peeking through a tangle of overgrown branches. Keeping the light steady, he worked his way through the ragged rocks and roots ready to trip his feet.

He shoved through the trees that seemed to push him back, finding what he had suspected—Jimmy's truck hidden away. A quick touch to the cool hood told him what he needed to know.

"He's got a good lead on us." He turned as his brothers pushed through the trees behind him. "He would have headed up, using the mountains as cover."

Luke nodded as he trailed the beam of his flashlight over the length of the truck. "I'll bring some of my men up here. Have them go over the truck and see what they can find. We'll keep going on horseback until the terrain forces us to our feet."

Cade would crawl if he had to. Whatever it took to find Cara before Jimmy had a chance to do to her what he'd done to the other women.

"I'll get Dad and Joe." Jake backed up through the large branches. "And bring our horses up. The sooner we head out, the less of a lead he'll have."

He gave a quick nod, all attention trained on the truck and the ground surrounding it.

"Over here." Luke's flashlight waved through the dark.

Cade rounded the front bumper and headed for the passenger side.

"Take a look at this." Luke aimed his flashlight down, illuminating small lines dug thinly through the hard dirt. "What do you make of it?"

He looked behind him where the lines started a few feet from the passenger door to ahead where they continued through the dense overgrowth crawling out through the rocks. "Looks like something was dragged."

Luke nodded, letting the beam of his flashlight reach as far as it could go. "From the looks of the constant lines, the distance between them, I'd guess it was more like someone rather than something."

"Someone…like Cara." Cade didn't know whether to cheer or cry. The idea of her needing to be dragged instead of walking on her own fell like a heavy rock in his gut.

The scenarios of why, of what she must be facing, played cruel games in his mind, shoving hard at his already frantic fear.

But there was also hope. Drawn forth by the understanding, whether she'd meant to or not, she'd left them a trail, giving him the first true relief that they weren't searching blindly.

The fear, he couldn't allow himself to deal with it. But the hope, he grabbed it hard, used it to keep going. Telling himself, as often as he needed to, he would find her before it was too late.

****

She'd pretended to sleep, leaving only mere slits under her closed eyelids. Watching Jimmy. Waiting for the chance.

It felt like forever before her opportunity came. Before he slumped forward, hands still wrapped around the knife, eyes closed.

Still, Cara waited. Trusting nothing. Knowing she had to be sure before trying her luck. So she kept her own pretense of sleep while watching him. The steady rise and fall of his shoulders and the low whisper of a snore escaping through his mouth.

Holding her breath, terrified of making even the weakest sound, she pressed her back firm against the cave wall and slid slow and steady to her feet.

He didn't move.

She dared a step, then another, tight against the wall, cutting a wide, safe circle around him. Fear urged her to run, but she knew the risk was too great. If the pound of her feet woke him, she would be done before ever having the chance to get away.

Her heart pounded hard against her chest. She was sure he'd hear it as she drew closer, inch by slow, steady inch. She prayed for even ground, terrified of tripping. Her eyes stayed on him, watching every breath he took, every twitch he made through his dreams.

She was so close. Only a few more steps to go. Though she was chilled to the bone, her skin was hot and clammy. Nerves and fear battled dangerously together, creating a disgusting, slick sweat dripping from her pores.

She could do this. She *had* to do this.

He'd set himself so only inches spread between him and each side of the mouth of the cave. It was a tight squeeze. One she dreaded. But it had to be done. There was no other way out.

She hovered close enough now to see him clearly, even through the heavy darkness. The wrap of his long fingers around the knife. The lines creasing around his eyes and mouth.

In sleep, he was still so much the Jimmy she remembered. She saw the young man, first hired on to the ranch. Her mind flipped through the images of him working with the horses, playing his guitar, offering a smile whenever she would pass by.

The truth of what he was proved hard to put to terms with her memory of who she'd believed she knew. How could this man she liked, thought she knew, turn out to be nothing more than a cold-hearted killer?

It didn't matter.

Chasing away the questions, she forced her focus on what needed to be done instead of on what could never be changed.

Sucking in a breath, holding it hard in her lungs, she kept her back pressed to the cave wall, eyes firmly on Jimmy until the moment her foot hit that first glorious line just outside the cave.

She was there, so close, when the unseen twig snapped under her weight, echoing like a gunshot through the cave.

Jimmy jolted awake. "What the—"

He turned, cutting his knife in a wild arc through the air.

Refusing to be stopped when she was so close, she pushed every bit of strength through her legs in desperation to get past him.

She'd almost made it when she felt the sheering pain stabbing into her side. Still, she didn't stop, adrenaline and fear pumping her blood strong and quick through her veins. Pushing her on. Refusing to let her stop even under the ache beginning to take hold below her ribs.

Behind her, there was a shifting through a scramble of pebbles. He was coming after her. She knew it but didn't waste the time it would take to look back.

Instead, she ran. Frantic steps pushed back a hard echo pounding through her head. Her lungs pulled desperately for every breath as she felt the warmth of blood streaming down her side, draining her strength with every drop.

Her sight blurred, her steps faltered, almost tumbling her to the ground. Still, she ran, sensing Jimmy was close, knowing she would rather take her last breath trying to escape than under his control.

She didn't know where she was headed. Where she should stop. She only knew to run and to keep going for as long as she could.

A part of her knew, dreaded the fact Jimmy would eventually catch her. Every second drained her more. Sharp pain burned through her side, sucking her under.

Thick roots, pushing through the hard ground, tripped her and threw her to her knees. Crying out, her side throbbing, head spinning, she fought back the piercing pain and struggled to her feet.

Blackness teasing the edge of her sight, she nearly fell back to her knees. Only the ominous thud of Jimmy's steps growing closer kept her upright, shoving her forward.

The frantic beat of her heart echoed in her ears. Every step was a fight, an effort to continue while her body screamed to quit.

She stumbled but caught herself. Fire burned through her side with every breath she pulled through her lungs. The tall trees and large boulders blurred into the night. Reaching for her. Threatening to take her down.

It was getting hard, so hard, to keep going. She gasped, desperate for air. There was spinning—so much spinning—leaving her lost in a long tunnel where nothing felt right or real.

Every step was like pushing through molasses, she

knew she was reaching her end. She tried grasping the reminder of why she ran, who she fled, but it all proved so hard to hold.

She was tired…so tired. All she wanted was to find a place to stop and sleep.

To simply drift away.

**** 

There were no words as they followed the drag marks over rough terrain and up the mountain. Cade refused to think about what would happen if, at the end of those marks, there was no Cara to be found.

He had to believe, desperately needed the anchor to keep him from completely losing his mind with fear and worry.

The beams of their flashlights forged ahead, cutting into the dark.

How long had they traveled this route? He couldn't be sure. It felt like an eternity even as it seemed only seconds passed.

A rustle in the towering knot of blue spruces ahead stopped them. Cade held his breath and then released a frustrated sigh when a large bull elk stuck his long, thick nose through the branches. He spared them a glance and moved on, feeling none of the urgency of the humans hurrying around him.

"Much deeper and we'll be off Grady land." Riding between his brothers, Luke looked ahead over the land before them. "Think there might be some kind of cave ahead. But that would be about it before we reach fence line."

Cade only nodded, seeing no reason to answer with the obvious. If they reached fence line, they would continue on. This side of the ranch had state park land past the property line. There was nothing stopping them from searching for as long as the tracks led the way.

Sweeping his flashlight over the rocks and through the trees, he caught another flicker of movement. It was too far ahead for him to be sure of anything. Kicking Midas into a faster step, he moved ahead of the others.

Even with the powerful beam of light, he struggled to get a good look through the darkness. He wanted it to be Cara. Ached for it to be her. But he couldn't get his hopes up until he knew for sure.

Wishing he could push his horse faster, knowing it was too risky with the uneven ground beneath, he strained to see the shadow swaying back and forth.

His breath caught, he held it until he drew close enough. Until the beam of his flashlight caught a face he knew as well as his own.

*Cara.*

She half ran, half-stumbled. Her left arm curved over her middle, both hands were pressed to her right side. Relief surged, only to fall away as another shadow shifted close behind. Though he shifted his flashlight to get a good look, Cade already knew who he would find running after her.

Jimmy was close. Too close. No longer giving a damn about the rough terrain or the risks it carried, he urged Midas into a run, seeing only Cara as he surged forward.

The hard fall of hooves echoed behind him. He refused to look back. To turn away from Cara, tripping over rocks and roots, barely staying on her feet. His heart pounding against his chest, every breath came through in a rough gasp for air.

The fear he'd felt up until that point paled

compared to the stark terror clawing through him. Time moved slow, every second an hour as he raced to reach her before Jimmy did.

He knew when she saw him. The lift of her chin. The flicker of relief in her deep blue eyes as the light passed over her. Clutching her side, barely steady on her feet, she ran for him, his name an achingly painful sound escaping from her lips.

Even with the obstacles under his hooves, Midas remained steady, leaving only a matter of minutes before he reached Cara. Cade didn't take the time to slow down before tossing his leg over the saddle and shoving free.

He hit the ground hard and spun around. He couldn't get to her fast enough. Every step felt like a weight holding him back.

Her blue eyes locked with his. He saw the desperation. The pain. Reaching for her, he wrapped his large hands around her slender arms and turned her, becoming the shield between her and Jimmy.

She collapsed, a lifeless tumble, into his arms. He heard the shouts, the confusion, echoing around him. None of it mattered as he cradled her limp body in his arms and saw the blood flowing over her hands.

"Cara." He shook her, desperate for a response.

Sinking to the ground, holding her close, he stared in horror at the dark red stains. The deep gash through her shirt and tender flesh. Ripping his own shirt over his head, he balled it in his hands and pressed it hard against the gushing wound.

"Freeze." Luke's deep voice barreled over him only a moment before the heavy burst of gunshots ripped through the air.

He didn't look back. Didn't need to see Jimmy meet his deserved fate. Only Cara mattered. Her blood seeped through his shirt while shallow breaths pulled painfully at his heart.

"No." Pain dragged heavy on Joe's voice as he pulled his horse to a stop only inches away. "My girl."

He looked at Patrick, no words needed. Seconds later, his old friend helped him to the ground.

Falling to his knees on the opposite side from where Cade held her close, he reached for her, grabbing her lifeless hand into his own.

There were no words to be said. They both knew it. Only desperate prayers. For her life. For everything they both loved and treasured about the fragile woman lying lifeless between them.

Everything they would give their own lives to save.

## Chapter Twenty-Seven

If there was a hell, he was sure he was in it.

Standing in the crowded waiting room with nervous, frightened whispers tumbling behind him, Cade kept his gaze locked on the emergency room doors.

They had offered nothing. Not even the simplest update in the hours since Cara had been rushed in, barely clinging to life.

The forced wait was agony. He wanted to rush the doors and demand answers, but he knew better. Knew it would only cause more trouble.

So, he waited. Impatiently. Harboring a fear hitting hard and deep.

"She's the most stubborn woman I know." Jake stepped up to his side, resting a comforting hand on his shoulder. "If anyone has the will to fight, it's her."

"And she will fight." Luke was there, on his other side, his rough nudge holding the love only brothers understood. "Cause she isn't done with you yet."

They stood there. The three brothers. Needing no words. No outward signs of comfort. In what was true—what was the way of the Gradys—they were support, and they were love.

The seconds ticked away loudly on the clock hanging above them. Cade wasn't sure if minutes or hours had passed. It felt the same to him. He only knew that moment when he saw the doctor pushing through the doors and heading his way.

He tried but failed to read his expression as he drew near. Thankful for his brothers at his side, he waited, stone-faced, until the doctor reached them and gave the slightest of smiles.

"She's a very lucky woman. Had you not gotten to her when you did, there would have been no hope of saving her."

"Is she—"

He couldn't bring himself to utter the question abusing him since they had rushed her back to surgery.

"She's alive."

Those two words nearly knocked him flat. Releasing the breath, held tight and painful in his chest, he allowed the first hint of relief. "How is she doing?"

"She's still under. Will be for a while. The knife hit just below her ribs, nicked a main artery, and grazed her kidney. Had you not slowed the bleeding when you did, had her kidney been punctured, it would have been a much different story."

"But, she'll be—"

He gulped in large drags of air, feeling weak and vulnerable. "She'll be okay?"

The man nodded, one short toss of his head. "As long as she allows herself time to heal, she'll be fine."

It was what he needed to know. Had prayed desperately to hear.

He could deal with the rest. Could deal with whatever else came his way as long as he knew Cara was alive. Would spend another day bringing to his life that special magic that only she possessed.

Everything else meant nothing in comparison.

\*\*\*\*

She floated. Like a cloud adrift in the sky.

There were flashes of memory, of fear and pain. Of running until she could go no more and then a gentle touch, a loving word.

None truly made sense. They served only as teasers to the reality hovering at the edge of her awareness, never truly giving her a chance to grasp it.

Then there was warmth. Strong and soothing, it flowed from her fingers and up her arm, surrounding her, pushing her to come out of whatever lazy drug held her down.

And then her name. A familiar voice calling out, encouraging her back.

The fog cleared enough for her to recognize it…Cade. His smooth drawl so familiar it tugged at her heart, pushing awareness even closer.

It hurt like hell. The pain threatened to take her under again. She fought, though, drawn to the sound of her name coming from his lips. Wanting to see him. Touch him.

Confusion still grasped her. She didn't know the where or why of what was going on. She knew only the need to open her eyes and respond to his desperate call.

\*\*\*\*

"Come on, Cara." Cade's hope rose at the slight flicker behind her eyelids. "Come back to me, sweetheart."

He'd sat there, tucked close to her bedside, from the moment she'd been brought from recovery. Holding her hand tight while he willed his strength to her.

The wait had drained him, left him fearful even with the doctor's reassuring words. His brothers and father had stayed until he'd reached the point of needing them gone, craving a peace they interrupted.

And old Joe stayed, his eyes dark and sorrowful. It wasn't until Penny and Hattie arrived, practically forcing him out the door, that silence fell, and he'd been alone with Cara.

Her small fingers twitched softly against his palm. "Yes. That's it. It's time to wake up. You've slept long enough."

A hint of blue peeking through her flickering eyelids pulled a relief so strong it nearly did him in. Though he wanted to urge more, push harder, he waited, giving her time.

She moaned. Mostly a whisper, barely heard. Her fingers moved quicker against his palm. Her eyes opened. Closed. Then opened again.

"There you are." He smiled as her gaze met his.

She tried talking, but all that escaped was a dry, hoarse cough.

Cade poured a glass of water from the pitcher sitting on the bed tray. "Here. This will help." With one hand gently curved behind her head, he used the other to guide the water to her lips, holding it while she sipped.

"Better?"

Cara nodded as he eased her back to the pillow. "It is." Her voice cracked from the dryness she fought off.

It was clear the two simple words drained her as he watched her struggle to drag in a breath. "I don't—"

She looked from him to the door and the wall of windows letting in the bright sun. "I don't remember—"

"Shhh." He rested a gentle hand against her cheek.

"It's okay. You don't have to remember right now."

If she never remembered the horror she went through, he'd be okay with that.

Though he knew she hurt, understood she needed to rest, he wanted nothing more than to gather her in his arms and hold her close. To finally see the spark of life back filled him with relief even as it surged the need to protect her from ever having to face such a horror again.

"I remember Jackie calling." Her eyes widened. "Jackie. The baby. Are they okay? I was supposed to be there. I promised her I would be."

"She had a bouncing, healthy baby boy a few hours ago. They named him Evan. He's got his mom's red hair, and hopefully, his dad's patience."

He helped her take another sip of water. "They're doing great. She's already kicking up a fight with the nurses, wanting to come to your room to see you."

Relief eased her. She pressed her head back against the pillow, staring up at the stark, white ceiling. He knew she searched, prodded hard for the memories she still couldn't draw forth.

"It will come, in time." He tightened his hold around her hand and dropped a soft kiss on her cheek. "Don't force it, Cara. Your mind will remember when it's ready."

"I remember some. Getting in the truck with Jimmy, reaching the hospital. But then it's nothing but darkness. So heavy it's suffocating."

"It's protection until you're ready."

Though she didn't look convinced, she didn't argue. Cade was thankful for that.

He wondered what else she remembered. What

about before? Did she still carry the knowledge of his proposal? Somewhere inside her head, her heart, was she aware he wanted her to be his wife and spend the rest of her life with him?

For now, it didn't matter. After the scare of losing her, it would never matter. She didn't have to accept. Just having her—over that terrible fear of losing her—was enough if that's what it had to be.

He hoped for more. But he knew having her near and part of his life was more a dream come true than anything else. If that was what he was forced to have the rest of his life without a true commitment from her, he'd take it.

It was, he understood now, much better than the alternative.

****

He was the cutest little bundle of joy.

Propped up in her hospital bed, Cara smiled down at the newborn baby she held tight in her arms. Jackie's baby...her son. It was a realization she still found difficult to wrap her mind around.

"He's perfect." She smiled up at her best friend, hovering at the bedside. "You did good, Mom."

"Of course I did." Jackie swept a soft hand over the feather-light dusting of red hair covering Evan's tiny head. Her gentle smile held more love than Cara had ever seen expressed from her friend. It was different. More intense than what seemed possible as one from the outside looking in.

She turned that gaze to the door, then back. "Course, if I get busted down here, I might not be considered a good mom by those nurses up on the maternity ward."

Cara laughed, enjoying the feel of it. "Who'd have thought, you breaking out of the maternity ward?"

"I'm telling you," Jackie thrust a hand through her long, red hair, "they're hardcore up there. There was no swaying them in getting permission for the two of us to come down here and visit. Felt like they all had their eyes on me when I snuck Evan and I out of there."

"You still have to sneak back in."

"Don't remind me." Jackie looked back to the door as if expecting a nurse to come charging through. "They'll probably have me on bed arrest if I'm caught."

The thought brought an even greater laugh, chasing away so many of the dark thoughts haunting Cara since memories started returning.

"You sound good." Jackie's eyes turned thoughtful. Her voice softened to concern. "I didn't know what to expect when I saw you. Wasn't even sure I'd know what to say."

Reaching up, Cara twisted her fingers with Jackie's, creating the bond only the two of them could ever understand. "You didn't have to say a word. Just seeing you and holding him." She boosted Evan closer, smiling down at him. "That's all I need to know that everything is right. As it should be."

"Is it? Are you?"

Cara didn't answer right away, putting her attention on the sleeping baby in her arms. "As hard as it might be to believe, I really am okay. I'm remembering what happened and it terrifies me. I won't lie. But knowing he's dead, knowing all the craziness is finally over, it helps. More than I thought it would.

"He was sick, Jackie. That's the only way I know to describe him." She stared out the window, watching the bright sun begin its evening descent as the terrifying images came back to her.

"Horrible things happened to him when he was a child, and he carried that with him. Wasn't able to work past the evils he faced. Evils neither one of us would ever be able to understand."

"You don't feel sorry for him, do you?" The disbelief in Jackie's voice drew her attention back.

She looked up into the comforting solitude of her best friend's gaze. Realized how much she was truly blessed with when so many faced such hell. "No, I don't. Not yet, at least. Maybe, in time, I'll find some kind of empathy for what he suffered. A better understanding of what he did. But that's not now, and it won't be for a while."

"For the record." Obviously needing the comfort of her son in her arms against the chill of what Cara faced, her friend reached down to gather him close. "I'll never have empathy, understanding, or any other feeling that doesn't involve pain and suffering. Every time I think of what he did, what he could have done, I have to hold myself back from losing it."

"And that's why you're the best friend a woman could ask for." Cara grabbed her hand and squeezed. "He's not worth worrying about now, though. Not when we have this handsome guy to spend our time on."

And with that, it was easy to slip into the innocent talk of new babies. Of diapers and umbilical cords. Overprotective fathers and well-meaning but pushy grandmothers.

Cara enjoyed the talk. The light-hearted back and forth. It was a good distraction. From what happened and from the thoughts running through her head, clearing more and more as the hours passed.

She remembered now. Saw the moment when she'd fled to her father's, leaving Cade and his proposal of marriage behind. It was that which led her right into Jimmy's hands. Her fear of committing to him had almost caused her death.

Not that such knowledge did anything to soothe the confusion still playing war inside her head and heart.

"Okay. Spill it." Jackie pushed when Cara fell silent, distracted from the conversation.

"I—"

Cara had planned to lie and distract the concern she saw on her friend's face. But one look at the pointed gaze shot her way told her it was useless. "Cade proposed," she gave instead, knowing the truth would be easier.

"What? When?"

Cradling Evan close with one arm, Jackie used her free hand to reach over the bed rail and grab Cara. Excitement danced in her eyes and lifted the broad smile spreading over her face.

"It was the morning before you'd called to tell me you were in labor. Before I was foolish enough to get in the truck with Jimmy."

"I could argue the foolish statement with you, but I prefer to concentrate on wedding plans instead." Full of excitement, Jackie nearly bounced in her chair with it.

Cara hated having to bring an end to it, but she had no choice. "I didn't accept. There isn't going to be a wedding."

"Why the hell not?"

Jackie held up a hand as Cara opened her mouth to explain. "No. Don't answer. I can already hear what you have to say. You've said it plenty before."

As Cara knew it would, the excitement faded. What wasn't expected was the anger taking its place. Anger falling directly on her.

And it wasn't the small tiff she was used to coming from Jackie's quick temper. It was more. Deeper.

It bubbled and brewed beneath the surface until there was no holding it back. "You are so damn set on this fear of losing your independence you're going to be left with only that by the time you're an old, shriveled lady. You'll be independent and alone. Terribly alone."

"That's one hell of a prediction."

"It's a true one." Pushing to her feet, Jackie leaned down and placed Evan back in Cara's arms. With one hard look, she shook her head before picking up a pace along the worn linoleum floor at the foot of the bed.

"Tell me this, who was it up there that got you out of that cave? Saved you?"

Cara watched her walk back and forth across the floor, trying to making sense of what she asked. "Nobody else was there. It was just me."

"Exactly." Jackie rounded on her, curling her fingers around the railing at the end of the bed. "Just you, saving your own butt. Something only a strong, independent woman could do. A woman strong enough she'd never allow a man to take that away from her, no matter who he was."

"Cade wouldn't be the one to take it. That isn't what scares me. It's that I'd be the one to let it go and slip back into that girl I once was with him."

Jackie's eyes narrowed, frustration clear in their dark depths. "A girl is exactly what you were." She waved a hand in the air and went back to her place at the bedside. "You really think you haven't lived enough, grown enough, to know better now?"

"I—"

Well damn. Her logic wasn't something Cara was prepared for. "I don't know."

"That's why you have me as a best friend. I know for the both of us." Jackie's laugh was soft as she reached over, placing her hand on Cara's arm wrapped around her son. "It isn't only losing your independence you're afraid of. Somewhere deep inside that stubborn shell of yours, you know that."

There was no bite to her words. Just truth. "You're afraid of being hurt again. Cade broke your heart once. Opening yourself up to the risk of him doing it again is part of your fear."

Cara's annoyance lasted for only a minute. Jackie's heart and thoughts were true. That much she knew. And, as much as she wished to deny what was being said, there was a part—a small part—inside, refusing to allow her to do so.

"You won't agree. I know it." Jackie let out a long, deep breath, settling back in her chair. "But as long as I've said it, it will be there, in your thoughts."

"And maybe—just maybe," she smiled at Cara before dropping a gentle kiss on her cheek, "I'll be able to say, looking back, that I helped spare you from a life all alone. From a life that wasn't true to your heart."

**** 

*True to her heart.*

The words repeated inside her head. Echoing and bouncing around until Cara found it impossible to think of much else.

Jackie had left. Cade had yet to return. And there

she was, her room quiet and still, alone with her thoughts and a head and heart full of more than she was ready to handle.

Her memories leaped, from that night long ago with Cade to what they had now. Back and forth they traveled, wearing on her, leaving her wishing it was easier.

But then that wasn't her and Cade. It never had been. Not even as friends. It had never been simple or cut and dried. There had always been more. More feelings. More complications than any one friendship should have known.

Was she afraid of the hurt more than losing her independence? Dancing around the suggestion brought more truth than she cared to admit.

And when she dug deep, searched further, she couldn't deny her independence had always existed. It hadn't magically appeared. It had been there, waiting for the chance to surface.

She'd allowed it, finding relief in it when she'd lived in Denver. It was the Cara she treasured in those first months back in Snow Ridge. The one she missed.

But looking at it now, seeing all that had happened and become a part of her since she'd been back, she had to admit there was more balance now. With her. Her life. Her need to exist within it while sharing it with others.

In Denver, she'd been hurt, so needing of space, she'd wanted only to be alone, craving it with every fiber of her being. It was healing, moving away from all the rumors and behind the back comments after Jacob's death.

But back in Snow Ridge, she'd again found the

connection, the need for people she'd grown up with. She'd needed it as much as she needed her alone time.

And she'd needed Cade as part of that.

The realization hit hard.

She'd needed him though she'd never realized it. And the idea of not having him was more than she wanted to think about.

The truth of Jackie's words settled in, finding strength. And in the mix of it, she saw what she hadn't allowed. While she had been sure he would hurt her again and take away everything she'd become, he'd been trying, changing one slow step at a time. Letting her know, even when she was blind to it, that he didn't want to take away from her, but only add his own heart to her life. In all her anger and fear she'd been the one who refused to change, holding desperately to a woman she no longer was. Forcing her to exist when there was no longer room for her in the present or future that lay ahead. Using it as an excuse to keep Cade from fitting deeper into her life.

Into the happiness and love he offered.

As if brought by her thoughts, he pushed his head through the cracked door. "Is it safe to come in?" He turned his gaze from one side of the room to the other.

"It is." The sight of him lifted her, reinforcing what she'd come to realize in the moments before.

She loved him. More than she cared to admit. And putting a commitment to that love didn't threaten her independence. It didn't change the woman she had become. It only enhanced it, adding to what she loved, cherished.

He reclaimed the chair he'd occupied when she'd come back from her injuries, gathering her hand into his. "You feeling okay?"

"I am." She beamed at him, feeling better than she had when he'd left. Much better.

"Good. Your doctor said you should be out of here in a day or two."

"I prefer to be out of here now." She twisted her hand, folding her fingers with his. "But I doubt anyone would go for that."

"No." He shook his head without hesitation. "And I was thinking, though you'll want to be back at your place now that the threat is gone, it might be best if you spend a week or so at the ranch until you're fully healed."

"I don't know." She tilted her head as if in deep thought. "That might not be the best idea."

She waited only a moment before looking back at him, the smile on her face reaching up to her eyes. "Staying at the ranch only a week or two might make it difficult to rent out my place."

"Rent out your place? What?" He shook his head, not understanding her. "Why would you do that?"

"Well," she tightened her hold on his hand and leaned closer, "last I heard, it was usually customary for married couples to live under the same roof. It'd be a bit difficult to do that if I was still living above the store while you were back on the ranch."

Confusion danced in Cade's hazel eyes. Cara stayed silent, letting him work it through his mind until understanding slowly dawned. "Married couples…such as you and me?"

"You did propose, didn't you?"

"I did." The smile on his face grew wider as he inched closer. "But I don't recall you accepting."

Reaching up, she traced a gentle finger down the curve of his cheek. "I love you, Cade." She pushed up from the bed to brush her lips against his. "I always have. Always will."

"But I was afraid." She looked the other way, hesitant now to share the truth she had just come to. "Afraid that by committing to you, I would lose me."

He pinched her chin between his broad fingers, turning her back. "I've only ever wanted to be a part of who you are, not take that away from you. Even when I was young and didn't realize what I did, it was never my wish to take, only to share."

"I know that now." She smiled softly, giving truth to the emotions she couldn't put into words. "We were, in many ways, still foolish kids, bound to make mistakes. And when I came back, when I finally found my way home, neither of us knew the way to get past those mistakes."

"But now." She curled her fingers with his, holding tight. "I think we're finally there. Or at least getting closer. I can be with you and still hold my independence. It doesn't need to be separate from you. It can be a part of both of us."

"I still have that overprotective streak inside me," he warned, pulling on their twined fingers to bring her closer. "I'm working on it. But I'm far from being perfect."

"I don't want perfect. I want you." Ignoring the pinch of pain in her side, she shifted and lifted her mouth to his, taking deep the kiss he returned. Knowing, finally understanding, this was what she needed. The last fit to her life to make it complete.

She watched Cade soak it in for as long as he

could. Finally drawing back, he cupped her cheeks in his palms. "Is that a yes, then?"

"It is." Her gaze bore deep into his, pulling at his heart and making it one with hers. "Our yesterdays have led us here…where we've always belonged."

## A word about the author...

Cassandra Bella is an author of romantic suspense novels and has been writing for as long as she can remember, and for as long as she's been letting others know. She completed her first book, *Dear Diary* in her grandmother's family room on a manual typewriter at the age of twelve—that manuscript still holds a place of honor in her home.

With Italian and Irish heritage, Cassandra was an only child who still managed to grow up in a large family and all the craziness that goes with it. Those unique, sometimes complicated, bonds often reflect in her writing. And growing up a Cop's Brat, spending many childhood days running around the police department, she draws on that experience now with many of her heroes who are also protectors of the law.

Cassandra was born and raised in Colorado, and currently lives there with her husband, who was her high school sweetheart, children, and grandchildren.

http://cassandrabella.net